Praise for

The Life List of Adrian Mandrick

"With a birder's eye for detail, White takes us on [Adrian Mandrick's] painful, near-death descent. . . . [Her] life-affirming conclusion reminds us that endangered species aren't the only ones that need to change and adapt in order to survive."

—*The New York Times Book Review*

"Beautiful and fascinating . . . *The Life List of Adrian Mandrick* is a riveting and heartrending book about birds, love, and the fleeting unknown."

—Sy Montgomery, *New York Times* bestselling author of *The Soul of an Octopus*

"*The Life List of Adrian Mandrick* is a poignant story of a man whose epic search for glory forces him to face his own human failures, all set against the backdrop of a stunning, natural world that there's still time to save."

—Courtney Maum, author of *Touch* and *I Am Having So Much Fun Here Without You*

"*The Life List of Adrian Mandrick* is impossible to put down: it's dramatic and fast-paced on every page, but still a poignant and intense look at a man and family reaching breaking point."

—Claire Fuller, aut
and *Ou*

"Stunning and lyrical, *The Life List of Adrian Mandrick* will make you want to both slow down to savor every elegant sentence and tear through for the heart-pounding plot—I couldn't put it down. A masterful debut from a profound talent."

—Lisa Duffy, author of *The Salt House*

"[An] intense, poignant debut . . . This engaging, unusual novel successfully combines the best elements of a psychological portrait, a travel adventure, and a suspenseful mystery."

—*Library Journal* (starred review)

"Far from an everyday bird book, *The Life List of Adrian Mandrick* takes our hobby as the starting point for a thoughtful look at how memory and the truth can be manipulated and sometimes ultimately restored."

—*Vermilion Flycatcher*

"An immensely affecting observation of human nature and foibles."

—*Chicago Review of Books*

The
Life List of
Adrian Mandrick

— A Novel —

CHRIS WHITE

ATRIA PAPERBACK
New York   London   Toronto   Sydney   New Delhi

ATRIA
PAPERBACK

An Imprint of Simon & Schuster, Inc.
1230 Avenue of the Americas
New York, NY 10020

The Life List of Adrian Mandrick was the 2016 runner-up for the Faulkner Society's Gold Medal for Novel.

First Atria paperback edition February 2019

For information about special discounts for bulk purchases, please contact Simon & Schuster Special Sales at 1-866-506-1949 or business@simonandschuster.com.

The Simon & Schuster Speakers Bureau can bring authors to your live event. For more information or to book an event, contact the Simon & Schuster Speakers Bureau at 1-866-248-3049 or visit our website at www.simonspeakers.com.

Interior design by Jill Putorti

Manufactured in the United States of America

10 9 8 7 6 5 4 3 2 1

Library of Congress Cataloging-in-Publication Data is available.

ISBN 978-1-5011-7430-8
ISBN 978-1-5011-7431-5 (pbk)
ISBN 978-1-5011-7432-2 (ebook)

For Cathy and Hal White,
who showed me the mystery and power of words,
and the sanctity and refuge of the natural world.

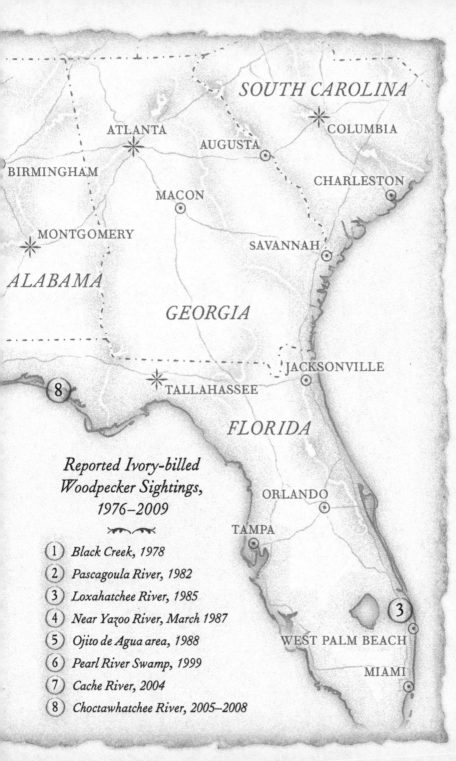

Reported Ivory-billed
Woodpecker Sightings,
1976–2009

1. Black Creek, 1978
2. Pascagoula River, 1982
3. Loxahatchee River, 1985
4. Near Yazoo River, March 1987
5. Ojito de Agua area, 1988
6. Pearl River Swamp, 1999
7. Cache River, 2004
8. Choctawhatchee River, 2005–2008

"The beauty and genius of a work of art may be reconceived, though its first material expression be destroyed; a vanished harmony may yet again inspire the composer; but when the last individual of a race of living things breathes no more, another heaven and another earth must pass before such a one can be again."

—William Beebe, *The Bird: Its Form and Function*

Prologue

Greenville, North Carolina, 1976. Everything Adrian needed had been loaded into his backpack the night before. He loved that. It was very early—that clear-headed part of the morning when plans were made and not yet botched. His mother took out the map and stood at the kitchen counter in a cotton shirt and jeans, brown hair pulled back in a ponytail, pushing her fingertip along the Carolinas, whispering where they'd go: "Forty south to Wilmington, Seventeen along the coast past Myrtle Beach, then west till we get to the swamp."

They passed through the living room with their coolers and bags, Adrian first—the TV silent in the corner, Adrian's father's BB gun mute on the mantel. And while Greenville slept, they backed out of the damp driveway and sped off.

Adrian's mother drove as the radio mumbled about a town called Love Canal, which sounded like a fairy-tale place where no one actually lived. Adrian sucked on Necco Wafers and studied her profile as she sang along with the song that came next, "Just slip out the back, Jack. Make a new plan, Stan," and "get yourself free." In a place called Sunset Beach, they stopped for boiled peanuts that came in steamy wet bags, and when they got back into the car, Adrian teased his mom about hiding behind her big white sunglasses in a voice like a guy from a cop show about to arrest her, till she laughed and slapped at his knee.

By late afternoon, they slid along the river in an old rented canoe, quiet, thinking their own thoughts, letting the sun and water press those thoughts into nothing. Spanish moss hung from the arms of towering cypresses like great loosely woven shawls as they floated beneath them. Adrian pulled the tongues out of his shoes so they'd dry better. His mother pursed her lips, scanning the trees, when—in a lightning flash of discovery—she gasped, mouthed Adrian's name, jabbed at the air, and hissed, "*Ivorybill!*"

There it was. Perched on a branch of a cypress on the far bank of the swamp, the Grail Bird, the Ghost Bird, the Lord God Bird—the feisty, war-painted Ivory-billed Woodpecker, the extinct, most impossible bird on earth.

Or so his mother said.

In that wide-open moment, Adrian slipped down in the cool water and sloshed in the direction of the bobbing, joyful nearly two-foot-high creature, the river parting before him, the bird piercing the old tree again and again, its crest dipped in a bright blood red. As Adrian turned back to his mom and gestured broadly at the ivorybill, water fanned from his outstretched arm. She snapped a picture, and the woodpecker began to lift from the tree into the sky.

When they arrived back at the hot tar driveway and whirring window fans of the Greenville house, Adrian's mother found the magnifying glass in the rolltop desk. They hunched together on the couch to compare her Polaroid with both a drawing of the Ivory-billed Woodpecker and a drawing of a common Pileated Woodpecker in the *Birds of North America* field guide.

"See?" his mom said, squinting at her photo. "*Yes*, Adrian, there is the red tuft on his head. There's the white on his face extending right down his neck to his back."

She pointed to the drawing of the pileated in the field guide. "And see that?"

Adrian nodded.

"That's called the trailing edge. It's black on the pileated. But see how on the ivorybill it's white?" She pointed out the difference in the two illustrations.

Then she pointed at one of the partially opened wings in her own photo. "Now, what color is that?"

"White," said Adrian, fingering the tight skin on top of his sunburnt nose.

"That's *right*."

The birds lifted everything up—outside in the trees or hopping around the grass or winging across the sky or down the highway by the bay or amid the live oaks on the dirt road by the Pamlico River. But inside the town with its concrete and its buildings, inside the houses with their rooms taped together like boxes, things were spilling, falling, gathering speed on their way to the ground.

Adrian's mom threw a mug of coffee at the entryway wall just as his father was careening out the front door—just as Adrian and his older brother, Evan, were coming in with Slurpees. Adrian's Slurpee spilled, and he stood there straddling it until Evan said, "Clean it up, nimrod!" His mom shouted, "Leave it! I'll get it later," but there would always be a stain under that welcome mat.

Then, a couple months later, pumping gas at the Shell station, Adrian's mom spilled petroleum all over the asphalt and soaked her shoes. She screeched like she'd been burned. "Stay in the car!" she warned Adrian, then she took off the sneakers and left them soggy and flammable on the pavement. Adrian still smelled gas all the way home, and when they came into the living room, his father smelled it too. He laughed, grabbed her by the arm, and marched her into the shower. The whole time they were in there, all Adrian could hear was the water running.

Sometimes they kissed right on the lips, their hands running up and under each other's shirts, glasses and bottles clinking late into the night with friends from the contracting company. His mom cried out, "Dean, *stop*," then they both laughed. Adrian snuck looks at them on the way to and from the toilet to pee, trying to identify them as parents. Other times, Adrian's father looked worried or sad when his mother left the room. (Adrian had caught him doing it.) The next minute, his dad would catch up to her and they would argue. His mom would shoo Adrian away, saying, "Go on! Go outside!" while his father watched him with eyes full of rage or something like it.

When Adrian and his father played Battleship, his father always won. The night that changed, Adrian was maybe nine. His father said, "One more!" but Adrian won two games in a row, and it was past midnight when the pretzels were gone and his neck ached before he lost again. During that final big game, his father hid his aircraft carrier, battleship, destroyer, patrol boat, and submarine all in the center of the board. Adrian found one, sank it, and started searching the perimeters. By the time he came back to the center, it was too late. He had been duped.

As his dad bolted up, victorious, he flipped the spindly table with his belt buckle and both boards fell so that all the pegs bounced and spread across the kitchen floor. "Pick up this mess!" he demanded, hands on his hips. Adrian didn't mind putting the red and white pegs and gray ships back in the box—he liked putting things in order—it's just that his dad had been the one that spilled them. Adrian's mistake had been winning.

Not long after, Adrian's father took his BB gun to the crows out the master bedroom window. He waited for their intermittent arrival like a sniper on a rooftop, while Adrian paced back and forth along the hallway, pausing in the bedroom door. The birds were tall and upright enough that he actually saw one of them topple over when it was shot, and by late afternoon, dusty black, square-tailed corpses littered the yard like fallen soldiers. His dad knew Adrian and his mom were crazy for birds. He knew they watched the sky and trees for them and listened for their sounds.

Late that night, she came into Adrian's room and shook him awake. They stole out into the dark yard, collected the bird carcasses one by one in a bucket they used for watering, then buried them in a mass grave along the back fence line. Adrian didn't remember going to sleep again when they came back inside, but the next morning, he woke up in a knot of blankets on the couch with his mother when his father slammed the front door.

That was about the time when Adrian's stomach started grinding. The doctor said he had a duodenal ulcer. It made his stomach hurt, and he had to take medicine and drink milk. The doctor also said he needed to relax, but nobody ever said how. A couple of weeks after he was diagnosed, a perfect ball of poop escaped from his intestines in the middle of the night without him knowing. When he saw it in his underwear, like some billiard-ball-sized egg he'd laid, he was so shocked he wadded his briefs around it and threw the whole lot into the laundry hamper. It was a month before he realized that his mother had certainly seen it or, worse, stuck her hand into it. She never said a word, just kept Adrian's secret to herself. The whole thing was so distressing, his stomach hurt even more.

It turns out crows are one of only a handful of species that hold funerals for their dead, which Adrian read in *National Geographic* magazine. He thought back to the night when his mom had come in to get him and they buried all the birds, and he wondered if they had disturbed the natural way of things, leaving the crows with no corpses to grieve—no dark-suited crow processionals marching around the yard, folding tiny flags into triangles, playing taps on tiny trumpets. Adrian never told his mom what he'd learned. He could keep a secret too.

Goose Creek State Park, 1980. Labor Day. Evan, Adrian, and their mom and dad were unloading their cooler and bags at the picnic table by the river. The air was tart with pines. It was the last day of the year for swimming. The last day for a lot of things.

Circling high above them, in a sky suspended in a fishnet of clouds, a Red-shouldered Hawk screamed its descending *"Kee-ah!"* like an announcement or a welcome or a warning.

Adrian and his mom threw back their heads to locate the bird, and with her blouse slipping from her shoulder, she climbed on top of the picnic table, squinting into the sun, and echoed, *"Kee-ah!"*

The bird answered, *"Kee-ah,"* and back and forth they called, *"Kee-ah,"* *"Kee-ah,"* until sound filled the river basin.

Adrian's dad shouted, "Get down from there!" for no reason anybody could see except that his mom was calling like a bird and Adrian was calling along with her. Adrian hadn't even known he was doing it.

His dad yanked at the leg of his mom's shorts, and she clambered down—their words sizzling like bacon in a frying pan, their backs shielding the boys from their faces—then he pushed her shoulder and she stumbled back, and he pushed her again so hard she fell to the ground. Adrian gasped. He thought Evan, fifteen then, might do something, anything, but neither boy moved.

His mom stood back up with little bits of gravel poking out of her palms, and to everyone's surprise, she slapped their dad's stubbly red face. Evan and Adrian waited for the explosion, but their father just looked down and nodded his head, too fast, like the quiet movement in the beginning of an earthquake.

They all walked back to the car in silence. Evan carried the heavy cooler by himself while Adrian carried the blanket and bags. When they were almost to the Pontiac, their mom stumbled over a railroad tie that separated the path from the parking lot. It wasn't like her to stumble like that, and Adrian reached out to steady her. But his father lunged for his wrist and held it up in the air like a prize, until Adrian relented. "Okay, Dad, I'm *sorry*."

That night, as the brothers lay stretched out in their beds, police arrived. They could hear their father and mother yelling, but they never heard the voices of the cops. They just lay there staring at the ceiling, occasionally giving each other a look to affirm they were not alone. When the police car drove away and its red tail-lights snuck along the bedroom wall, Adrian got into Evan's bed.

Outside, the cicadas began chirping again. Measuring the night. It was late.

Finally, Evan said, "That one girl, Cindy, called me on Friday."

"Who? The one from the pool?" Adrian balled a pillow up under his neck.

"Yeah, the one who takes a Walkman everywhere and actually listens to Steely Dan and Boz Scaggs."

"Who's Boz Scaggs?"

"That's not the point, a-hole. She's totally cool. You've seen her. Plus she won the talent show freshman year."

"Doing what?"

"Gymnastics." Nothing more needed to be said.

"I'll never have a girlfriend," Adrian stated simply.

"Yeah, probly not. *A-hole*."

Adrian shoved Evan playfully by the shoulder. Evan shoved him harder. Then when Adrian was keeping himself from falling off the bed, Evan gathered him up and tossed him back down like a pile of dirty clothes and pinned him, eyes screwball maniacal, inches from his face.

"*I am not going to hurt you*," Evan wheezed like the guy from *The Shining*, then went in for a grinding, head-to-head noogie. "I'm just going to bash your brains in!"

"White man's burden, Lloyd, my man!" Adrian screeched, trying to twist out of Evan's hands. "White man's burden!"

Evan heaved himself forward so his whole weight mashed into Adrian's shoulder and, in his most sadistic Jack Torrance, whispered, "It's his mother. She . . . uh . . . *interferes* . . ."

They both laughed hysterically, jabbing each other in the ribs, whipping the sheets onto the floor, swatting at each other's heads with pillows, breathing hard. Soon they lay on their backs again, smiling into the darkness, and before long, Adrian fell asleep against his brother's cool, pimply back.

Adrian woke with the gnawing of the ulcer in his stomach in the wee hours of the morning. He got into his own bed and pulled the covers up over his head, lying out like a cartoon character that had been run over by a road paver, head to one side, feet pointed down. He tried to stop breathing. In times like these, he liked to imagine that if someone came in, they wouldn't even notice him there, he was so flat and still. But the grinding in his stomach only grew worse, so he decided to go for a glass of milk.

Just the little light over the stove was on when he turned the corner into the kitchen. There was his father—his large body curled up on the Formica floor, collapsed against the cupboard, crying.

He hadn't heard Adrian come in at first, and he looked up suddenly.

Adrian tried to make himself invisible again and hurry away.

"Where you going?" his father demanded, hoarse. "You don't just *leave* people like that."

Adrian opened his mouth to try and say something—he didn't know what—but his father shouted, "Get out!"

A week or so later, that's just what they did. Evan, Adrian, and their mom drove north from North Carolina to New York State in their forest-green Pontiac in the middle of a workday and into the night, with boxes and bags overwhelming the back seat and his mom's easel jutting over Evan's head.

Adrian was instructed to sit in front with his mother and was put in charge of the map. He'd never know why he was granted this honor, but it was the most important job of his life. In spite of all the rushing and shoving and open box flaps and garbage bags and slamming doors that had characterized their morning, examining the map made leaving seem crisp and orderly, like a beginning.

That long drive was thrilling, in fact, with their lives suddenly crowded ahead of them and the map telling Adrian precisely what came next—what river, what crossroads, what mountain, what town. They drove past the battlefields of Virginia and along the busy highways around Washington, DC (Evan kept repeating "the *nation's* capital" as if he were making a joke). They drove over long bridges crossing the Chesapeake Bay and the wide Delaware River, and they got so close to New York City they could picture the skyscrapers rising into the clouds.

When they arrived in Kingston, the map went back into the glove box. They had nowhere to go. There had been someone their mom was going to call, some long-lost uncle, but whoever it was, he never answered. They stayed in a Howard Johnson's for three nights, swimming in the pool in their shorts and crunching on ice from the machine, but that all cost too much money, and with no alternative she could see, their mom moved them into a building where they slept in a dorm full of people in bunk beds with two bathrooms at the end of the hallway—one for men and one for women. They ate breakfast and dinner with strangers at long tables in another building two blocks away, and all the food, including what turned out to be "mustard greens," mashed potatoes, and sloppy joe meat, came out of stained silver tubs. Most of their clothes and toys and books and belongings were forever stranded in the house they'd left behind. For a while, Adrian couldn't quite remember who he was.

He stood with Evan on a street corner watching for a school bus that would take them to other school buses where they would go their own ways. Their mom looked, every day, for a job, trying everything, coming back haggard, asking the boys what they'd learned in school. Adrian learned that their new town, Kingston, was the first capital of New York, where the NY state constitution had been written. Then the British burned it to the ground. That's what they got for waving their independence around like a flag.

At the end of his first week of school, Adrian's mom took him with her to sell her wedding ring, which a fat, bearded jeweler put onto a scale and weighed like a grape.

"Not worth much to me," the man said. "Guess it's not worth much to you either," he smirked, but his mother didn't smile or laugh. Neither did Adrian.

As they walked out onto the street again, she folded thirty-five dollars into her wallet, and Adrian found himself peering into alleyways, half expecting his father to burst forth and demand to know why his ring was lying at the bottom of a yellow plastic bowl.

"Dean is capable of anything," he had heard his mother say.

Within the space of a few weeks, Adrian's mom secured work at the brand-new Hudson River Maritime Museum, at the information desk. It wasn't a *real* museum, she told them, just a historical one, but Adrian was deeply relieved. Even Evan hugged her and said, "G' job, Ma." The first Saturday she had a day off, she brought both boys for a visit, and they saw intricate models of ships, a real, life-sized tugboat, and Adrian's favorite, tools for "harvesting" ice. The museum seemed like a victory they'd all won, and soon they were living in a house again.

Their mom drank wine in the evenings instead of whiskey; she bought oil paints and brushes and turned out paintings one after another—sunrises on the water, fruit in a bowl, roses on a table—mustard yellow, cadmium orange, cobalt blue, deep red. She made a close friend at work, Suzanne, with hair like a well-made brown hat, who began coming over to bring little tables and pots and pans and blankets and folding chairs and food, until everything was new.

Before Adrian even learned Suzanne's last name (Bingham), she had moved in with them. His mom subtly stroked her forearm at the dinner table and left notes for her on the refrigerator when she left for work: "Can't wait to see you tonight—xo June." The two of them made meals with courses and desserts. They bought a new television. Evan was allowed to bring home friends (girls as well as boys). Adrian read for hours without ridicule and set up a bird feeder so he could watch pigeons loiter outside his window. His father would never have allowed any of it. And though Adrian was pleased by all the new freedoms, he feared things were *too quiet*. Like they said on the cop shows. Too quiet wasn't good.

In the late afternoons before the women came home from the museum, when he sat working on his fractions and division at the

kitchen table—any pop or crack in the yard, low noise, or familiar motor sound from a passing car made him breathe shallowly
and his heart pump in his ears. He leapt up from his work to peer
through the curtains at the front window, imagining the possibility of standing opposed to his father, should he find them and
come to call—imagining his father stalking around the corner
of the house, BB gun braced against his shoulder, ready to take
back what was his: his wife, the Pontiac, the small TV from the
kitchen, and the two boys.

None of this plagued Evan, who sat hunched over in his bed
with a jar of beef jerky at his side and a roach clip around his
neck, playing the Doors, the Stones, Santana, and Dylan's *Blonde
on Blonde*. Evan wanted to stay sane until he got through high
school, he said. He had no interest in writing a part for himself in
the family's little suburban drama, just wanted out of the whole
fucking movie, "no offense." He wanted to be an easy rider, like
Dennis Hopper.

Stakes were highest at night. How could his mom hear the
sounds on the street or in the yard when she was making so many
sounds of her own? Adrian had heard night sounds plenty of
times between his mother and father—repentant, punishing, or
triumphant sounds. When his mom and Suzanne were together,
though, the sounds were different and went on longer. Sometimes he couldn't distinguish between the voices at all, which
sounded like two starving women feasting at a dinner long denied
them, or like the cooing of pigeons, or like two people breathing
one breath, over and again.

Why couldn't his mother have found another man to be with?
The strangeness and exclusivity of two women together wasn't
lost on him, but men were, Adrian assumed, impossible to live

with (at best) and unpredictably violent (at worst). It was just that unpredictability that he couldn't forget.

His father didn't like to lose. So Adrian stayed up as late as he had to, sometimes past midnight—listening for the creaky front door, the sticks in the yard, the passing cars and trains, and the boats chugging and yawning a half mile away out on the Hudson—so they wouldn't all be shot down like a murder of crows.

Chapter One

Adrian's got his Ray-Bans on, lurching along a desolate two-lane road northeast of Valmont Reservoir. He's gripping the steering wheel so tight his knuckles bulge, craning his neck to see if there's *really* a yellow patch on the head of the bird flying ahead of him or if it's just some prank of the light.

This morning he explained to his audience at the main branch of the Boulder Public Library how migratory birds get back home—over thousands of kilometers of land, by way of the sun, the constellations, and genetic imperative. A kind of warm-blooded, feathered compass (that's how he described it this morning), a migratory bird feels the pull of the earth's poles in tiny grains of magnetite under the feathers above its beak. Using the olfactory organs in, mainly, its right nostril, it's able to *smell* geography into some kind of full-blown, retrievable map in its brain, a map it never loses sight of, no matter how far it gets off track, even if it were to be shuttled a thousand miles off course.

"Not to say birds don't get lost," Adrian had chuckled, the notes he didn't need folded on the podium. And if there is really a Golden-crowned Sparrow winging along in front of his new 2009 Saab, *it is definitely lost.*

Birds go missing, he told his small audience, mainly because of factors outside the realm of navigational error, "unlike *us*," he joked. They fall victim to genetic mutation and can't decipher the clues in the landscape. They happen onto environmental degradation. They're socked in too long by fog or blown off course by storms. Which of these may apply to the Golden-crowned Sparrow in question, Adrian doesn't know. He ticked his in Oregon years ago. But Colorado? No. Right now, this bird should be somewhere en route from California to Alaska, not a hundred feet in front of his car, a few miles east of Boulder.

At the age of forty-one, Adrian has sighted, correctly identified, and catalogued 863 species of birds, many more than reside on the continent. He lays claim to the third-longest "life list" in the North American birding region—the sweat-and-blood register of bird species observed over the course of a lifetime: a chronicle of loons, hawks, waterfowl and perching birds, tubenoses, grebes, shorebirds and pigeons, owls, goatsuckers, woodpeckers, kingfishers, vultures, herons, and cranes. Just two autumns ago, he saw the mega-rare Brown Hawk-Owl on St. Paul Island in the Bering Sea (displaced from Japan, or maybe Siberia); early last year, a White-crested Elaenia on South Padre Island, Texas, all the way from Chile.

Now, without warning (and why would there be one?), the sparrow makes a sharp right-hand turn across an open field. Adrian hits the brakes so hard the shoulder strap flattens him against his seat, then he squints to follow the bird's flight— against a backdrop of plains stretching to the horizon, toward an abandoned cadaver of a house—disappearing.

He's out of the car in seconds—five feet, eleven inches tall, brown-haired, lightly tanned, and bright-eyed—wresting open a barbed-wire fence so he can squeeze through, sprinting into the open, soggy field like a soldier on reconnaissance, dragging his feet one at a time out from under his weight to keep advancing. He should have changed his shoes. And his pants. *It doesn't matter.*

Binocular up, he bends to one side to try and zero in on the light patch of feathers on the bird's head. It may or may not be too close to the eyes, split into two white sections instead of one the color of mustard. (It could be a White-crowned Sparrow, common as a saltine.) The heel of his right shoe slides on a spate of horse manure, and when he scrambles to catch himself, the bird startles and ruffles right in through the gaping doorway of the house.

"*Nice,*" Adrian says aloud, then sprints to the threshold, teeth to the wind. There, he hesitates with that tugging feeling that he's forgotten something—left the car running, or the window open in the rain—and when he can't think what it could be, creeps inside.

This is a first: venturing *into* a domestic dwelling in search of a bird. He's used to going into the wild, not away from it. He smells humanity. Motor oil and old woodsmoke and . . . sulfur or uncapped sewage.

Before he's taken three steps more, a musical phrase bubbles through the room—a sweet, descending lament that sounds like, "*Oh.* Oh, dear me." The call of the Golden-crowned Sparrow. He's next to certain, but that isn't enough for him, can't be. So he proceeds in slow motion toward the sound, softly humming, "Mm-hmm," passing his hand along a crumbling plaster wall.

In the kitchen: the western sky, purple through a fist-sized hole in the door; the ghosts of wild horses careening across the wallpaper over the sink; a rusted-out stove; an old Frigidaire; a muddied floor scattered with bits of rubber, twisted aluminum shards, broken glass, and so many tiny metal balls Adrian could fill his pockets with them. Shot—from the exploded, shredded shotgun shells of some vandal.

He tilts back his head, allows his eyelids to drop, and listening acutely for the call that will lead him to the source, hears instead the *ding* of a text.

Stella saying:

Where are u? We need to leave

Adrian takes in a pull of air. There's the squeeze from the wife he loves.

It's nobody's fault. Maybe he's minutes from seeing the bird— but he is late. He promised the kids he'd be there for Halloween, and he doesn't want to disappoint them. He *could*, if he were a certain type of person, call and tell Stella he has to attend an emergency C-section, and it wouldn't exactly be a lie; an hour ago, he was turning off the inhalation agents and laying a reassuring hand on a young father's shoulder. Stella and the kids could trick-or-treat without him, he could keep searching for the bird, and Zander and Michaela would be counting out Nerds Ropes on the living room floor by the time he got home. He'd report the golden-crown to the Colorado state listers, if he could confirm it . . .

Nah, he thinks, he's got to let this one go.

Back at the edge of the pasture, he searches his pockets and retraces his steps, unable to find his keys before realizing he left them in the ignition. He tosses off his matted shoes and pulls off his muddied pants, then changes into his hiking boots and scrubs.

He slides back into the driver's seat and eases back onto the road, disappointed, sure, but not exceedingly so. Drinking sake from the thermos, watching the kids parade in and out of the stores along Pearl Street, and feeling Stella's hand in his back pocket sounds pretty good. As he turns into town, he calls her, his spirits still high.

"Hi, honey," she says too loud. "You should see this place! It's *insane*. Because of the Pumpkin Run."

"What do you mean?" Adrian knows the Pumpkin Run: a Boulder Halloween tradition, when a hundred and fifty people jog naked but for shoes and the pumpkins on their heads down four city blocks. It's too early in the evening for that nonsense.

"Michaela!" Stella calls. "Stay with us."

"What's going on? Where are you?" Adrian asks, unable to hear her well, unable to turn from Pearl Street to Fifteenth Street, finding it inexplicably lined with orange warning cones.

"They outlawed it," Stella says. "Said if people streaked again, they'd all be arrested and registered as sex offenders."

"Well, what's that have to do with us?"

"Nothing, the police are just trying to make a point."

"Police?"

"Just park somewhere and meet us, okay?" she says. "We'll wait."

"Stell, why don't—"

"We're at Fourteenth and Pearl," she says. And clicks off.

Adrian squeezes into an illegal parking spot on Pine and hurries along the sidewalk into what looks like an affluent, militarized Hollywood Carnival. Wooden blockades manned by SWAT troopers line Pearl Street with costumed Power Rangers flanking them like backup singers. Boulder city police cluster at the corner of Broadway and Pearl alongside the Joker, Freddy Krueger, and Jack Sparrow. In his sky-blue hospital scrubs,

Adrian jogs, on and off the curbs, past blinking red signs that all say Don't Walk.

Amid a boisterous crowd, across the wide, bricked thoroughfare of the outdoor mall, he searches, suddenly frantic. Not for the Stella who looks like his wife, but Stella as Marilyn Monroe— standing about five ten in her tight black skirt, stilettos, and cheap blond wig; Michaela, his youngest, as a Native American scout in buckskin pants with a feather poking up from her headband; and Zander as Frodo from *Lord of the Rings* in linen shirt and short trousers, thigh-high cape thrown back over his shoulders. Though Adrian's precisely at the corner of Fourteenth and Pearl, he can't see them.

He takes out his binocular and hovers on the edge of the sidewalk, peering through the revelers, just as a troupe of jack-o'-lantern-headed men and women begin to spew from the alley. The Boulder Halloween pumpkin runners. Dozens of them, clothed at the moment in zippered hoodies and running jackets, jeans and sweat pants. They usually come out only in darkness. They usually trickle along in a mild naked rush under a canopy of trees and darkened storefronts, when the town's children are long since back in their beds. Now they look both rowdy and organized, organic orange faces carved into masks of outrage, and there are still pockets of light in the sky.

Adrian texts Stella:

Better get the kids out of here.

He spots a tall blonde tottering toward the far corner, turning back to wave wildly at him, exaggeratedly mouthing something he can't make out—but it's only a man in drag—as the pumpkin heads form a mumbling circle in record time, from the gyro place to the kite store, along the courthouse lawn, spilling onto the sidewalks and the curbs, blocking his way across the mall.

Cops unclip walkie-talkies from their belts and pull billy clubs from their holsters.

Suddenly, there is Adrian's thirteen-year-old son, Zander, cell phone in his hand, standing alone atop a bench, at the opposite side of the restless circle, longish hair uncharacteristically in curls.

"Dad!" he yells blindly into the crowd, as Adrian's iPhone rings in his pocket.

Adrian snatches it out. Without looking at his screen, without taking in the number carved in sharp pixels across the glass, he waves toward Zander and says into the phone, "Hey. You see me?"

"Adrian?"

In a sudden rash of goose pimples, he hears his mother's voice for the first time in years. His Adam's apple lifts against his will. The commotion of the scene thrumming all around him, Zander included, stills and distorts, as though he's plunged under deep water.

He pictures June sitting at her kitchen table, nervously running her thumb along the edge of the wood, until, when Adrian doesn't talk, she stills her fingers and stares straight ahead, barely breathing, as if stillness will make a response more likely. What is she staring at? The collection of petrified flies and bees caught between the closed window and the screen, the rectangular bits of fried egg left on her plate from the morning, her change purse sitting out from paying a boy to rake the lawn this afternoon. Knees knobby through green or brown slacks.

Adrian is unable, unwilling, to speak, so she does.

"Adrian. Are you there? It's your mom," she says. "Listen . . .
I just . . . I want you to know I'm si—"

He jabs at the animate screen, disconnecting, and the pande-
monium of the mall rushes back louder than ever.

Before he can rebound or react, before he can feel relief or
remorse, before he can even locate Zander again, the pumpkin
heads begin whipping off their jackets, shirts, and sweaters en
masse—exposing bras, bare chests, camisoles, nipple rings,
tattoos—followed in breakneck speed by their pants—flashing
thongs and boxers and buttocks, pubic hair like clumps of sea-
weed or nests of silk or shaved into indistinguishable shapes or
shaved off altogether, penises flinging loose or bobbing at the
root or shrinking deep into their ball sacks, pumpkins lolling on
their heads, while the mall erupts with hooting and whistling,
bouncing and unzipping, all caught, as in a corral, in an encapsu-
lating ring of escalating hooves.

Mounted police gallop onto the scene from three directions.
For a split second, Adrian thinks it's one of his nightmares, where
everything is animals and creatures with the wrong heads and
he's some apocalyptic Alice slipped down into a manhole. But
there is Zander, still standing above the crowd, not thirty feet
away, trying not to look turned on or grossed out or embarrassed
or panicked, like he's trying to resist the pull of the Ring.

As Adrian tries to bolt for him right into the naked throng, a
burly cop seizes him by the arm. "Hold up."

"Just let me grab my son, all right?" Adrian urges, pulling
back to test the earnestness of the hold, cursing himself, cursing
his mother. "He's right *there*."

"Hang on a minute, buddy," the cop says almost casually. "Let us get these idiots out of your way," like a couple of pranksters are knocking the lids off trash cans.

Adrian watches, helpless, in his Armani jacket, hiking boots, scrub pants, and Swarovski binocular, wondering where Stella could be, while people dart around for their clothes, cuffs snap closed around wrists, masks spatter to the ground, and mounted police clatter down the bricks giving chase.

Zander disappears from the bench. In a hurried blur in the mayhem, Adrian makes out Stella, looking like Marilyn after a bender. She holds on to Michaela with one hand and grasps at Zander with the other as though they're threading their way across a collapsing footbridge.

"Stella!" Adrian yells, waving his free arm high above his head, then "Hey, Zander!" hoarse and raw, but they're gone, disappeared into the crowd of half-assed disguises.

When the cop finally releases him, Adrian lumbers into waxing darkness. He takes out his phone again to discover a red "1"—a voicemail from his mother—but he clicks off it. Dials Stella.

Waiting for an answer, he slaps unconsciously at his jacket for his old pillbox. Its absence is suddenly palpable, like a veteran's missing limb when the weather starts to change.

Chapter Two

In the straight-backed chair in the corner of the master bedroom, Stella sits long-legged in her "I love Paris!" nightgown practicing her fingering on the oboe, still in the wig. Outside, someone shouting runs along the street, while Adrian watches Stella from their bed, messing around distractedly on his phone. It strikes him as odd when she practices like this: her fingers are rushing around, but there's no music, only a sort of muted typewriter clacking. The nightgown is ironic too, with its floating pink hearts and miniature Eiffel Towers. She's not the type; they both laughed when she brought it home. He wants her to come and lie down.

Zander and Michaela are fast asleep now, exhausted from their brief stint at nomadic life—the Native American and the hobbit off on adventures far from home, hoping for the blessing of their elders, ambushed by an angry mob. Michaela had decided to dress as one of her "ancestors." When Adrian reminded her she was only one-eighth American Indian (from the Catawba tribe, his mother's side) and was mostly French, actually, plus Scottish, English, and God knows what, she was undeterred. But when they got home from trick-or-treating, Zander hunched at the dining table playing Mario Kart on his sister's DS, and Michaela blew fraying colored feathers aimlessly around the room. No one spoke of the night's events, as if somebody had died. Later, when Stella went in to say good night to Michaela, she stayed a particularly long time, speaking low. Now she turns off the light and slides in beside him smelling like somebody else's cosmetics.

"Nice wig." Adrian smiles, a little aroused, a little bewildered.

She lifts her knee up onto his thigh, moves in closer so her breasts surround his forearm. "You should have seen Zander with the curling iron."

Adrian chuckles. "I'll bet."

Stella chuckles too, and kisses Adrian's clavicle. "I thought he looked pretty good like that, actually."

To convince himself that nothing's wrong, that he's being superstitious, that he's making something out of nothing and the phone call from his mother can be safely contained, Adrian regales Stella with an account of the evening's high-jinks adventure—the sparrow that flew like a heat-seeking missile, him sloshing across the field in his good shoes, sliding into horseshit like it was first base, the bird flitting right into the broken-down house like it was coming home from work. The whole thing was pretty funny.

"*Into* the house?" she asks, with exaggerated incredulity. "Come on."

"It was crazy." He cups the soft weight of one of her breasts in his hand. "You should have seen it."

She slides her leg up over his hip and says, "So, *that's* why you were late."

He hesitates. Unclear as to whether he's being chastised, he moves his hand from her breast to her shoulder, just under the foreign blond hair. "I wasn't that late. Plus I had an emergency C-section this afternoon."

"Don't worry about it. They were only bodies."

She means the pumpkin heads. They were only bodies the children had seen. Adult bodies. In handcuffs.

"It's nobody's fault," she tells him, but she backs away, takes off the wig, and tosses it onto her bedside table. It's nobody's fault.

Then she places her head on the edge of his pillow. "Everything okay?" she asks, looking for an answer he's never been able to deliver. "Early day tomorrow."

The years have amassed between Adrian's mother, June, and him like thick cotton padding around a wound. June had seen her only grandchildren, Zander and Michaela, more often in their early years, on and off, always with Adrian present, watching her, trying not to watch her. He wanted to keep the relationship with his mother alive, in spite of his confusion, but it had slipped away from him, little by little. As the years progressed, he returned fewer of her phone calls, found less time in his schedule to visit with her, claimed they hadn't room for her in Boulder for more than a day or two. When she asked if the kids might fly out to see her on their own, Adrian said he'd rather they didn't and, not long after, told her it was probably best for her to stop calling for a while. Maybe he would call her, he said. There was a terrible silence on the other end of the line, then he heard her crying. "I'm so sorry for everything," she said, pleadingly, and Adrian felt something drop away. "I should have put an end to it all sooner," she said, then he hung up.

A couple of months ago, without warning (and why would there be one?), she started calling again. Adrian didn't answer until tonight, didn't hear her voice again until tonight. She didn't leave a message, until tonight. He says nothing more to Stella, just pulls on deep breathing like an invisibility cape. Soon she's curled into an S-curve not six inches away, as blissfully unaware as one of his anesthetized patients under the knife.

Adrian strains for sleep.

He's got work in the morning. He's got to talk to patients, review charts, and look for danger signs. He's got to administer propofol and sevoflurane in appropriate doses, at the appropriate intervals. He's got to monitor his patients' journeys like the guy whose name he can't remember who ferries the newly dead over the River Styx (Charion, Chairon, Clarion?) carrying them over whirlpools of amnesia and hypnosis, bailing the boat, watching for rocks, and, with his oar, pushing away from the shore until it's time. That's what he does, stays vigilant. Does no harm.

He's thinking about the tiny metal balls on the kitchen floor of the abandoned house, and the mud that had leaked in from under the blasted-out kitchen door and dried along the bottom corner cupboard like waves frozen against a shoreline. He's thinking about the pumpkin heads and how such a mass of people could all be so fucking stupid. He's thinking about his mother's voice on the phone when she said, "I want you to know I'm si—," running his fingers over the gnarled skin of his elbow, considering the possibilities: "I want you to know I'm sincerely sorry." "I want you to know I'm sick of you." "I'm sixty-five." "I'm sinking." "I'm sick." He's thinking about her voicemail blinking in the memory of his phone, which maybe he will listen to in the morning or tomorrow after work. And about how, when he'd finally caught up with Stella and the kids on the street, Zander said, "God, why did we even wait for you?" as though it had been his fault the cavalry had descended on the squash heads in the middle of the marketplace.

He edges back away from Stella, feels for his laptop on the bedside table, then lifts it onto his thighs and flips up the screen.

He skids through passwords and pages and postings. Onto the Cornell Lab of Ornithology site. And North American Rare Bird

Alert. To the Cornell Ornithology Lab's eBird site. Then Back-yard Birder's chat room. His article on thrushes was published here some months ago, and his blog piece on hummingbirds, last week. He'll check for comments or questions, one in the morning now, and nearly the instant he logs on, some backyard birder's post blooms onto the page like a parachute opening in a pale sky.

4601 (11/1/09): About 6:20 a.m. I saw a Northern Cardinal out in the yard by the hedges by the mess. They are bright red which every-body knows. When I was trying to think how to describe the color I thought of fruit but I couldn't think what kind then I thought pome-granits (sp?). Its back wing and tale feathers are also red except like they're antique. It has a black mask over its eyes and throat and over its beak which is more orange and looks like it was stuck on with glue for Halloween. I almost forgot they have a crest on top of there heads also red. Everybody likes the males but I also like the females because they still have red but most of there body is like this old sweater I had I left somewhere I wish I still had. Which I think everybody has a sweater that faded brownish green color. Its a fuck-ing circus around here today because we're getting a new batch of boys from Georgia. The north field is like grand central station.

Hah. Pretty hilarious, Adrian thinks, this *cardinal* posting. Under his breath he says, "Oh, please."

In the moment that follows, though, somewhere between in-somnia and self-declared banishment, he's plunged into a kind of heartsick melancholy by the naïve passion with which the man described his acquisition, one of the most common birds in the hemisphere, as if it were the most extraordinary find.

The house quiet, Adrian pulls himself from under the covers

and steals down the hallway into Zander's room. In the soft light from the closet, he lowers himself onto his bed. Listens to his steady, gentle snoring. Kisses his hair. Breathes in his smell of sun, dirt, and baked potatoes.

These are the times when the anxiety is strongest, when the past comes rattling at the door. Anything can happen at any time. When the children were young, it was the fear of hot pots on the stove. Hotel windows. Rabid dogs. Flying rocks. Steep stairs. Thin ice. Sharp-cornered tables. Swimming pools. Pointy sticks. Fast-flowing creeks. Certain nightmare scenarios got stuck in his head on replay: he's bathing an infant Michaela when the phone rings. He looks away, starts reaching for the phone, she sinks down into the water centimeter by centimeter as he's trying to nudge the phone down from the sink, her lips wet then submerged. When he looks around again? She's bloated and still. Like that. Now that they're older, it's bullies. Apathy. Terrorism. Meth, heroin, crack, shooters, twisted Internet porn. Shame, failure, belittlement. The limp-dicked, pig-headed government. Incurable illness. The dark. And Adrian's own accountability, that too—for leaving them where maybe he shouldn't have, for ignoring his instincts, for trusting his instincts, for the unpredictability of even he, himself, how he could be a danger to them in ways he only imagines in some narrow, hurtling shard of consciousness. How do children live to become adults? Who the hell knows.

"Dad? What are you doing?" Zander turns to squint up at him. "What time is it?"

"Hey, buddy. It's late. Just checking in." His heart palpitates, a little startled too, to find himself here.

Zander looks up at him a minute.

"What were they going to do to us?"

Adrian is at a loss. "What was who going to do?"

"The people with the pumpkin heads. If the police didn't come, what were they going to do?"

"They weren't going to do anything, buddy. They already did it. Took off their clothes. That's why the police came."

"Oh." Zander twists his mouth over to one side then moves something around under his blankets.

"Didn't mean to wake you up," Adrian says, and the boy turns back over to close his eyes again.

"'Night, Dad . . . Go to sleep."

Adrian makes his way down the stairs, across the dining room, and into his office. Clicks on his desk lamp, pulls out the shoe-box-sized safe lying on its side behind the bottom row of books. He finds the key hanging on a pushpin on the underside of his desk and unlocks the safe.

Here is what remains from his difficult days with pills—the caramel-colored cylinders, the odds and ends.

- A snack baggie of Vicodin—10 mg / 325 mg tabs
- An original bottle of Klonopin he'd abandoned after finding he preferred Xanax—about half full
- A few Thorazine from the time he had hiccups for seventy-two hours—useless
- About twenty 2 mg tabs of Lunesta in a bottle along with about the same count of 2 mg Xanax bars
- A sticky bottle of codeine cough syrup—half full (prescribed for Zander)

- His old wood and metal pillbox with the hummingbird carved on top

This was the comfort. The liquid honey. This was the way alienation was obliterated and the fire started in the damp cave. This was how, for nearly a decade, he had protected his family from his own jaggedness and endured. Or so he told himself.

Stella and the kids never knew. Which is, he likes to think, what separates the men from the boys. Take your medicine if you must, but avoid impacting the ones who depend on you, avoid going off the rails, avoid losing your job and becoming a homeless person under the overpass, huddling under a piece of plywood. Because Adrian has seen it all. Once, just a couple of years ago, a man threatened a doctor with a raised metal stool, demanding a prescription. Every day, desperate patients of every stripe sob and beg, faces contorted, bent over their bellies in anguish. Every day, they roll in on gurneys with their eyes facing backward in their heads, skin and bones, shivering, brain-dead, or DOA. Controlled quantities, that's how Adrian accomplished what he had—never fully losing hold but enlarging himself with a little optimism and peace. Science. And magic. He would take a series of generous doses over the course of a couple of weeks, titrate down a bit for two or three more to keep dependence from seizing him, then edge his way back up, etc. In this way, he tried to keep the process clean and, mostly, manageable.

The fact is, he came to believe Stella liked him better when he was on Vicodin (and maybe a little Xanax). He was often more talkative (sometimes *too* talkative), more easygoing, less controlling, less irritable, less socially anxious. Sexually, not so much. He could last forever but couldn't ejaculate. Or he couldn't get hard. Or he got hard but couldn't stay hard.

One summer night, maybe three or four years into all this, when he had only recently stepped into the deep, soft water of Vicodin, he spent an hour in the sweaty darkness with his wife. His penis was a Nerf Dart version of its former self. His ejaculation was ten steps ahead of him. Stella had taken him in her mouth a full fifteen minutes before, sucking and circling him as if cleansing a wound—to no avail. All Adrian wanted was to fill her mouth as he always had, to push out his fluid onto her tongue with a full-throated cry (sometimes that happened). She just curled away from him, a victim of chemistry. She slid her hand between his legs and gathered him in her palm like something dying she'd found on the shoreline. Then she sobbed. He wasn't attracted to her anymore, she said. What was she doing wrong?

"*Nothing*, Stella, please," he whispered. "I'm coming down with something. I'm sorry . . ."

That was the moment he came closest to ending the bullshit (before it had even fully begun). It wasn't her fault *at all*, he wanted to say. It had nothing to do with her, only with him. He'd always desired her, always wanted to please her. It's just he was weak and selfish and steadily going *off the rails*. Instead, within twenty-four hours, he obtained a script for Viagra, which pretty effectively solved the problem, if he thought to take it ahead of time. He came to live with it, all of it—the benefits and the inconsistencies, the dreams and the cravings, the occasional sickness from going too far and the process of weaning back off, only to begin again.

Then, two years ago, he fell asleep in the middle of jury duty, drooling all over the halls of justice. When the DA nudged him awake with a file folder and a lifted eyebrow, Adrian promised himself *nevermore*.

Now, he doesn't touch any of it. Just recalls the grueling afternoon he stood here at his desk and made the choice to keep the pills but bury them like treasure he'd find years later. If he's honest, he had hoped it would be a lot more years than this. Even to him, it sounds like some juvenile deception; already his heart is higher in his chest, closer to the skin, and the sense of his body as something in precarious balance gives way to the sharp, one-pointed craving. He doesn't want to start the whole cycle over; of course he doesn't.

He will not take the pillbox. That would indicate a full recommitment, a lifestyle reversal, and he's not doing that. He'll only take a couple of pills with him back to bed and a few to tuck into his wallet, to short-circuit the anxiety and the sleeplessness, then he's palming the lid off the Xanax and tapping one into his hand. He's unscrewing the top from the cough syrup to take a deep, cherry-flavored swig.

Adrian finds himself on his back in the weak morning light, eyes open to the high window across the room, the shimmering red and yellow leaves floating noiselessly as confetti.

He hears the clank of plates downstairs, Michaela announcing something about muffin tops, chanting, "Daddy, Daddy, Daddy," and Stella responding in a stage whisper he can't make out. He's groggy, heavy-lidded; there are several seconds in which he doesn't recall the events of the previous day—the pumpkin runners or the call from his mother or her voicemail—but the moment he does, he's surprised to arrive at a sort of clarity.

If he hadn't decided to abandon his search for the sparrow in the old house, Stella and the kids would have gone on trick-or-treating without him. If they'd gone on without him, they would never have been waiting for him at the corner of Disaster and Idiocy. If he hadn't been searching for them there, he would never have been so distracted as to answer the call and hear the long-ago voice in his ear, consequently landing both him and Zander knee-deep in cocks and balls, then descending, himself, into an irrational state of paranoiac dread.

June's voicemail, her insistence, will wait. He should never have stopped pursuing the bird.

Chapter Three

Twenty-four hours later, Adrian's killing time, blowing a few short, hard breaths through his nose like a fighter circling his opponent in the ring.

Perched at the edge of his ergonomically brilliant black mesh chair, he inspects the objects on his desk, making order of them in his head: a leaning tower of (twenty-three) unread copies of *Anesthesiology*; a box of envelopes with little plastic windows (bought by mistake, never used); November's (twenty-one) bills; two empty grande-sized Starbucks cups; a set of (six) antique ornithological tomes (a gift from Stella); and dozens of postage stamps in a heap—antique cars, ruby-throated hummingbirds, Navajo jewelry, Christmas trees, flags, the Wildlife Conservation Society wild-turkey stamp, the Lewis and Clark Expedition stamp, the Booker T. Washington log-cabin stamp, and Adrian's personal favorite, Atoms for Peace, which shows two globes circling like particles within an atom and reads: "To find the way by which the inventiveness of man shall be consecrated to his life."

Adrian takes an Atoms for Peace stamp and sticks it to the back of his iPhone with Scotch tape, just as Michaela comes padding in carrying a plate of pancakes with a strawberry on top.

"Want it, Dad?" she asks, holding it shakily out in front of her.

"Hey! My goodness, thank you," he says. He takes the heavy plate. She finds her way into his lap.

The first bite goes to her.

"Want the strawberry?" Adrian plucks it up between his fingers. "Going . . . going . . ."

"Come on, Micki! Mom says your pancakes are getting cold!" Zander yells from the kitchen table.

Michaela lets Adrian feed her the strawberry, kisses him sloppily on the cheek, then rustles out again in her robe. "You can come out if you want to."

"One sec," he calls after her. "Be right there!"

Yesterday evening, Adrian got a call from Jeff, his best friend, attaché, and partner in the crime of the birds. Jeff told him that Henry Lassiter—inveterate birder and longtime captain at the helm of the American Birding Association (with the second-longest life list)—had died near the cliffs at San Juan Capistrano watching the swallows evacuate the mission on their way to Argentina. This morning, when Adrian called Lassiter's birdwatching companion, Will Marienthal (the birder with the fourth-longest list), to express his condolences, Marienthal presented him with an unexpected gift: news of a Siberian Accentor (extremely rare) right here on the continent. Just as Marienthal was about to say more—where the bird was, how long it had been there, under what circumstances—he had to take another call. It happened to be Lassiter's widow, and he said he'd phone or text Adrian straight back with the details.

Since then, some forty minutes ago, Adrian has waited like a sprinter for the sound of the pistol. He finds no Internet buzz about the accentor yet—this is fresh news—so he cleans the tops of the keys on his keyboard with spit and the tail of his undershirt. He shuffles the stacks of stamps and drops two stuck-together waving American flags into his water glass to loosen them. Much of the activity of birding is waiting, after all. Planting your feet and waiting. Listening. Alert.

Adrian has held the *third*-longest life list for three straight years, which he's achieved in spite of the fact that he lives in a semiarid desert, a thousand miles from the nearest border, with only 489 bird species native to his state. He's convinced that if he lived in a state near a border or coastline (as most of the top birders do) like Arizona or California or Texas, where vagrant and accidental species tend to drift over (or if he was retired!), there would be no contest.

For the past dozen years, the top two listers (Shell Eastman and the late Lassiter) have held on like pit bulls. The whole top ten is nearly ironclad. There is some occasional shifting about—say, number five will trade positions with number six. There is the very occasional quitter who, for personal or political reasons, withdraws from the game. Once in a great while, someone will shoot up into the higher ranks from below, having completed a highly exceptional Big Year or committed themselves to lengthy pelagic trips. But at this level of competition, each of the top ten has seen so many species, opportunities for new lifers—birds extraordinary, birds unexpected—are exceedingly rare. The lists sit waiting too, open like the beaks of baby chicks, hungry for another entry.

Adrian trails the newly deceased Lassiter by only three species and, as it happens, Adrian has already added a notable three species this year. Usually, Lassiter would also be adding species. But if Lassiter had been ill, and unfortunately he had, it occurs to Adrian that *maybe* Lassiter hadn't added many new life birds this year, and this could be his time to rise to the very top. Adrian wouldn't wish sickness on anybody. He drank bourbon with Lassiter on Attu, sea-watching at Murder Point. And who knows, maybe Lassiter had added another four species and Adrian will continue to trail him. (Adrian's pretty sure Lassiter added a Thick-billed Vireo in the spring, at the very least.) If he hadn't added *any*, though, Adrian and Lassiter would be tied at this very moment; and if Adrian could add one more species before the deadline at the end of December, he could overtake Lassiter, whose impressive list (which continues to stand after his death) includes a Bachman's Warbler and, miracle of miracles, an Ivory-billed Woodpecker (the only current list that does). The fact is, there's no sure way of knowing what Lassiter's year looked like without begging Marienthal for information. But the course of treatment—the way forward—is the same.

Adrian clicks onto the major bird posting sites to check again for signs of the accentor, but he finds nothing. When he goes to Backyard Birder to check on his articles, nothing requires his immediate attention, but there, just posted, is the same novice birder from the other night.

4601 (11/2/09): At 11:17 a.m. I saw a American Kestrel on some electrical wire while I was loading pipe. They are a really good looking bird. They are the smallest falcon. Blue gray wings and a brownish orange body and tail. It looks like a woman with smeered blue mascara coming down and it has more blue where its ears would be if it had ears which I guess it does somewhere under there. The rest of the face is white. It just sat up there and after a while I had dto stop watching and go back to work.Then it lifted up to look for pray and hovered over the field like a chopper. It got so cold I put

on a jacket. The new guys are breaking down getting their hands
burned and black. I've gotta get something to eat before they clos
down.

Tilting back in his chair a moment, Adrian grins, finishing the
last dripping bite of his pancakes. American Kestrel. It's a step up
from a cardinal, anyway. Guy's such a newbie, he doesn't even
have a username, only a number. Adrian wonders how "the new
guys" are getting their hands burned and black. He clicks on to the
member profile to find a photo—a man, silhouetted black by sunset, sitting on rocks beside a warmly lit body of water—clicks off.

He plucks up the now parted, floating stamps from the slick
of his water glass and tosses them into the trash; then he pops a
Vicodin into his mouth and drinks.

Cut through by a lone road like a wavering jet stream across a
vast sky, North Cascades National Park consists of over five
hundred thousand naked acres swelling up to the bosom of British Columbia. The Siberian Accentor, a vagrant species blown
over from Russia, has been there twenty-one hours by the time
Adrian, Stella, and Jeff pack their bags and drive the kids to
Stella's German mother, Oma Gertrude. She'd do anything for
Zander and Michaela, but she finds Adrian's passion ludicrous
and has never pretended otherwise.

Standing now in front of her condominium off Twenty-Ninth
Street, gray hair spiky, housedress down to her calves, she waves
him off like a bad joke, saying, "Bon voyage, Birdman." Zander's
already made his way into the house, but Michaela stands waving
alongside Oma, laughing, "See ya later, Birdman!"

Stella hasn't gone birding with him in years. They had bought tickets to the Philharmonic for the weekend, and Adrian knew she would be understandably disappointed when he wanted to leave town instead, so when he went to deliver the bad news (saying too that the only flight into Seattle-Tacoma was canceled, and the one into Vancouver was such a complex web of flights with inconvenient departure times, it was faster to drive) he found himself tempting her with walks in view of the glaciers and crackling fires outside their cozy tent.

To his surprise, she was moved. She said, "You sure? Maybe I could give it another try . . ."

"Besides"—he took her head in his hands, kissing her—"it's a Colorado day," and it was, and it is, and they push off now, barreling forward, everything in HD. The sky is blue as a cornflower, every crag and tree of the Rockies stark to the eye.

All night and into the morning, they take turns driving and sleeping. Adrian drives the longest stints while Stella plays Yahtzee on her phone or naps and Jeff reads *Sausage-Making for Idiots*, then complains of motion sickness. The car is one of Adrian's favorite places to be—contained but utterly free. Sometimes when it's particularly sunny, even when it's raining or snowing, he simply sits inside, charmed by the sun on his face or the tapping of rain, protected by shatterproof glass, rubber, and steel.

"That's why he's number *one*," Jeff insists, his balding head concealed under his Tampa Bay Rays cap. He picks little cotton pills from his fleece vest and flicks them onto the floor of the car, rain now dashing across the road before them as they wind, small, against the backdrop of the forested mountains. They refueled about forty-five minutes back. Forty-five minutes ahead, they'll hit Coeur d'Alene and its illustrious lake. Beyond that, Spokane.

"I could be number one too, if I listed every bird I *thought* I heard. I'm not the only one that thinks this, Jeff. His reputation is plummeting."

"But it's legal," Jeff says. "I don't see what's wrong with it."

"I haven't listed a single bird on call alone," insists Adrian. "I still can't believe they changed it and Lutz is going along with it. The ABA just wants higher numbers."

"I guess," Jeff says, losing steam.

"'Cause you've got to *see* it to believe it, my friend."

"You're the expert."

To lighten the mood, Adrian asks, "So, how's A Good Sport?"

"Happy to have the flexibility," Jeff says, and taps meaningfully on the cover of his book.

Jeff works part-time at a sporting goods store, having recently quit his decadelong career in heating and cooling to pursue his dream of writing a how-to book. Adrian's known Jeff some six or seven years now, and it was the first risky move he's ever seen him make. They met when Jeff came to Adrian and Stella's to look into replacing their old furnace. Jeff started asking Adrian about his antique binocular collection, and next thing you know, the two of them were out looking at Horned Grebes at Valmont Reservoir, Jeff saying, "Touchdown!" every time one landed. Stella and Adrian became the proud owners of a larger-than-life furnace with a blower so loud, you sometimes have to raise your voice in conversation when the thing kicks on.

Meanwhile, Jeff pushed off from the shore of conventional, full-time income along with half the population of Boulder. During a conversation Jeff had had with a friend who had worked at

Wiley Publishing, the company that puts out the *For Dummies* series, he was encouraged to believe that he could find something to write about, make some money, and establish himself as a how-to writer, instead of digging around in overgrown backyards and musty basements into his middle age. Apparently, the friend told Jeff that he was a naturally interesting and interested person, that people know about lots of things, and that sometimes the things they could be writing about were obscured to them.

For example, Jeff's friend said, a man who grew up hunting and skinning his kill might fail to realize that not everyone knew how to do these things, and with a little additional research could write a book called *Animal Skinning for Dummies* or *The Idiot's Guide to Fur Trapping*. Jeff became convinced there must be a number of these veins of knowledge running though his experience that he simply had to mine and exploit.

Now, thumbing distractedly through *Composting for Dummies*, Jeff says he's pretty sure everything's already been covered. In addition to all the big subjects—*Divorce for Dummies, PCs for Dummies, Bartending for Dummies*—there are very specific titles long since published, like *Acne for Dummies, Beagles for Dummies,* and *Building Chicken Coops for Dummies.* There's even a book called *C. S. Lewis & Narnia for Dummies.* Though Jeff is someone who's worked some twenty different jobs over the course of his life (which Adrian didn't know), perhaps he is an expert on nothing.

"How about *Heating and Cooling for Dummies?*" Adrian suggests.

Jeff says, "Way too late for that, bud," and they soon become spellbound by the white lines and the rain.

Adrian slips a Xanax onto his tongue with its benign, almost imperceptible taste, as a billboard advertising a Native American trading post whizzes by. A coyote dancing in a cloudless sky.

His mother's call swishes about in his head like tea leaves in a cup, with her half-finished sentence. Her voicemail remains a tiny red 1 on his home screen that won't go away until he checks or deletes it. This morning, in the wee hours, he set his cell phone to silent to be sure she couldn't surprise him with another call.

"She still asleep?" Jeff asks.

Adrian's head snaps to look where Stella should be—but finds only an empty expanse of palomino leather and her cell phone gone to black.

When the Range Rover speeds over the freeway and back toward De Borgia, an hour and fifteen minutes have passed from the time they stopped to get gas. They can just make Stella out, trudging alone on the westbound shoulder of the wide highway, her backpack drenched across her back, holding her hands over her eyes like a visor as she scans both sides of the road. When Adrian honks the horn ever so briefly, she squints in his direction, looking truly amazed, like a woman witnessing some sort of natural disaster. As he speeds by, she spins. He can't get to her. He wants to, but he can't. He has to keep going to find a place to turn around. Seven long miles he and Jeff say nary a word, until Adrian finds an exit and squeals away from the stop sign shiny with rain.

He drives within arm's length of her. Jumps out, slipping on the pavement, supporting himself on the hood of the car to keep from falling. The windshield wipers whip fervently across the glass and rain bounces onto his trousers from the road as he rushes to embrace her, swiping dank hair out of her face. He looks manically into her eyes then steers her by the elbow up and into the passenger's seat, as though she were a wounded soldier being loaded into a medevac. What has he done?

"Jesus," he whispers huskily, breathing heavily, throwing himself into the car, and again there is that flat brutal rhythm of the wipers.

"You okay?" he asks, clutching her jacketed forearm.

She just looks at his hand there, panting mildly.

"We are so sorry, Stella," Jeff says, flushed.

"I just . . . ," Adrian begins, "I got into this whole thing about how the Ancient Murrelet spends its nights on Vendovi Island and flies over to feed during the day, blah, blah, blah, it doesn't matter. Then we . . . got into this whole thing about Michael Lutz and *Chicken Feed for Dummies* and Jeff asked if you were asleep and I just, you know. Fuck."

Her face pressed against the door, Stella says, "I smell Armor All," which leaves them speechless.

Adrian edges back onto the road, his jaw tight and high. Jeff shakes his head over and over again.

"Can I just ask," Adrian finally says, gingerly, "why didn't you stay at the gas station?"

"I don't know, Adrian! I went in to pee and I came out and you guys were gone! I kept calling you and you didn't answer, and I didn't know *what* to do. I figured if I started walking, maybe I'd run into you broken down on the highway. I didn't know you just completely forgot me, for a fucking hour and a half!"

"Fair enough," adds Jeff.

"Why didn't you answer your fucking phone?" she howls.

"It was turned off," Adrian says. That's his mother's fault too.

"*Why?*" she demands.

Because he's a coward.

"Probably didn't think to try me, I guess," Jeff ventures.

"I didn't have my phone, Jeff. I don't have your number memorized."

Jeff places his hand on Stella's shoulder.

"Even my underwear is soaked."

Adrian makes amends as best he can. He stops at Coeur d'Alene to get her into dry clothes, buys her blueberry scones and café au lait, sits in the back seat with her while Jeff drives. They put in Malcolm Arnold's *Fantasy for Oboe*, which comforts her, then listen to her Joni Mitchell CD, the one with the symphony when Joni's had too much Paris jazz and late-night painting and cigarettes. They listen from cover to cover while Stella looks out her window or closes her eyes with her head back, every few minutes whispering, "Christ."

"Looks like it's going to be a slam dunk, though," Adrian finally says, checking the Rare Bird Alert as they pass through Spokane. "The accentor's been perched near this 'marker 12' on and off all day, like he's waiting for us."

He turns to smile at Stella, but she's asleep. Her expression is so mild he almost believes she's forgiven him.

North Cascades National Park, Washington. Stella, Jeff, and Adrian wait for the accentor all day from two o'clock on, standing, sitting, and circling the trees around marker 12. That night, they set up camp by a nearby stream, the water fast and cold. They eat and sleep, walk back the next morning, and wait again—the wind now relentless, the sky a sea of clouds.

"He's still around here somewhere. Let's find him," Adrian tells Stella, tugging her to her feet.

"How are we supposed to do that?"

"This is what I do, honey. Just let me show you."

Adrian begins reloading his pack, so Jeff does the same, peering from under his ball cap. "Where you thinkin'?"

"Up the pass." Adrian gestures with a stiff hand as if saluting.

"Seriously? Don't accentors like a nice little meadow or, you know, backyard?" Jeff ventures. "You really think it'd be farther up the mountain?"

"It blew all the way here from Siberia, Jeff," Adrian instructs. "The wind's now blowing thirty-five miles per hour due north. We follow the wind."

Adrian leads Jeff and Stella up Cascade Pass—over cracks and crevices filled with snow, amid western red cedar, Douglas firs, devil's club with its trippy, oversized leaves, and something Jeff calls bunchberries, turning red from green. They spot a Clark's Nutcracker, a raven, a female White-tailed Ptarmigan, and a fat, pink-red White-winged Crossbill, but no Siberian Accentor.

Three hours and four blustery miles from the foot of the pass, Jeff says, "That bird's just gone, man," stopping to breathe.

"I told the kids I'd call," huffs Stella. "Come on, Adrian, it's snowing. Let's go back."

"That bird's up at the lake, I'll just bet ya." Adrian sniffs and begins re-Velcroing his boot. They are now thirteen miles from where they arrived the day before. He's back in his element, gathering steam.

"What lake?" Jeff asks.

"Up Sahale Arm, that way. It'll be a great place to camp.

Come on, Stell, you'll love it. Plus maybe we can get up above the snow." He can salvage this thing. He can salvage it all.

Jeff says, "This wind's nippy, though, man, seriously," but Adrian keeps working at his boots.

Stella takes her upper lip between her teeth, turns, and walks up the trail.

Adrian calls, "I'm right behind you!" chucking Jeff on the back on his way toward Stella. "You with me, bud?"

They continue on through vine maple, stinging nettle, tangled growths of alder. Every so often, Adrian takes out his MP3 player and sends the bird's call into the air—*ti-ti-ti*—hoping the Accentor will be duped into looking for a counterfeit mate, lost in the same place at the same time, miles and miles from home.

At some point, Stella calls out, "My ears are killing me, you guys."

Adrian hears it as a sort of accompaniment to the wind, but no one responds, not even Jeff. Adrian only barks an occasional comment or command now, hunching his shoulders against the blowing snow, setting an unwavering pace for all their sakes—consumed with the punishing ache of his muscles, the numbing cold of his face and fingers and toes, the whiteout bliss of the increasingly impossible task at hand.

When they finally come upon the alpine lake, they halt at the sight of it. It ruffles with the wind, then stills in seconds, only to ruffle again—a shelf of shining water in the eaves of a rugged cathedral surrounded by a snowfield—and in the next thirty seconds, before they resume movement, the swirling snow begins driving down harder, thicker, and wilder, in a stinging milky squall.

Adrian screams, "*Unbelievable! Get the tarp, let's get the tent up!*"

In some burlesque pantomime, they grab and fall upon each

other, trying to unload poles and cords from each others' backs, uncoiling flying ropes with tarps nearly lifting them from the ground then folding around their bodies like capes—finally whipping out of their hands entirely. When they try to secure the tent, they can't. It's all they can do to keep their belongings from blowing down the mountainside.

"*Over there!*" Jeff points, trudging toward a huge lone rock, a stain of gray, near the lake.

Stella doesn't move, just bobs in the sea of snow, barely moored. Adrian reaches out to pull her through the storm by her jacket, both their hiking boots brimming.

Jeff shouts, "We're just going to have to wait it out! There's nothing else we can do!"

"Just stay with me, okay?" Adrian wails to Stella. "*Stay with me.*"

Mount Terror, Mount Challenger, Mount Fury, Mount Despair, Mount Torment, Desolation Peak: these are the names people have given this place. Once the blizzard has passed, they set up the tent (though the tarp has flown away and can't be found), then crawl one at a time into its dark womb. As the wind rushes outside, they pick through their belongings to see what they can use. Is there a shirt left dry? A pair of socks? They take off what is soaking and put on what is salvageable, and in the blue-green light of the lantern, Jeff is asleep in minutes.

Stella wriggles herself into her sleeping bag and downs a handful of almonds while Adrian gathers everything wet into one nylon bag and tosses it out the flap into the snow.

When he's zipped up the tent again, he stands over her, the approaching weight of defeat tugging him by the kneecaps.

"Stell, I'm so sorry about the gas station. I don't know what happened in my *brain*. Can you forgive me?"

Either she doesn't hear him or chooses not to respond, only curls up like a potato bug and closes her eyes.

When she opens them again moments later, Adrian is lying beside her in his own bag, peering at the fleshy rise above her nose, beneath her eyebrows.

She says, "Tell me, okay?" Her lips are slightly parted. Her eyes are watering from the wind and sun.

Adrian unzips his sleeping bag and pulls her hand to his chest. Tell her.

She whispers, "I walked on the highway in the rain, Adrian. I waded through the blizzard. I'm *with* you, right? I'm with you right now."

Outside the tent, the wind kneels down to the blue silence of snow. Something breaking echoes from the distance.

"Did something happen?" she asks, her voice like a slowly opening palm.

"Nothing happened," he lies. "I really wanted that bird," which is true. "That thing with Lassiter passing . . . I mean, this could finally be my time, you know?" What can he say? *I've been a freak since I was thirteen years old but somehow forgot to mention it?*

She withdraws her hand from his chest, her expectant face suddenly lax. She mutters, "Okay, Adrian." Then she douses the lantern, turns toward the rustling tent wall, and zips the sleeping bag over her head.

This is how disappointment looks from the back.

Adrian closes his eyes. The echoing *crash* sounds again. The glaciers. They can't re-form in winter anymore. There isn't enough snowfall to offset the spring melt.

He lies anxious, listening for another crash that, for the moment, doesn't come. There is only the hard ground beneath his hip through the mat. Stella's breathing. The cold and ache. The miles they'll travel tomorrow across Desolation Peak Trail.

He finds the tiny zippered bag in his vest pocket and fishes out a Lunesta, identifying it by its familiar size and shape—small, like Xanax, but a bit flatter, harder—and a Vicodin for his legs and back. That's what it's for, after all. It's so fat and white it gleams in the dark. He gropes around the tent willy-nilly for his pack and finally locates it only a foot or so from his head, where he finds his water, frozen. He doesn't need water anyway.

How could he have forgotten Stella on the road? How could he so easily accept there were two in the car when there should have been three? She *had* slipped out at the gas station without anyone noticing. Plus these days it's always just Jeff and him, and he was ridiculously groggy from lack of sleep. Worthy justifications, all. He vows to try and believe them.

He takes deep, conscious breaths and waits for the pills to enter his bloodstream. Like a priest presiding over some strange mass, he silently recites:

Accípiter coóperii.

Accípiter gentílis.

Accípiter striátus.

He summons to mind the three auklets and the Red-winged Blackbird (*Agelaíus phoeníceus*), and by the time he gets to *Ánthus hódgsoni*, the Olive-backed Pipit, his life list is corporeal and firm, the subtle weight of it like a companion on his arm.

Sun in his eyes, he sloshes through warm swamp water, the canoe rocking behind him, the huge woodpecker hammering, hammering, hammering, then silent as a pool cue. His father stands on the riverbank, steam rising from his shoulders, with a briefcase dangling from his hand like a Bible salesman. His mother crouches naked, dripping wet, in the boat—not like a mother at all—as mounted police crash through branches and stalks, collapsing a path from the forest to the waterside. Their enormous snorting horses back up, inch forward, back up, inch forward, while the police train their guns at the arm of the cypress.

Adrian's pants are frozen to his ass. He liberates his thighs from one another and creaks open his jaw. He chokes back the snippet of a dream that jabs at his throat like an ice pick. Maybe it's the frozen zipper of his jacket, jutting into his neck.

Stella's head is heavy on his belly. He carefully lifts it, as he would a patient's when he unhooks the breathing tube from round her ears.

"Don't," she says, before she's even fully conscious.

Adrian slides out from under her with his lips blubbering out of some primal emotional reflex and crawls along the ground to the opening.

When he emerges, Jeff is shuffling around in the snow. Chipper, he calls out, "'Morning, Colonel!"

They pack up, nothing fitting back into its container right, too many things wet or frozen, too stiff or dripping to pack, and they look like three nomads—pieces of clothing hanging from bungee cords on the outsides of their packs, tent poles slick with ice protruding from their carriers, sleeping bags and mats in haphazard clumps, scarves encircling their faces.

As they slog through the clouds down the mountain, Stella finds it.

"Adrian, Jeff." She pokes her toe at the snow. "Look at this poor guy."

She bends to pick up a stiff sparrowlike bird the colors of butterscotch, cherrywood, and sandstone. She turns it over in her gloved hands. Its eyes are milky brown and staring from a black mask under yellow brows, with a bill like a finely sharpened lead pencil.

"That's him all right," Adrian says, looking down on the creature. "That's the Accentor." His sinuses start to fill with pressure, but he shakes it off and walks away.

"I can't list it, though, Stell," he calls back, watching his step over a patch of uneven rock, willing himself forward. "Dead birds don't count."

Chapter Four

4601 (11/7/09): Yesterday I sat on a log and smoked a cigar after work (5:45 p.m.). I was watching a blue heron fishing on the SR sound. I don't smoke cigars much any more because it usually makes me want to drink. But this time it didn't. Blue herons have yellow eyes that shine like they have a fire in there belly. If there is one they act like they don't want anybody to know about it because they act so cool on the outside. I talked to one of the new boys when I was patching a sidewalk out by the bowling alley. Said he was pretty impressed by the reservation. Real nice guy. Even asked if he could help me out. Thats a first. Down here from one of the Carolinas I forget which. Nice to have a conversation.

Adrian sits at the kitchen table in front of his laptop eating a whole-grain English muffin with butter and grapefruit marmalade, shaking his head at this increasingly pathetic excuse for a birding post. When he checks his own account on the site, he finds that this man, this amateur, is the most frequent visitor to his page. There you have it.

Honestly, at this point, it *would* be nice to have a conversation.

"All you ever care about is your list," Stella said when they got home from the Cascades. "Where are your priorities?"

She'd made implications like this before—that he was obsessive, that he had trouble seeing the forest for the trees (or, in this case, the trees for the forest), but he won't apologize for his one strength. Besides, no one finds nearly nine hundred species of birds for the sake of a number. If she can't see this about him, she doesn't know him at all.

He clicks onto the new Audubon study. He used to find respite in the traditional, almost nostalgic feel of the site, but these days it's nothing but an early warning system. Based on forty years of data, the study says global warming is driving 60 percent of the 305 bird species found in North America in winter far from their normal wintering grounds. A continent of species is moving, year by year, decade by decade, as far as four hundred miles north—from Kentucky to Minnesota, from Louisiana to Wisconsin, Montana to Alaska—out of environments they've adapted to for centuries, eons, to escape the unseasonably warm and rising temperatures, into ever less suitable, ever narrowing habitats.

It's code red, like the disappearing frogs, the diminishing colonies of bees, the lifeboat polar bears. Adrian imagines the birds winging, branch to branch, feathers ablaze, pushed finally to the Arctic Sea, oil floating in great slicks across the waves to greet them.

He slides his phone toward him on the table like a deck of cards he's about to cut. Picks it up. Slides his thumb across the glass. Hits voicemail, finally deciding that it can't hurt to listen to the damn thing. He hopes June's all right, actually. He certainly doesn't wish her harm. It's just the landscape of his mother is too vast and strange for him to traverse. He isn't her caretaker, after all. He isn't her steward.

Cowardice twists in him. He spins the phone. Can't do it.

A subtle ringing in his ears, he returns to the laptop. One click away like a bleating siren: "Common Birds in Decline," saying the average population of North America's most common and beloved birds has fallen 68 percent since *Star Trek* first aired. This, while Adrian was buying winter jackets, memorizing the states and their capitals, learning to use chopsticks, and getting married. Where there were thirty birds—Eastern Meadowlarks, Field Sparrows, Snow Buntings, Whip-poor-wills—now there are six. Like a POW bracelet around his wrist, Adrian wears the sickening awareness that every time he eats breakfast, one endangered species of bird—the Prairie Chicken, the Tricolored Blackbird, the Mottled Duck, the Whooping Crane—vanishes from the world. Where there were 400,000 birds, there are 1,000. Where there were 60,000 birds, there are none.

Adrian looks again at the phone. Reanimates the screen. Hits voicemail and presses the arrow.

June's voice starts, "I think we were disconnected, but . . ."—hesitates—"Anyway, Adrian, I really need you to come home." There is a short silence. She hangs up.

Kingston. The nonhour of four in the afternoon, the day before Thanksgiving, 1981. In school that morning, Adrian had celebrated the great mythical coming together of the Indians and the Pilgrims. There was disagreement among historians about when and where the holiday had first been celebrated in the Americas, Mrs. Garvey said, though it had been celebrated by European Christians since the sixteenth century and by European pagans and Native Americans for millennia. Anyway, Thanksgiving is about goodwill, trust, and gratitude. Gratitude for family and the plenty of the earth, Mrs. Garvey said. It's so great when everybody gets along!

When she asked if anyone in the class had ever met a Native American, Adrian kept his hand down like everybody else. He hadn't really, because his mother's father, a full-blooded Catawba, had died when his mom was small. Adrian and Evan didn't even know about him until they moved to Kingston, when June mentioned this in a way that made them feel they didn't need to talk about it again. Adrian didn't know if she'd hid it because she was mad or ashamed or if she just forgot. They had thought their mom was just a regular American and that they were regular Americans. Plus, she didn't look like an Indian. It was easy to forget. At the end of the day, Mrs. Garvey gave out caramels. *We're thirteen-year-olds, not little kids*, thought Adrian—still, he stashed one in his pocket for later.

Adrian had taken over the snow shoveling (and mowing) from Evan, who recently graduated and left for Jackson Hole. Evan went to see the West, to work with his big hands and strong muscles apprenticing with a master log-house builder his mother's partner, Suzanne, had known from an old stint at tile work. Their mom didn't tempt Evan to go to college. She let him leave with her favorite sleeping bag, Toll House cookies, her almost-brand-new skis, and three hundred bucks. Adrian had admired the whole thing. It wasn't something he himself would want (he wanted to go to college and preferred lemon-meringue pie to cookies), but it was admirable from all sides.

Evan had pulled tight onto his neck when they hugged goodbye. When their eyes locked, Evan looked like Adrian felt in the night—very small in a world unbearably large—but when Evan released him, he had that same old "fuck you" face on. He strutted out the front door, parted the Hudson Valley air with the exhilaration of the Wild West, and filled the yard with waving and yelling. Gesturing all about him like a rogue prince, he called back to Adrian, "Hey, you're in charge!"

Now Adrian grasped the handle of the snow shovel with both hands. Since he hadn't shoveled yesterday, the snow had melted in the heat of the day and refrozen again in the afternoon, so he had to gouge. That was okay; his mom had promised to make spaghetti for dinner that night before some gallery thing she and Suzanne had to do.

With an uneven vibration in his arms, slush jumping into his boots to melt into his socks, he shoveled all the way up one side of the driveway toward the curb: gouge, gouge, shovel— throw . . . Gouge, gouge, shovel—throw . . . Then he turned, straddling the outside line of the jagged aisle he'd just created, breathing heavier, exposing sparkling concrete, scraping his way back toward the house, singing—

"I wish that I had Jessie's girl! I wish that I had Jessie's girl!" Pivot 'round the corner, and one "Where can I find a—"

His father stood before him.

Adrian's feet sunk deep as he stared at the apparition puffing steam like himself. His thoughts flew to the garage, the kitchen, the tools, the cutlery. He was off guard, impossibly small, and dressed like a child gone sledding.

"You look at me like I'm some kind of monster," his father said, low. "Do I look like a monster to you?"

A blood-red cardinal rushed to a leafless magnolia. That's exactly what he'd heard his mother say to Suzanne: *Dean is a monster.* He acted like one, and his hair was long now, and he had a stubbly beard and no jacket even though it was freezing.

"Nah," his father answered himself. "Just surprised to see me, I bet." He had some kind of briefcase.

Adrian swiped at a drop of sweat that ran into his eye in spite of the cold.

"Are you crying?"

"It's *sweat*. I'm working." Adrian held himself up against the handle of the broad shovel.

"I didn't know where you guys were. Did you realize that?" his father said, flicking ice crystals from Adrian's chest.

Adrian shrugged out from under him. "Quit it."

His father let his hand fall to his side, and he stared a hole straight into Adrian's chin.

"Just . . . why are you looking at me like that?"

His father shook his head, hitched up his pants, and turned toward the house.

"Leave her alone!" screamed Adrian.

Adrian's father stalked along the path Adrian had just cleared. "You think she's so fucking innocent?" he called back. "You got no idea!"

"She doesn't want to see you! I know that much."

As his father knocked on the front door, Adrian loosened his feet from the snow, shouting, "She's blending spaghetti sauce! She won't be able to hear you!"

His father slowly turned the knob on the door, peered in, and stepped across the threshold of Adrian's new life.

Adrian ran.

He ran down the block and took an immediate left on Walnut Street. Ran two more blocks and turned onto Abruyn, slipping and sliding. The pain in his lungs and legs was already killing him, from crying and gasping and running.

Another long block more and he turned left again. Forgot to look at the street. Lost track of the blocks and turns. His mom and Suzanne would be home in less than an hour. Would his father wait that long?

At the front door of a random brick house, Adrian knocked. Waited four seconds, knocked again. Scrambled back down the steps, skipped a house, and went to the next. *Knocked*. Waited, peering back and forth from one end of the street to the other, fearing his father's brown car. *Was it brown?* Or dark blue. Pounded six more times.

"God, who is it?" A timid human voice inside.

"Please," Adrian gasped, "help me. I'm . . . I have to call the police."

There was a pause. "Are you a little boy?"

"No. *Yes. Someone might be following me!*"

The lock in the door tumbled open and a girl's face appeared between Adrian and safety. She frowned at him and stepped aside. "Come in, hurry up."

He scrambled inside and fell back against the door, slamming it, his breaths coming so fast and out of control he thought he might throw up.

"Calm down, okay?" she said, no more than a teenager herself, maybe sixteen, seventeen. "What's wrong?"

Adrian scanned the room. "*I've gotta use your phone.*"

She stepped back and motioned to a phone by the couch.

Adrian ran to the phone, picked it up, and sputtered, on the brink of tears, "I don't know the number. I have to call the police."

The girl trotted from the room and quickly returned flipping the pages of a phone book—"Hold on a second"—and gave him the number.

He dialed, spoke into the mouthpiece. "Hello, yes, a man's in my house. He's a monster. *He already went in* . . . No, I . . . ran away, but my mom will be home soon." He glanced quickly up at the girl. "Six twenty-nine Lindsley Avenue . . . Adrian Mandrick . . . Well, I'm not calling from . . . Just a minute." He put his hand over the receiver, quietly pleading, "Can I have the number here? They can't file the—"

Ellen Rason gave him her name, her number, her address.

When he'd given the police the information, Adrian hung up, sat heavily down upon the couch, and dropped his head into his hands. "They said they'd check it out."

She didn't speak then, just sat gently beside him. Adrian heard her swallow and the air puffing from her nose, the beautiful creature.

Thirty-five minutes later—Ellen watching through the curtains in the front window, Adrian drinking a Dr Pepper, his socks drying over his boots by the door—the phone rang. She bolted to it, then handed it over to him like they were in this thing together.

"Hello?" his heartbeat speeding up anew. "*Mom*. Are you okay?" He looked at Ellen's soft white hands with the tiny blue veins. "Is he gone?"

Ellen stood waiting, her mouth slightly ajar, her light hair gathered into one of her hands.

"Divorce papers?" Adrian didn't understand. "Oh. I didn't— Huh? I just . . . ran. Some girl . . . I mean, Ellen Rason's house. She let me—" He looked at her, sheepish. "It's five twenty-seven Ponckhockie."

Ellen gave him a little half smile and released her hair. Then she held out her hand for the phone and, when he gave it to her, placed it on the cradle, like a period at the end of a baffling run-on sentence.

"So, everything's good, then," she said.

He knew he should feel relieved, but he felt tiny on that couch. Like a very young child whose feet barely touched the floor. His father hadn't done anything wrong.

"I guess he just left some divorce papers on the kitchen table. Nobody got hurt or anything."

"It's sweet you were so worried about your mom like that."

"She's coming to pick me up."

"Cool."

"I should probably just wait outside."

"If you want," she said, and gathered up his soda can and the phone book.

Adrian stood. "I guess you thought some crazy man was screamin' through your door."

"If you ever need a place to hide out again . . . ," she said. Adrian thought she'd just walk into the kitchen with the can and the book, but she tucked the phone book under her arm and opened the door for him.

As he stepped out onto the icy landing, he remembered the caramel in his pocket and thought to offer it to Ellen. He twisted around toward her again, but he slipped and skidded on his knees, and as he tried to right himself with his other foot, the first nonexistent step seemed to disappear from underneath it, and his boot, ankle, and knee followed it down into a jagged heap.

He let out a muffled, startled scream.

There she was, in only her skirt and tee shirt in the cold,

kneeling beside him, knuckles blanching white, palms down on the frigid concrete. "Is it your ankle?"

Grimacing into the shimmering air, his breath coming in rasping bursts.

"Can you walk?" She forced her forearms under his padded armpits as Adrian pried off his boot in a firestorm of pain.

"Is that my . . . *bone?*"

It was his tibia. It was fractured.

His mother rushed him to the hospital, where everyone came to his rescue with haste and few words, gesturing like in a silent film. The pain was way beyond anything he'd experienced before, but his doctor was unfailingly kind, with his cool, dry hands and perfect fingernails, all of which made Adrian feel safe. Adrian was "so brave," the doctor said, he wasn't even going to put him to sleep when they screwed him back together. Instead, he gave him a "nerve block" so he wouldn't feel anything and a pill to make him sleepy. (Adrian hoped he'd be able to watch, but no such luck.) After the procedure, the doctor prescribed Tylenol #3 and put a brace on his leg, which would be replaced by a cast once the wounds had begun to heal. As Adrian was being wheeled out, the doctor patted him on the shoulder and said, "Nice work, little man."

Adrian's mom drove him home spread across the back seat, helped him into the house on his crutches, then laid him out in his bed. She and Suzanne debated hotly about whether they'd go to the gallery opening they'd planned to attend as they tore apart pieces of bread for the next day's stuffing, and finally Adrian broke in and said, "Just go, okay? I'll fall asleep as soon as I eat anyway."

He meant it, and they finally drove off and left him in peace, though with no spaghetti on the stove, only a bed tray with Campbell's tomato soup and a rat cheese and Miracle Whip sandwich.

He'd been given a Tylenol with codeine pill when he got home from the hospital. Now, lying in the privacy of his own sheets, he experienced the sweet, numbing relaxation of the drugs tilting through his body like a cruise on a breezy sea, and he, a bit of cocoa butter on a hot deck chair. He was thinking of Ellen.

As he was summoning the image of her tongue moistening her own lips and taking another sip of his ginger ale, he noticed something alien on his bedside table. It was an envelope with his name scrawled on it, tucked between his lamp and his globe.

He picked it up, feeling as though he were about to be a part of some espionage—thinking for a moment, nonsensically, that it might have been from the girl. He felt its dry, smooth face, ran his finger along the almost-sharp edge, then ripped it open, all at once placing the familiar handwriting.

I know your mother talks shit about me to you but you don't know. When you were little she had you naked in the bathroom doing something to you. You understand what I'm talking about? Don't ever forget it. Stay as far away from her as you can. Never trust her.

Adrian reread the message.

Naked in the bathroom. *Doing* something.

He flinched unconsciously with the weightless note in his hand. The light in the room shifted, as though a shadow were passing over the sun, and a high whine lodged itself behind his temples. He was alone.

When he bowed his head, images began amassing in a heap in his mind like rubble—out of context—

A steamy bathroom. Round, brown nipples dotted with swollen bumps. The fear of discovery. His mother's face flushed. The sickening humiliation of something running uncontrollably down his leg.

He shot up in bed.

You think she's so innocent, his father had called out as they stood in the driveway, staring at Adrian like something terrible was inside him he couldn't let out. *His mother?* Impossible. But the obsessions, the scenes, of two hours before—his father's brown (or blue) car, the mad rampage through the frozen neighborhood, the senseless police call, and the mortifying fall onto Ellen Rason's icy welcome mat—were nothing now, hollowed out by those few words on a page.

He pulled himself from bed, his ankle stitched and fat, and hobbled into his mother's bedroom on his too-tall crutches. He stood queasy, helpless; then he approached her dresser and began rummaging through the drawers—cautiously, then recklessly, through stockings and slips and bras and socks, through nightgowns and buttons and ticket stubs and safety pins. He didn't know what he was looking for, but in the bottom drawer was the family photo album.

Blood pooling in his ankle and foot, head spinning, he flipped from page to page. Her face and body language in the pictures seemed strange, grotesque: her blank expression as she lit the candles on a birthday cake while Adrian sat in giddy anticipation; her guilty turn from the camera, holding a hand in front of her face at their spring garage sale; her lopsided grin as she draped an arm around Evan's shoulder by the balloon man who made animals into party tricks at the Kingston city park. Even the smell of perfume that hung in the room, the amber that had always comforted him, was suspect, past sweet, like flowers left too long in a vase.

He called out, "Mom," his voice not yet changed, his chin hairless and soft. She was his mother, his life raft, his home. How can this be turned upside down, flooded, and ruined?

He knew his parents hated each other. Who could know what was true and what was false, where there was so much loathing? But no person would lie about such a thing, and those bathroom images had come into his mind with such insistence, images he'd never before recalled. He shook his head to try and clear them. His throat grew tight and hot, but then his eyes lit on a fat red book—the *Physicians' Desk Reference*—lying open on the bedside table.

Within those unfamiliar pages, there was a pharmacological solution for every disease, a tonic for every ailment. There were photographs of thousands of pharmaceutical drugs in exquisite Technicolor, beautiful and diverse: tiny pills—delicate and powerful; huge pills—jellied and thick; tablets and capsules; octagonal, oval, circular, triangular. Resting on the armchair beside the bed, Adrian lost himself in contraindications, dosage, and administration. He read adverse reactions, even waded through a bit of clinical pharmacology. Then he looked up Tylenol #3 to determine how much more he could take. Here, he instinctively knew, was the antidote to his father's letter. It was both science, he thought, and magic.

He unfolded and read the note again.

Don't ever forget it . . . Never trust her.

Adrian should tear it up. If his mother saw it, she would be devastated, wouldn't she? He should save her from even being on the edges of an accusation so perverse. But he couldn't tear it up, because what if it was evidence? What if it was the truth? So he hid it underneath her mattress, urging it along the rough ticking, pushing it back, as far as his arm would reach.

He hopped on his wooden crutches into the kitchen and pulled a Yoo-hoo out of the fridge, teetering dizzily at the counter. He washed down a second tablet of Tylenol #3, the drug's chalky aftertaste pleasant in his mouth (or was it the Yoo-hoo?), then made his way to the bathroom medicine cabinet to see what else he could find.

"Adrian. *Adrian . . . Adrian!*" It was pitch-black outside as Suzanne crouched over him.

"Honey, are you all right?" Adrian's mother trotted across the room and dropped onto the couch against him.

"Get away . . . ," he said, his mouth full of cotton wool, and pushed at her hip with his knees.

"You scared us to death!" she said. "When we got home, we thought we'd let you sleep. But we've been trying to wake you for the last ten minutes, and you have been dead to the world. We were this close to calling an ambulance."

Her thumb and her forefinger almost touched, as her face twisted just outside his eye slits.

She tried to take his head in her hands but he pulled out of her grasp. "Look at his eyes, Suzie. We're going to the hospital!"

"Stop. I'm not going to the hospital. I . . . bet you I shouldn't have taken two of those Tylenol pills. My ankle was killing me." (The Seconal hadn't helped matters.)

"Don't ever do that! Please don't ever take any more medicine than you're told to. You can overdose on those pills. Do you understand?"

"I understand."

Adrian spent the next week in a carnival of medicated splendor. Suzanne, it seemed, had a lot of invisible ailments. (Surely she had been the one to bring the PDR into the house.) The peas left over from Thanksgiving dinner wouldn't stay on his fork on the two-Dexedrine day; they kept jumping up and off with the twitching of his hand.

On the day of the two Valium, he stopped taking his Tylenol #3 to get a more pure reaction from his body and noted a deeply relaxed response. His limbs were draped across the pillows of the couch as he watched *I Dream of Jeannie* and *Bewitched* reruns. The old programs were uncharacteristically sad, but his best old favorite, *Dragnet*, sent him into an amused delirium.

Darvon was a challenge. He didn't have any idea what to expect. According to the PDR, it was a painkiller, but Adrian took two Darvon at nine thirty in the morning and started hallucinating on the couch around ten fifteen.

All around him things were shimmering: the alabaster lamp, the *TV Guide*, the candy dish, the little brass teapot by the fake fireplace. His pajama pants took on the shimmer of satin and began to shake, right on his own body, and when he pulled out his elastic waistband to look inside, his penis was vibrating into a little mound of molten wax.

He *screeched* and stood up, pants dropping to his knees, and balanced precariously on one foot and a cast—waiting to become

himself again, a part of a family. He imagined his mother standing over him, shaking her head, then kindly reaching down to re-
arrange the pillow under his ankle, as she had done a dozen times
in the last days.

His father's note seemed to make sense of a splinter of pain
that had always been lodged in him. Gave it a reason, provided
some semblance of proof. Even now, as he swore to forget it—
to think, instead, of Ellen Rason's sand-dollar-sized breasts—
the words of the letter were reproducing in his subconscious
like mutant cells, tapping tiny sharp nails into the house of his
identity.

———————

Stella speed-walks into the kitchen waving some kind of document, and Adrian startles, clicking off his phone, standing, escaping toward the stairs. *Come home*, his mother's message said. *We
got disconnected.*

"Adrian, wait," Stella calls.

Now he remembers, that same night, under the tent of his
rough sheets, during the time of his father's letter, still high on
Darvon, he began the first species list of his life. He wanted to
keep the birds but separate them from his mother somehow, to
define the birds for himself, to begin to unravel the seemingly
inextricable braid that was his mother and the earth and sky.

"Hold on!" Stella says, yanking him back toward the kitchen
by the shirt, a grin pulling at her lips for the first time in days.
"You've got to read what I'm going to show you." She holds the
written side of the page of paper against her chest. "Ready?"

Adrian still holds the monolith of his phone in his hand.

The names on that early list . . . House Finch. Chickadee.

"*Adrian*." Red-tailed Hawk, cardinal, turkey vulture, whippoor-will.

"Just read straight down the page," Stella says. "You ready?"

Robin. Crow. Pigeon. Goose.

"This'll take two minutes. Now, don't *examine* it, just read it."

She flashes the paper, but Adrian sees her only peripherally, like an extra in the background of a movie scene. Ibis, wood stork, ruby-throated hummingbird.

"What'd it say?" she asks.

(Pelican, sandpiper, swallow, sparrow.)

"Adrian?"

"Yeah." He rubs the heels of his hands into his eyes. Ivory-billed Woodpecker.

"What did it *say*?"

"I didn't see it," he admits.

Stella laughs, heartily. "Fine. Are you *really ready* this time?"

He didn't know whether to write the ivorybill down that night in his bed. He can't remember if he did.

"Here we go . . ."

Stella flips the page into view. Adrian tries, now, to focus before she retracts it again.

"Okay," he musters. "I see it. 'A bird in the hand . . . ,'" smiling weakly, and turns again toward the stairs to get to a Xanax. "Funny," he tosses back.

Then he'll get out into the sunlight, drive, and take another one. "'Fraid not."

Or a Vicodin. "What?" he asks. He'll take a Vicodin.

"That's not what the paper says."

He looks back, obligatorily. "Well, that's what's *written* on the paper." Xanax, Vicodin, Klonopin, codeine.

"No, actually, it isn't." She chuckles and squints up at him. "Would you like to try again?" She raises her eyebrows in anticipation.

"Okay, whatever. Just . . . *go ahead*."

Stella flashes the paper again, then thrusts it against her chest. Yes, he sees it perfectly.

" 'A bird in the hand,' Stella." This is ridiculous. "What are you trying to prove?"

"That your brilliant brain and superior eyes are, quite simply, deceiving you."

"Give it here." He attempts to snatch the paper from her, but she sweeps it behind her back. "I hate shit like this. Stop."

"No, *read the words. Read the letters*. Read them. *All*."

"Okay, I'm not *deaf*." She is a bullying, self-satisfied stranger. "You don't have to be so fucking mean."

She shoves the page just inches from his face. "What's it say?"

"A, bird, in, the, hand!" He bats impotently at the paper.

Stella pokes her finger at it. "XXX, okay? First it says, XXX. *Then* it says, 'A . . . bird . . . in . . . the . . . *the* . . . hand!' Two *the*s." She barks with bitter laughter.

"Let me see that!" Adrian lurches at her, holds the page in his hands, examines the double-crossing words.

We got disconnected.

"You're the slowest one yet," she says with a condescending pat on his shoulder. "Slower than the entire woodwinds section."

He makes for the hallway. Adderall, oxy, morphine, fentanyl.

"Oh, now he's mad." She trails after him. "Just thought I'd turn the tables on you for once, you're always so—"

"Don't *you're always* me!" he shouts, wheels around. "I'm not *always* anything. Why do you *always* say that?"

"You can't even see whether your own wife is in the car with you!"

"I'm sorry, okay? I'm guilty! *I'm fucked up.*" He's in her face.

"Get away from me!" She shoves him by the shoulders, her nails skim his chin.

"You gonna fight with me now?" he says, stumbling backward, and starts to laugh.

"You asshole," she breathes.

Come home.

Stella seizes her keys from the kitchen counter and storms out. "I'm *never* going on a fucking birding trip with you again."

Chapter Five

Two hours later, Adrian's going nowhere but away. He floats along the Peak to Peak Highway in his Saab, north from Nederland through Ward, the isolated town of eccentrics already packed with snow: bare-bones old shacks, rusted-out pickups and SUVs, cords of firewood piled against every lean-to and shed, houses and cabins clinging here and there to the rocky landscape like barnacles on the back of a gray whale. Two gnarly dogs sit on a weathered porch with bandanas around their necks, whistling a happy tune.

Decidedly high on three Vicodin, he's pretty sure he could be perfectly at home with these hippies and rebels. They make their own warmth. Do what they need to do. Doesn't matter what it looks like or what anybody else says. They're a hell of a lot closer to what matters: staying warm and dry, stockpiling their supplies, gas, food, and water, living and dying. It's a paradise up here.

The clarity of the mountain air is *transcendent*. The branches of the trees have been etched into the sky. He opens his window just a scratch, so he can feel the cool air lick his face and—there is the smell of woodsmoke. He can see it, actually. Trailing from a handful of chimneys into the air. This air is so thin, and so sparklingly transparent—like the world's best lens—it gets him remembering, suddenly, the first time he did acid, which he hasn't thought about in years. LSD did not become his drug of choice, obviously—too much loss of control, too much psychic danger, too many variables (like the pharmacology, for instance!), plus almost nobody looks good in light that bright—but he loved the neon, the slow dance of the arms of trees, the complete freedom from the demands of the body.

He was in college at UVA, years from meeting Stella, miles from his mother. He was "friends" with this older guy who hung out in the student union, who always wore threadbare clothes with a permanent smell of sandalwood in his dreads. This guy said he'd give Adrian (and his buddy, Freemont) a hit of LSD but he said they had to swear an "oath of respect": they couldn't smoke pot or drink beer (to tamp down the high), couldn't sit around laughing their asses off all night (to ward off deeper insight), couldn't drink Coca-Cola products or eat shitty food (to destroy the purity of the "vessel"). This ended up being somehow correct, as it turned out.

Adrian was crying uncontrollably in the shower, foreseeing his own death in an alien landscape, as Freemont tended a small fire they'd made in a cast iron skillet that was part of the kitchen décor, when the bird god appeared. Initially, Adrian was frightened. The creature doesn't exist in literature—either biological or mythological—but it had great, long red legs like a huge chicken, black-and-white downy wings, and the head and shoulders of a pit bull. Adrian tried to step around it to slip out the shower door, but it was too big, and he soon realized he wouldn't be able to escape the beast. So he bowed down to it instead, theoretically; he treated it with sober respect, compassion, care, and by the end of the long shower, Adrian was sitting on the tile floor of the cramped stall with his knees up, letting the now-cold water cascade over his head and his balls get hammered, with the bird god curled tame and ghostlike at his feet. When Freemont showed up, it disappeared down the drain.

Being in the high mountains is like an acid trip. If you don't give it the respect it demands, it can (and will) maim you, what with the sharp rocks, icy-cold water, and dizzying heights. It will take you down. Adrian's got to be especially respectful right now, actually, because he hasn't driven high in two years, and it's a long trip over the guardrail.

Adrian wants to go see Jeff, *that's* what he wants to do. Sometimes talking to Jeff, even when it's not about the subject at hand (and it clearly won't be) is comforting, and right now Adrian is full of a sort of liquid glee but a little bit lonely, so before he gets to the town of Raymond he turns around and drives back the way he came. Faster this time. Whooshing around the bends in the road, now that he has a goal in mind. He can talk to Jeff about the Lassiter memorial he's inviting him to in Orange County, show him photos on his phone—the mansion, the mission, the hotel where Adrian usually stays—pick up a couple of coffees on the way.

Ten minutes or so south of Ward, he comes upon a woman just off the pavement wearing a colorful scarf, waving her arms in the air, while her red Volvo waits patiently on the side of the road. He slows, so as not to frighten her, and waves at her through the glass. Friendly. Beautiful. Everything beautiful.

When he rounds the last curve into Nederland, he brakes a little too hard and turns onto 119 to take in the view at Barker Reservoir for a minute, thinking maybe he'll see some birds, nothing too special probably, though a couple years back he saw three Trumpeter Swans up here, which is pretty crazy. When he's approaching the water, he makes out a man instead, small against the amphitheater of the valley, painting a picture on an easel, and Adrian just fucking pulls over. Pulls over to the side of the road. Scoots the ass of the Saab back into a gravel path. Takes his last slug of the codeine cough elixir and watches the guy paint, though the canvas is too far away to make out the subject (presumably the water). He remembers his binocular, though, after a moment, and whips it out to see if he can get a glimpse of the painting itself. Yes. Sort of. It appears to be, as predicted, the landscape before him: electric-blue sky above, Barker Reservoir deeper blue and wide before him, and the valley sweeping back and up into mountains of green.

The car still running and the light in the sky waning, as he's watching this timeless scene—the easel, the painter in a hat and jacket, the sky, the water, the world—the story of Alexander Wilson comes to him, the story his mother told him the night after the two of them thought they saw the ivorybill and couldn't sleep from excitement. Adrian knows all about Wilson now, of course, and it's a true story, about the renowned, if mediocre, Scottish draftsman and painter on a quest to chronicle in watercolor every bird species in America.

This is the story June told. One day in the early 1800s (right near where they lived at the time in Greenville) Wilson shot at a male Ivory-billed Woodpecker to make a painting of it. That's what the guy did. Shot birds, then painted them. For posterity. And science. But Wilson didn't make a clean shot and only wounded the bird in the wing, and when it didn't die, he thought, *Excellent, now it'll be even more lifelike when I'm painting it, because it is actually alive, but conveniently crippled.* Then he wrapped the bird in a blanket, tucked it under the seat of his carriage, and drove to a nearby hotel to set up shop.

The next part of the story is about the sound the bird made when it was being carted away like a prisoner, which was so eerie and mournful that it made Wilson's horse rear back and just about throw Wilson out of the carriage. It sounded so *human.* Why is this required for true empathy—a human sound? Isn't it enough to sound like a captive bird who's bleeding to death? Adrian's never understood it. Nevertheless, "a humanlike" cry, a childlike cry, in fact, is what Wilson reported, and that's how the story goes and likely always will.

Next thing, Wilson is checking in at the hotel front desk. He's got the bird hidden under his coat because he's afraid the hotel manager won't let him in with an enormous wild bird, and the ivorybill lets out another one of these unworldly, childlike cries, and the manager is like, "What the fuck is that?" and Wilson pulls the woodpecker out from under his cape like a bunch of flowers. This is what June said. Adrian has never forgotten the image. "Like a bouquet of flowers." Well, Wilson and the hotel manager have their laugh, because they're both fucking dweebs, they exchange money and keys, and Wilson takes the bird up to his room like it's Lolita.

In the room, the ivorybill lies there on its side on the hard floor, its chest rising and falling fast, and after a couple minutes, Wilson feels thirsty and thinks his horse is probably thirsty too, so he goes back out to feed and water his horse and drink a beer and maybe eat a brat, and when he comes back, twenty, thirty minutes later, the ivorybill is *wailing* and flapping its wings, way up on top of the window. Curtains are flying, chunks of plaster are scattered all over the bedspread, and a two-foot-square hole has been blasted through the wall all the way to the weatherboard. Wilson is in awe that this bird with the wounded wing is so strong and resourceful, but he also thinks, maybe this bird is hungry too, so he ties the ivorybill to the table by its leg so it can't do any more damage and goes off to find it some grubs. When he comes back again, with what grubs he might have found just out in the yard there, the ivorybill has essentially destroyed the table.

Now Wilson is a little pissed, and he knows he'd better get to work painting, and fast, because he's no match for this bird, and that's what he does, while the ivorybill stabs at his wrists and fingers with its sharp keratin bill, staring him down with cold yellow eyes.

Adrian remembers how when June told the story, he hoped the ivorybill would break free and blast its way out into the night, with the painter's book spoiled forever, always missing one bird. But no.

Wilson finished his precious painting, still one of the most famous illustrations of the ivorybill in existence. Later that night, and the next day and the next, he tried to feed the wild creature, but it refused to eat and refused to eat and, on the third night, it died in a corner of that little room under the hole it had made in the wall when it still held out hope of escape.

June said Wilson was terribly sorry about the death of the bird, that when he'd written about the experience, he said he'd loved and admired the ivorybill and would never forgive himself. Then June said, "But listen,"—swiping Adrian's tears away—"I think that's the bird we saw."

It's a sad story. Adrian sits in the idling Saab, the empty cough-syrup bottle in his hand, having forgotten what it was he was so intent on doing earlier. He licks the inside of the rim of the bottle, just for the musky flavor. He almost wishes he had a hit of acid right now. But not really. He takes one more Vicodin instead, pushing it to the back of his throat, eyes comic book wide as he swallows with the familiar jab to the throat. He wishes he could paint, like the guy standing out in the brisk weather with a brush in his hand. Maybe he'll go talk to him. He looks lonely too, out there all on his own, with that chill coming off the reservoir—though, for all Adrian knows, somebody's probably making him lentil soup and homemade bread, feeding logs into the woodstove in the soft light of their stained glass windows, in a house just up the road that the guy built himself, something like that.

Adrian does not know what his mother wants. He doesn't know why *now*. He doesn't want to find out. And he's *not* going to fly out to Kingston and show up at her front door. Clearly, there's something she wants to tell him in person, or show him, but he's no longer at her beck and call. If it's important enough, she'll leave another message, one that actually says something. "I want you to know I'm s—" she said. *I want you to know I'm setting up a trust fund for your children. I want you to know I'm stripping for young boys in the afternoons and starting my own website. I want you to know I'm straight. Stranded. Stuck in a briar patch.*

That woman on the side of the road, the waving woman, Adrian thinks suddenly, had been having car trouble, *you idiot*, and he slams the Saab into gear, pulls out onto the road, and speeds north again. Probably too late now, but it's worth a shot.

———

When he climbs a little light-headed out of the Saab, the auburn-haired woman blurts out, "Dr. Mandrick?"

Her nose is running. She clomps toward him exaggeratedly, as if to say, *Thank God*.

He's startled at first, because he is not, in this moment, Dr. Mandrick, not the Dr. Mandrick he wants anyone to recognize, because this Dr. Mandrick is too *high*, but he realizes this woman works at the hospital, and nothing can be done but smile broadly.

"I am so sorry," he says. "Did you see me whiz by you earlier? I was listening to a podcast." No idea why he said that.

"I'm just happy to see you now!" she says. Deborah. It's Deborah.

"I actually thought someone was just waving to be friendly, but of course I didn't know it was you, Deborah." He points at her like she's won a round of a game show.

She chuckles. "It's no problem, Doctor. Thanks for coming back."

"You bet. What's going on? You didn't call anybody?"

"Phone's dead. Perfect for a hospice nurse, right? Let's hope nobody dies before sundown."

"Right?" he chimes in, standing with his hands on his hips for support.

"I was just about to start walking. I thought somebody would stop, but three people dissed me. Sorry, not you." She smiles like she's drinking a hot toddy in front of a warm fire, and it makes him smile too. "I'm just out of gas. My gauge is screwed up."

Adrian nods, then throws open the passenger-side door to the Saab. "Hop in."

During the ten-minute drive to Nederland to purchase a can of gas, Adrian offers to plug Deborah's phone into his car charger, which she accepts. They're both giddy for their own reasons, Adrian can only assume, yet they are giddy. They make some slightly off-color jokes about the town of Ward. They laugh about how Adrian waved to her when she was broken down, like he was saying, *Hello! Tough shit about your car!* Deborah says she used to be a certified nursing assistant, then volunteered in hospice, then decided to get her RN, and is now a hospice nurse. She spends a decent amount of time at the hospital, where she interviews with potential clients and their families but does the bulk of her work in-home, for hospice. When the hospital "can no longer serve." Adrian's experience with hospice people has been varied. Occasionally he finds them a little self-satisfied, but Deborah has a sort of devil-may-care attitude that cheers him.

At one point she says, "You have to attend to your own joy," not in relation to him, but to her own assertion that she's going to get a fish tank. She says she refuses to apologize for it, and why should she? Attend to your own joy. Adrian can't argue it. He doesn't mention the birds, but he tells her he loves the outdoors, even the cold.

When she's inside paying for the gas, he rereads the text that came in from Stella hours ago, before he even left Boulder.

Hey. I don't know where u are. I've been thinking about this morning. You need to do what you need to do but you're very far away and I'm locked out. Michaela said it too. What's wrong with Dad? I'm sorry if you don't like hearing it but it's true. I'm sorry I pushed you. . .Come home okay? Can we talk??

As Adrian is again considering a reply, Deborah comes back, the car floods with cool air and happy noise, and he pockets the phone. She says she'd like to buy him a drink for helping her out. A drink sounds so good to him. He says he should probably get home, though, and she says they could go somewhere for just one drink.

Adrian sticks to his guns and starts back to the highway instead, saying no thanks necessary, he's just glad he happened by.

Once they're driving north again, she says, "Tell me what made you want to be a doc. Unless everybody always asks you that."

A doc. He likes that word. Like a man of the people—a mechanic or a bricklayer. Everybody does always ask him that, and he has a rote response: something about his deep respect for science, and the importance of modern medicine in an increasingly complex world. But that's the Twitter answer, the 140-character response.

"You know, I've never cured a single patient," he begins, twisting the steering wheel with the palm of one hand.

"Well, but—"

"It's true. Never cured anybody. Never saved anybody's life. Never made a brilliant diagnosis. I rarely even get blood on my hands." These aren't admissions, they're facts. "I knew I'd never do those things. I deal *exclusively* in the avoidance of pain. That's what matters to me. And the alteration of consciousness. I make it possible for braver doctors to work," he says, simply. He glances at her out of the corner of his eye, but her head's inclined, looking up at the stars. "I'm not brave, but I am precise."

He can smell the gas sloshing around in the can in the back seat.

"And humble too," she says, without a trace of sarcasm. "I'm with you, about the avoidance of pain. Morphine's my manna from heaven."

People often use religious metaphors when talking about opiates.

"My patients tell me all about their spouses and kids and grandkids and great-grandkids," Deborah says, sliding her hands between her thighs to warm them. "Sometimes, when I'm alone with them, when their spouses or kids are at the grocery store or taking a walk, taking a minute to themselves, they tell me what they wish they'd done different in their life. They tell all these old stories in supersonic detail. Then at a certain point, they get so bad off they can't make sense of any of it anymore. That's when they need the focus to go soft. So they can move toward the light, you know what I'm saying, without the distractions."

"And by distractions, you mean their lives."

"Right. Their lives. Their regrets. Losses. Attachments. Loves. That's where the morphine comes in. We've got a lot in common, actually, me and you. We both make the hard shit easier."

When she's getting out of the car, she flashes another one of those toasty smiles and says, "You're the greatest. Thanks, Doc." She tosses the empty cough-syrup bottle onto the passenger seat from the floor, startling him, then says, "Get well soon," and opens the back for the gas can.

Adrian jerks into action, unfastening his seat belt, unlatching his door. "Let me do that."

She tells him it's fine, she's got it.

"No, come on." He reaches her, and they wrestle gingerly with the handle of the can, the flammable liquid gurgling again inside.

"If it makes you feel better," she relents, wryly.

Adrian cheerfully empties the gas into her tank, while Deborah stands by, arms crossed and one leg extended.

Zander and Michaela are watching *America's Funniest Home Videos* in the den when Adrian gets home. A young man in Bermuda shorts zips along on his banana-seat bike and crashes into a riding mower.

"Dad," Zander calls over his shoulder. "You missed tacos. Mom's got rehearsal."

Adrian can hear the sound of banter punctuated by musical starts and stops from the front living room. He had sort of expected Stella would be waiting for him.

Crouching with his bag over his shoulder, he kisses the kids, but their eyes are plastered to the flat screen. A scrawny teenager leaps from a toolshed roof onto a trampoline, then catapults into an empty wading pool.

Adrian ambles along through the hallway. The sounds swell louder as he approaches, pausing by the curtained French doors.

"Drummers don't eat!" Stella declares in a high-octane voice. Adrian recognizes this woman. The one with a sense of humor. The flirt.

Then a male voice: "I *know*, then he was like, 'Food is fuel to me, nothing more.'" Maybe that guitarist from Denver.

Two male voices laugh along with Stella.

"Well, he's a friggin' athlete, basically. He's a machine," Stella counters.

"But he's *kind* of an ass," says the second man—that Asian violinist, probably. "You're just too nice."

"I am *not*," Stella faux whines. "That's a terrible insult."

"Doctor's wife," the guitarist says, like it's an old joke.

"Stop!" Stella says. "Not *that*."

"Five, six, seven, *and*—" Frantic guitar strumming joined by purposefully squeaky violin. They all laugh.

"Hey, wait a second!" Stella bellows. "Wasn't I supposed to solo over that?"

Again, the boisterous laughter. The guitarist says, "I'm going to solo over something here in a minute . . ." Something knocks against something else and Stella squeals.

Adrian's head has been pressed against the wall, and he draws back.

"All right, let's *do* this," declares the violinist, and there is general agreement and the rustle of pages and throat clearing.

"Two, three . . ." The music begins again, straight as an arrow—the timing, perfectly in sync, everything subtle and un-rushed.

Adrian's heard enough.

He is on a straight trajectory to the bedroom, mouth pursed, when Michaela swerves down the hallway and thrusts out her arms like a traffic cop.

"Stop! I'm going to be on the swimming team."

Adrian obliges, pauses, swallows the bile in his throat. "Hey. You are? I thought you were a little bit afraid of the water, no?"

"Not really."

"Well, good. I think that's great. Wanting is half the doing."

Michaela puts down her arms, saying, "Go!" and Adrian con-tinues on to the bedroom.

She trails him. "Mommy says I'm a water girl. Because I was born in the water."

"Ah. That's true," he says, tossing his robe from the bed to the chair.

"And I have to go to bed early. 'Cause I have a *swimming* test tomorrow."

"I guess you'd better." Adrian holds out his hand in the air, and she slaps him a high five. "You should get in the bath and practice holding your breath."

"Yes!" She runs away. Easiest bath he's ever talked her into.

Adrian climbs onto his bed and sits with his hands over his belly, then picks up his laptop, waiting for the woman he's been avoiding since morning, the one he'd been waiting for all of his life.

——————

Summer of 1996. Adrian sat at a desk in a classroom in CU's Old Main with his knees jutting out, pink from his early-morning bike ride, waiting for the workshop instructor on Western Raptors. Up to that point, there had been no surprises, just the usual bird nerds of varying ages with their bright eyes and dull hair who always found their way into ornithological gatherings, a trio of hippies who looked like they'd smoked a joint on the way over, a couple of fit lesbians in belted shorts, shining with health and solid as rocks. So when the ancient mahogany door creaked open and a tall, ashy blond–haired, graceful young woman entered carrying a tray of muffins with a sunny expression on her face, Adrian was delighted.

She set down the tray on the middle desk of the front row and spoke warmly into the sleepy, fractured group. "If anybody wants any, I made some banana-nut muffins. So, help yourselves."

This gesture of goodwill automatically changed the uncertain, careful aura around the small assemblage, and individuals became couples and groups of three, lifting crumbling confections out of their tins and hypothesizing about the day ahead.

She sat down a couple of rows from the back, took out a book, and began reading. Adrian cocked his head to see the cover, Thomas Mann's *The Magic Mountain*, and surmised she was probably a graduate student. He edged his way over, awkwardly standing while she finished a muffin she'd made, licking the sweetness from her fingers.

"That was nice of you."

"People feel better when they eat something."

He waited a moment, hoping for something else to say. "Thomas Mann, is that for a class?"

"Hah! I'm way past that phase. It's just an incredible book. Have you read it?"

"I don't get as much time to read as I'd like to. I'm a doctor so I've got a crazy schedule."

"You don't look old enough," she said. "Maybe it's just the setting, with the desks and everything."

Adrian laughed. "Right." They both looked down at the floor like teenagers.

"I'm Stella," she offered.

He held out his hand, told her his name, then gave a firm squeeze.

"You're not a student," he said.

"Just interested in observing . . . life. Wildlife, night life . . . life life."

"An artist."

"I play the oboe. In the orchestra. Give lessons. I do a little studio work but of course I don't make any money." She placed a finger between the pages of the book to hold her place. "Are you married?"

He shook his head, grinning.

"I just figured, doctor, big house, wife, and kids."

He chuckled, "You've been reading too much fiction."

A tall graying man entered the room with an urgency that seemed to say, *I am your leader.*

Stella said, "This must be the guy," and after a half-hour lecture, the group moved outside to a couple of waiting vans that drove them in search of a Prairie Falcon or Golden Eagle.

Adrian and Stella hung together all day like pants on a clothesline, blowing in the breeze, soaking in the sun. They each saw the eagle at the same moment as it flew over their heads and away, screeching in that way that obliterates time but not place.

The café where they went for dinner smelled like cinnamon, and Adrian found himself confiding in her about the inherent loneliness of his work. He asked her where she was from, and she said nowhere, that her mother was from Germany and her father had been an American military man. He'd died when Stella was ten, falling from a pier during a fishing trip in Michigan, off duty. When she talked about her father, her duty-bound, good-hearted father, Adrian took Stella's hand, pressed her fingers against the table, and stroked them with the belly of his thumb. They both sat and stared at their hands touching.

"It was just my mom and me forever after that," Stella finally said. "She lives in town here now. Drives me nuts with her five-minute eggs and her hand-painted Bavarian trash cans."

"My mother's messed up too," said Adrian simply.

They kissed after dinner in front of Stella's Honda. She had parked on a dark street along the backside of the campus protected by the cottonwood trees and the solid structures of the university. Adrian felt his mouth yield as it never had. She asked if he wanted to come with her.

When they got into her car, she told him, "Look away. Close your eyes."

He did as he was told. He could hear her rustling, climbing over into the back seat, making an occasional exclamation, the seat creaking.

"Hold on," she said. "Just one more minute," and when he was permitted to open his eyes again, she had on a little black silk dress and sandals, reclining across the back seat as if it were a limo.

Twenty minutes later, she was leading him into a basement club called the Upright Grand, carrying a case she'd taken from her car.

The place was dimly lit with pools of maroon and blue light, and people stood around a snaking bar with drinks in their hands while a thirtysomething bearded man played a sort of jazz-classical hybrid on piano. Stella and Adrian sat on the same side of a booth tucked into the corner of the back wall and ordered drinks. There they were, the woman in the black silk dress and the guy in shorts and hiking boots, talking animatedly about the books they'd read in college and the places they'd lived and the reasons they did the work they did.

People clapped lightly as the bearded musician finished an up-beat piece, then he took a mic out of a stand, pointed toward the back wall, and said, "You're on, Stella for Star."

While people applauded again, Stella said, "Be right back," and walked up to the little stage with her case, which turned out to be an oboe case, and assembled the instrument right there on stage, saying, "Thanks, Jack. Good evening, everybody. It's a great night, isn't it?" while the pianist went to order a drink at the bar.

Soon Stella held the oboe in both hands as the pianist began to play. She opened her lips to take the slim reed in her mouth, and the next thing you know, they were playing a jazz duet. *Who knew the oboe could even be a jazz instrument*, Adrian thought, but Stella sure as hell made it sound like one, and it was a miracle, the acrobatics she was doing, with the most intoxicating mixture of precision and abandon—the one he had never himself achieved in life—making the night seem festive and full and Adrian feel drunker than he was, forget what time period he lived in and what he had to do the next day.

When Stella came back to the table amid robust applause, she dismantled her oboe and packed it in pieces again like an automatic weapon she'd used on his heart. He told her she had been wonderful, and she thanked him and took up her wineglass.

"To the bald eagle," she said, and they toasted.

She finished her wine in that one gulp and moved closer to him. They were suddenly intimate in a way they hadn't been before—now that he'd seen what mattered to her, now that he knew what she had devoted the hours of her life to—and they began talking as though they were going to be together, stay together, and Stella said they should make disclaimer lists of all their faults, so as not to surprise the other down the line. They would get it all out in the open now, before it mattered so much. They would tell the truth, the whole truth, and nothing but the truth—laughing, touching, jostling each other like old pals, drinking, eyes twinkling in the club lights the way they were meant to.

They each got a bar napkin and pen and wrote intently, took intermittent sips of their drinks, and pretended to steal glimpses of each other's lists. It seemed dangerous to Adrian but thrilling.

When they were finished, they traded napkins, looking at each other from under their eyebrows and grinning. Adrian wrote:

> Have been called a tight ass. Not true!
> Claustrophobic
> Owe a load of $ on med school loans
> Too neat
> Can be freakishly awkward in social settings
> A little obsessive about certain things
> Can be short with people without thinking (shitty trait)
> Sometimes can't sleep
> Probably should not have kids
> Would always rather be outdoors
> Never even knew what music was until tonight

It was more truth at one time than he'd ever been prepared to tell anyone, much less someone he'd just met. He'd left things out too. Of course he had. It was a cocktail napkin, and there was plenty of time.

Stella's was written paragraph style and said:

> I don't have any money at all (so sorry), can be emotion-
> ally demanding (not that sorry!), don't clean my sheets for

several weeks in a row (occasionally), smoke cigarettes (lights, only sometimes), bouts of insomnia, hate a lot of rock music and almost all of pop, often flirtatious without meaning anything by it (unless I do mean something by it), needy when insecure (trying to get over this), drink red wine when I'm sad/happy/melancholy/celebrating, sometimes pee with the door open. ☺

They laughed at the similarities, joked and commented, and said they actually liked a lot of what the other classified as faults and none of it mattered anyway. It really didn't.

Adrian said he had something he wanted to show her.

"This is all so beautiful," Stella said, when she entered Adrian's apartment. "Very grown-up. You should see my place."

A wooden sculpture of a hawk in flight stood on a podium in the far corner of the living room. There was a series of walnut bookshelves, a looped rug, a light-charcoal leather armchair and sofa. The lighting was subtle and warm; the air cool and still.

"Thanks. I like . . . beautiful things," Adrian said. "I'm going to get us something to drink." He went into the kitchen and poured wine, calling back, "I bought a whole case of this merlot."

When he returned, she was lying back against the pillows. "What did you want to show me? I hope you don't mind I took off my shoes."

He handed her a dog-eared book.

"Should I read it?" she asked.

"If you want to."

Thumbing through the tattered pages, she saw each contained

at least one handwritten entry. Some of the entries were short and concise; others were more intricate, some with sketches, some with bars of color drawn on with marker or colored pencil in small squares at the top corners of the pages. All birds.

#203, Sunday, August 6, 1989, 1:20 pm: Scarlet Tanager, Piranga olivacea female – I saw it in Ragged Mountain Park (southwest of Charlottesville, VA) on a hickory tree near a dry creek. Beautiful sunny day (my first day off in three weeks). Olive green body (thus, the name!) – more yellowish on throat and rump. Wings and tail a deeper green. Pretty face. Clear little tune – "tchuh tcheowee tchuh, tcheeohweet tchee tchwee." I think that's close?! Sounds like summer.

The journal continued on, through many years and dozens upon dozens of pages, in blue pen, black pen, red pen, pencil, some hurried, some careful, some water-stained or ripped or turned down or frayed—

#328, Tuesday, May 19, 1991, 6:45 am: Abert's Towhee (Pipilo aberti), female. – Gila River valley, Arizona (with group). This is a large, plain, dusty-colored sparrow with a long, rounded tail. Black face with much lighter grey bill. Nesting! Unobtrusive. Rare bird now. We are lucky. On our way to the cliff dwellings.

#411, Wednesday, May 23, 1993, 8:15 am: Golden-cheeked Warbler (Dendroica chrysoparia), male. Edwards Plateau, Texas, perching on a live oak. Amazing color, bright-yellow face with black stripe running through the

eye to the nape. Black bib, crown, back and bill. Two white wing bars through grey wings, white belly. Very rare now (30,000) . . . Texas is the only place you can see them. Storm coming.

In 1993, the entries stopped.

"I started doing it on computer after that," Adrian said. "It didn't end, though. See?" He showed her a section toward the back of the book that continued the list but with only list number, species name, date, and location. "I'm not doing the detailed entries in here anymore, but I still want it to be complete."

"This is amazing," she replied, her thumb running along its cracking spine. "And here I thought we were equals earlier."

"Just wanted to show you," Adrian said, sheepish as an altar boy. He took the book from her hands and set it on the coffee table to put a stop to how much he wanted her.

Her green eyes liquid, she took his hand and said, "I have something I want to show you too."

———

Stella walks into their bedroom with her phone tucked between her cheek and shoulder, carrying a glass of wine and a music stand. "I should go," she says, and hangs up, setting down the stand in the corner of the room.

Still lying on the bed, Adrian doesn't look up from his laptop. "Who was that?"

"Claire." Her best friend. Pianist. Lives in Greeley. All Stella's prior frivolity has evaporated. She nudges closed the closet door on her way by it and says, "It's dark in here." All the lights in the room are off but for the glow of Adrian's computer illuminating his face.

"We were talking about Matthew's wedding. Now he says he wants me to play for the ceremony."

"Ah," says Adrian.

A short silence while she slips off her shoes. "I really am sorry about this morning," she says, cautiously. "Why didn't you text me back?"

"I was driving in the mountains. I didn't have a signal." Adrian watches her from under his brow as she settles on the bed and pulls the throw around her shoulders.

"I shouldn't ever have pushed you. I'm truly sorry."

"Appreciate you saying that."

She grimaces, "Do you smell like . . . gasoline?"

Adrian flips the laptop off his legs. "I'll wash my hands." But she tugs him back down.

"It doesn't matter. Just . . ." She takes a deep breath but doesn't say more. Adrian smells the gas now too, wafting from his fingers.

"How was rehearsal?" he asks, tight-lipped.

"It was fine." Life should all be so fine. "Adrian, can we talk for a few minutes?"

"Sure. We are talking, aren't we?" All day, in Ward and Nederland, at the reservoir and the gas station, he knew this would come, but it's spoiled, disingenuous.

Stella leans against her pillows and rests a forearm on her brow as if protecting her eyes. "Are you unhappy?"

"Are you?" he asks, petulant.

"I am unhappy right now, yes. Because I think there's something going on with you."

"I was driving in the mountains." And he was driving in the mountains.

"I don't mean today, Adrian, I mean lately. You know what I mean."

What can he say? "I feel bad about the Cascades, I've told you that."

"No, come on. I *know* you."

"Nobody knows anybody completely, Stella. It's not even healthy to try," he says. This is leading, but he doesn't care.

"Don't give me that."

"Maybe I'm just fucked up," he taunts her. "Like you said this morning."

"Like *you* said . . ."

"Like we agreed."

"We're all fucked up, Adrian. But sure, yes, let's say you are. Let's say you're fucked up." She watches him intently. "In what way do you mean?" Her eyes narrow.

"Some things people just don't say to each other," he says— again, so leading.

"Such as?" she asks, quieter.

If he did tell her about his mother, about her phone call, about his father, about the letter and how, though it's been so many long years, he's still weak and anxious though none of it should matter anymore, true or false, she would never look at him the same way again. She'd pity him. Feel betrayed. Fear for her own children. Some things people don't say to each other, even when they're still a little high.

"Such as what?" she repeats, impatient now, almost goading him.

"I don't know, Stella. Such as how belittling and banal it is to be a 'doctor's wife.'"

Adrian watches the tumblers of her brain click into place, while he inflates himself with indignation.

"Next time why don't you just come into the fucking room?" Stella says, throwing off the blanket to stand beside the bed.

"Like it's some kind of insult or *joke*."

"Oh my God, Adrian, I'm not a doctor's wife. I'm a musician."

"I know this, I didn't—"

"A musician basically functioning as a single parent. Trying to fit in rehearsals and gigs and sessions between dinner and homework, married to somebody who . . ." She shakes her head at what must be the cruel irony of her life. "I didn't sign up for this."

It could end but Adrian haughtily demands, "Married to somebody who's *what*?"

"Somebody who's emotionally *absent*, Adrian. Who forgets. Who thinks only of himself and his precious *list*."

"I help *constantly* with the kids, you just don't see it. I worry constantly about their well-being, you just don't know it, and Jesus, Stella, of course your career matters, I just don't fucking . . . *say* it all the time."

Stella bites her lip, shakes her head. "I think we should see someone. I know you don't approve of that sort of thing—"

"What sort of thing?" It's like she's not listening to a word he says.

"Therapy, counseling. Have you been drinking?"

Michaela eases open the door. "It's really dark in here."

Stella claws her hair back off her face. She nods bitterly. "Yeah, it is."

"I was supposed to go to bed early, so . . ." It's after nine. Even Michaela wants it to end.

*   *   *

Stella and Adrian gather themselves quickly and see to the rest of the evening, walking in and out of rooms like Sims, little tornadoes in the air over their heads, moving computers and phones and hairbrushes and keys and book bags around, holding their mouths closed and eyes averted. In bed, Stella listens back to a recording of the rehearsal on her headphones, teeth gleaming in the light, and falls asleep.

Adrian swims in a shallow pool of fading Vicodin, dipping in and out of wakefulness—through slips of color, mild nausea, and the repetitive jingling of a sound he can't identify. The itching's gone. He wants more. Maybe he should take more. He wants deeper, warmer, richer, because by now it's only the dim memory of an event, it's only the shadow of a shape. It's an echo. An echo of a previous sound. Like the creaking of the massive planks against the waves. And the uneven rustling of the great sails. Shrieking gulls circling high overhead. Legs wide apart, knees bent, he stands on deck with his comrades, whose voices are virtually lost in the wind, when all at once he realizes: he has to get off that ship. He is going to change. The ship is coming into port—on dry land, oxygen rises from huge swaths of hardwoods in visible waves. Adrian thunders down the swaying gangplank into the forest. And as he runs, he turns easily, simply, into a wolf, nothing painful or frightening in it; now he's off the ship. He lopes on all fours, the ground secure in his hands like a rope. All he knows is hunger. Pure purpose. Scent of dark earth, wet leaves. Night. The air.

Adrian had promised himself to never write a dummy script again.

Four years ago, he tried the super-opiate fentanyl, in lollipop form at the hospital—it had been ordered for a patient who died before using it—and he was pretty damned keen on it. But he knew he shouldn't mess with fentanyl (which skyrockets your tolerance for all opiates and is way too readily available at the hospital), so in an effort to get a little bit closer to its unforgettable high, he wrote a dummy script for morphine, which is the closest thing. He wrote the prescription for his brother, using Evan's birth date and name, then picked it up at the pharmacy, showing his own ID. Just picking up meds for a family member, thank you. So simple, it was ridiculous. He liked the morphine, of course, too much. But it wasn't like the fentanyl: nothing is. So one day, walking with a syringe of fentanyl on the way to a cancer patient, Adrian veered into the men's lounge prepared to take a little off the top. He glanced at himself in the mirror— the syringe in his hand and desperate gleam in his eye—and couldn't do it. He went back to Vicodin. He chooses it because it's imperfect. Because it's not easy or uncorrupted, because the acetaminophen in it will make dog meat of your liver if you go too far. He believes this awareness is partly what's kept him from increasing dosages enough to develop an extremely high opioid tolerance—this, and the subtle titration. But Vicodin's not that easy to get, not even for doctors. Missing pills must be accounted for, and you can't write a script for yourself. The easy thing is what Adrian avoided in the men's room, and that's a step he found himself unwilling to take. He once had a genuine prescription for Vicodin, however, from when he tore a ligament in his wrist playing racquet ball, and for years a doctor friend from med school liberally refilled it for him. It wasn't exactly morally upright, but Adrian felt it was a lesser crime, and it flowed like a well. Then the guy moved to Saudi Arabia.

This is the hateful part of it all—the scheming, the counting, the scheduling, the fear of loss—but he's determined, this time, to stay completely within the law. He will dole out four, maybe five tabs at the most per day (plus a Xanax or two) to get him through until they're all gone, then that will be that.

He begins rousing himself at six instead of six thirty and going to the gym: that's helped in the past. Sometimes his body just needs the extra attention, the extra burn. He says yes to coffee with Chip from the lab and Claudia from oncology to try and take the edge off the alienation and anxiety. Nights he lingers at his desk at the hospital until seven thirty or eight, avoiding the discomfort and frustration of his dynamic with Stella. He pours over the ABA website and the North American Rare Bird Alert for current sightings, reading birding blogs and tweets, listening to Tom Waits on his headphones, praying for his next chance at a bird, checking and rechecking his phone to be sure his mother hasn't called again.

Meanwhile, scenes from his youth begin sinking into his awareness like flashing lures floating noiselessly down into a lake—choosing a woman on a whim, fondling in inappropriate places, entering in wee hours and backing onto a couch or bed with musky hands, sprawling into late, hot mornings. He finds himself fantasizing about women he sees on the street, in the used book store, in the Trident coffee shop—the young waif wandering the Pearl Street Mall with a clove cigarette in her hand, the older woman with short graying hair who teaches at the university, the woman with honeyed skin and black glasses typing in the public library. He identifies a whole species of woman with muscled shoulders and thick waists who lift weights at his gym, another with pale skin and prominent veins who swim at the pool, and another with furry boots and backpacks crossing the lawn in front of Old Main.

When he's home, the children are more difficult to deal with. Not because they actually are more difficult to deal with, but because his wandering thoughts seem related to them somehow and the juxtaposition makes him a little ill. When he watches them playing together, wide-eyed, consuming *How I Met Your Mother* or zigzagging around the basement, knocking into the Ping-Pong table, and laughing and teasing, his heart shudders. Their innocent expectations of happiness and safety seem inevitable and right, but so dangerous, like crossing a four-lane highway. He doesn't want to be the semi that mows them down.

Deborah begins stopping by to talk when only his desk lamp is burning at the end of the hallway. Why should he stop her, when she is so kind? There is an exoticism in her "every woman" sensibility that appeals to him in ways he can't explain. She attends to her own joy, for one thing. And he's compelled by the fact that she spends her days sitting with people who are dying. Caring for them when no one else will.

It must be strange to work for someone you know will be dead soon. That someone is often in a morphine dream or sick with dementia or fear or regret; perhaps they've achieved a measure of acceptance, but they can't hold you accountable for your current mistakes or weaknesses in the future. Certain people might take unfair advantage of a situation like that. Though Adrian doesn't believe in God, the phrase "with God as our witness" comes to mind: sometimes it's only Deborah and the walls who know if she is kind, if she changes the bedpan when it needs to be changed, or listens, quietly attentive, to the story that must be told before it is too late, when everything that had once seemed so important has dropped away (the mail and the debt and the headlines and the parties, the drink and the pills and the tools and the mirrors). He envisions Deborah sitting quietly supportive in an uncomfortable plastic chair, her hand cupping his, listening to his own deathbed narrative: the story he's never told about the thing he can't remember that may not have even happened.

One evening, when they've talked and joked like the friends they're becoming, and she's left, he's checking his email, wading through his Twitter feed, scanning the week in weather, reading through *Orion*, logging onto Backyard Birder, curious. And there's the guy.

4601 (11/11/09): I saw a duck this after noon but wasn't sure which one at first. Pretty sure from the book now it is a Ring Necked Duck. Didn't look real it was so much like a decoy . They are a black and grey color with a little white. The head looks like its got a black light shining on it kind of a purple velvet look. I got up pretty close and saw the grey black and white stripped bill also great. It was floating around in a pond while I was clearing brush. Eye looks painted on!

Adrian laughs out loud. He's got the duck ID'ed right, at least. It's true about the purple velvet look, and, yes, it does look like a decoy. (That's why decoys work.)

Then, just as he's about to pack up and go home, he logs on to the Rare Bird Alert.

An Ivory Gull has shown up in Cape May Harbor (he got his on St. Lawrence Island in the early nineties); there is also a Pink-footed Goose (which he ticked in Pennsylvania in '99); but on the Texas Rare Bird Alert, he finds notice of a bird he's never seen—a Ruddy Quail-Dove flown over from Mexico. Bentsen–Rio Grande State Park. Now.

Chapter Six

Tapping neatly on a hollow door of an apartment building just off Walnut, Adrian is conscious of the soft tissue on the insides of his cheeks and of the harder ridges just behind his teeth. If he presses his tongue into any one spot too long, he discerns a tinny taste. Saliva is building up in his mouth.

The husky voice sings, "Washing my hands!"

Adrian steps back to wait. He clears his throat. Dabs at his brow with the sleeve of his jacket. And swallows.

After a long moment, Deborah opens the door a crack so the smell of fresh coffee seeps out to him like steam from a hot shower.

"Hey!" she says.

Adrian strains a little toward the opening in the door then steps back again.

"Come on in."

He enters but doesn't take off his jacket.

"When did you get so quiet?" she teases.

He shrugs and chuckles, "*Sorry*." Nothing else comes out.

"Why don't you take a load off?" Deborah suggests, gesturing to the armchair. "I didn't think you'd take me up on it. You want regular or decaf? It's French press, so no problem either way."

Adrian scans the apartment, a studio, her futon bed where the living room should be. It looks like a place someone's grandmother would live, if that grandmother were a graduate student—a lacy doily on the end table, a no-nonsense mini dining table with a plastic covering, three six-packs of Red Bull stacked on the kitchen counter, the only chair, a recliner.

"Nah, I uh . . . I probably shouldn't. How's work?" he asks, still standing.

"People are dying every day, I can tell you that much. Check out my *fish*," she says, gesturing to a ten-gallon Wal-Mart special on a corner table containing a half dozen orange-and-blue neon tetras.

"I'm going birding in Texas," he says bluntly.

She crosses her arms and nods. "Oh, very cool."

"Yeah. Thanks."

She smirks. "Just what is it about those birds?"

He nods a bit gravely, then the words spew out of him. He tells her humans have always watched birds and that it's a deep, primal impulse, more than just the sum of its parts. That detailed observations of birds and their characteristics show up in the illustrations and writings of all ancient societies, from Greece to China, Japan to Persia, Assyria to Mesopotamia and Egypt. Drawings and paintings of birds as old as the late Paleolithic period, some 45,000 years old, have been discovered on rocks and cave walls around the world. Birds are the direct descendants of the dinosaurs, he says, mummified in ancient Egypt as representatives for the gods, where their images came to represent letters and *words*. They have hunted our game, fought to the death for our amusement, fed and adorned us, delivered our most urgent messages. They herald our mornings, alert us to the presence of dead things, announce the change of seasons, and predict the weather.

She had said she was interested in birding, and it's a time-honored tradition for experienced birders to mentor those who genuinely want to learn. He's mentored several people in the past, including his friend Jeff, who didn't know a cockatoo from a peacock when they started, so she is absolutely welcome to come along. If she'd like to.

"I . . . ," she begins.

"But you'd have to be ready to go to the airport in an hour and a half."

She is silent another moment, as Adrian looks down at the floor again, shaking his head at himself, for so many reasons: the robust sheen of her hair, the generous swell of her hips, her good-natured throaty laugh, the terror and inevitability.

She's off for the next couple of days, she finally says, and she'd love to come if he can pay—which he can, he says, and he will.

While Deborah packs, Adrian drives home to find the Range Rover gone. This could mean any number of things, including the distinct possibility that he won't have to face Stella and the kids. He parks the Saab on the street and steals up the eastern edge of his lawn past the juniper shrubs.

Once inside, he finds no one in the kitchen, no one in the dining room, no one in the living room—just the sanitizing hum of domestic, upper-middle-class silence. He takes the stairs and creeps along the upstairs hallway and peers through the cracked door of Zander's room.

Earbuds plugged into his ears and eyes closed, Zander lies on his bed, one leg crossed over the other in the air, his foot flopping rhythmically to some song playing on his iPhone, only a tinny scribbling leaking into the room.

Wincing at his own deception, Adrian tiptoes away toward Michaela's room, and peeking there, finds it empty. Michaela has probably gone out somewhere with her mom, to get some last-minute ingredient at Alfalfa's or buy the khaki pants she needs for her school recorder recital Saturday afternoon.

Adrian writes a note for Stella on a piece of paper from a pad advertising digoxin, telling the truth: that there is a bird he must see and that he has to leave immediately. He packs quickly, stealthily, all the things he'll need; then, carrying his suitcase close to his body, he edges again to Zander's door, just to see him a second time.

Things are much the same, but now he has his sister's Etch A Sketch in his lap, dialing something out with tiny bits of aluminum powder, and he's begun that type of singing exclusive to those listening through headphones—the odd half phrases that dip in and out, the sense of confidence derived from the false sense of seclusion, always out of tune. Though the sweetness of this image is enough to make Adrian throw down his suitcase and run to his only son, he knows he can't.

Yesterday, when he was driving, he passed the same carcass of a house where he'd chased the sparrow on Halloween. This time, though, from the road, he saw a face in the abandoned window, a jaundiced, outsized face moving inside the house. He pulled over onto the shoulder again, raised his binocular, and the looming image sharpened into the wagging head of a horse. Adrian got out and sprinted across the pasture, much as he'd done before, even risking his shoes again, though this time the field was dry. When he approached the house, the horse disappeared and he followed, entering the living room of the house yet again, walking back through the dark hallway to the kitchen. There it was, the mute beast, shifting unsteadily on the tiny metal balls, hips high above the countertops, ducking its head to stumble past him across the threshold, thundering along the floorboards.

That's how Adrian feels now. Too unwieldy for the house.

———

"Have you got any water? I thought I . . ."

Deborah's entire arm disappears into her backpack, resurfaces, and then thrusts back in, as Adrian attempts to settle into his seat. (He had paid an elderly couple a hundred dollars each for their places on the stand-by list.)

"No, but I'm happy to get you some," Adrian says, cramped.

She twists open a bottle of pills she pulls from her bag, says, "Don't worry about it," and pops one into the back of her throat.

"Headache?" he asks, hoping she's not sick.

"It's Wellbutrin."

"Oh, really?" Adrian asks, distracted by a woman crisscrossing the aisle with a cat in a bag.

"Yeah, really," she slings back, a little loud. "Is that a problem?" She smiles, but it's a bitter one. What did he say?

"*No.* I just meant, you know"—lowering his voice in hopes she'll follow suit—"nothing. I just wasn't aware."

"You can't be as naïve as you sound right now." She turns toward him full on.

"What do you mean? There is absolutely no judgment," he says, and he obviously means it.

"Oh, absolutely," she parrots. "Good thing you're an anesthesiologist, not a psychiatrist."

She immediately takes up with the round-faced man sitting next to her on the aisle, ignoring Adrian. He wants her to look him in the eyes and say something unexpected and straightforward, so he'll remember why he's doing this, why he really *must* do this.

But he plugs in his headphones and listens to Bob Marley: "Baby, don't worry . . . 'bout a thing . . ."

She's on medication. That's fine. Who isn't? They'd met a couple of times at the Trident Café, talked in his office in the evenings, said hello here and there, at the cafeteria, the parking lot: he'd never pissed her off until now. Truth is, it *is* a good thing he's not a psychiatrist. He briefly careened into the discipline his third year of undergrad when he took a class called Psychoanalytic Theories. Adrian had thought, Educate yourself on the human psyche. If you want to be a doctor, and you do, don't just take premed classes in chemistry and biology. Acknowledge the implicit importance of the mind on the body, the nurture-and-nature relationship. These seemed like honorable aims.

The class was held in an ancient building that smelled permanently of formaldehyde, though science labs were no longer held there. The professor, Dr. McQuown, wore a squared-off pubey beard that made him look like he'd been dispatched from Vienna circa 1885. The first few classes were perfectly fine, though a little dull, and Adrian listened with half a mind. But at the end of the second week of the semester, the professor gave a lecture on

Freud's Oedipus complex, which Adrian had heard of, of course, but only in vague, layman's terms.

In Freud's model, McQuown explained, it was normal for a young boy's early sexual feelings to be unconsciously directed toward his mother. To dream about her, to love her like a goddess, to crave spending time with her, to want to sleep in her bed, to want to protect her from his father, even to fantasize doing violence to him. All that was normal. It was as if the professor had Adrian's very life in his hands.

"*Then*," McQuown said, pressing his beard together, pacing the floor, "the next stage *must* occur." A healthy boy begins to repress his "incestuous" inklings, to experiment with other children, play a little doctor, and to identify with his father, sensing that only by doing so (halting his competition with him, joining his team) would he ever have a real lover to take the place of his mother. At this juncture, the "healthy boy" (he kept saying *healthy boy* like that, *the healthy boy*) experiences a temporary renunciation of the mother while he undergoes "individuation by his father's side." (Dear God.) After completion of this final stage, the son "rediscovers" the initial relationship with the mother in the form of an adult female sex partner, and all is well, blah, blah, blah, blah. But if this transition is not accomplished, not "resolved," *fixation* will result, McQuown said, and adult neuroses of all types can follow.

Adrian was tortured and confounded. He spent the class not raising his hand, biting on his pencil, trying to shred it into sawdust. The professor took great pains to explain that although Freud had illuminated some foundational truths (that there is an unconscious mind, for example, or that people are often unable to report or even see the deep psychological issues that reside there), his theories must be taken with a "grain of salt." They can sometimes be used to *explain* behavior, but they cannot *predict* it.

McQuown clutched his folded glasses in his fist. "Formulated subjectively from a tiny sample, including Freud *himself*"—he chuckled a little, irreverently, and looked directly at Adrian— "the theories cannot be proven nor disproven. In fact, recent, more objective researchers have discovered little to support 'the Oedipal conflict.'" *Why then?* Adrian crushed his hand between the hard cover and first pages of his textbook. Why teach it *at all*?

Adrian *had* felt like his mother's companion. He had literally wanted to kill his father. And once they'd moved away from him to Kingston, and June had fallen in love with Suzanne, he was sometimes wounded by the attentions she heaped on her female lover, wanting his mother only to himself. But if a mother actually committed an incestuous act? (This was never mentioned or even hinted at, either in the lecture or class materials.) If such a thing happened to this hypothetical "healthy boy," combined with a father whom the boy had never respected and refused to emulate, what then?

Sitting in that classroom, feet shoved under his desk, Adrian was surrounded by three blackboards scratched white with the facts of his own annihilation. And whatever excuses and caveats the professor was making for Sigmund Freud, whatever question marks he occasionally added to the boards, whatever hastily circled material, Adrian couldn't help but feel—like an allergic reaction spreading across his face—he was an Oedipal complex to the power of ten. All this while resolutely wanting to prove fucking dickhead Freud wrong about his categories and his castration anxiety and his narcissism, wrong about children and their futures. He dropped the class. He took intramural tennis on indoor courts that echoed like canyons with the *thwack* of the ball against his racket, and he developed a killer serve. Psychology, psychoanalysis, case studies, theory, and practice in therapeutic settings? No, thank you.

Adrian skims the airline magazine, reading about a woman in Idaho who made a quilt for recent earthquake victims; thoughtful, he thinks, but not really helpful. He looks out the window at the reflection of his own face. He glances surreptitiously at Deborah, who is reading something her new friend is showing her, which looks like an interoffice memo from the days of the dot matrix printer. Her mouth is partly open in a smile, nodding. Adrian's pretty sure the man just spoke the words "sales index." Jesus.

They land in Harlingen, having been offered no pretzels and nuts, no shortbread cookie, and no Ketel One. (Is this how they do things in coach?) The Charlie Brown–headed man next to Deborah is now pointing something out to her through the window. Adrian can't imagine what it could be; he can't hear him now. *See all the big planes? There's a man with a fluorescent jacket!*

When they stand up, Deborah looks at Adrian as if he's just materialized and slaps him on the back. They deplane, barely speaking, then duck into their rented Explorer and head out into the warm Texas evening.

Deborah is hungry and wants to stop for dinner at a Red Lobster. She says she loves the stuffed flounder, and who is Adrian to argue, so they eat their popcorn shrimp appetizer as Deborah becomes her fully animated self again, giving him bawdy smiles behind the waitress's back. Adrian takes on the role of straight man, acting blameless and surprised like a kid passing notes at school when the teacher catches someone else. At one point, he takes out a Klonopin (he's out of Xanax), holds it up like a specimen from across the table, then swallows it. She laughs, genuinely delighted. It's the first time he's ever given a woman joy by taking a pill.

Adrian steps aside to allow Deborah entrance into room 378 at the Courtyard Marriott, holding back the door like a valet. It's the classic two queen beds with floral paintings and dark wood and minibar and flat screen, but it all feels alien and strange. There's a sudden sensation in Adrian's gut of having eaten too many potatoes. He places his suitcase against the wall and turns on the bedside lamp, fluctuating wildly between titillation and the fear of prolonged unproductive foreplay during which the self-lubricating gears of his body are clogged with guilt.

He's always been loyal to Stella, other than the time he kissed a woman, an artist, in Aspen's Hotel Jerome late at night after a fundraiser for PETA. There had been a silent auction, and Adrian had won her painting of a fat nesting grouse. When he came to collect the painting, he cordially introduced himself. She was French, and she took him by the shoulders and kissed him on both cheeks. He'd been drinking with a bit of Vicodin, and to his genuine surprise, his mouth slid across her tight, plump cheek to her lips, and her mouth softened, before he quickly pulled away, grabbed up the painting, and said, "Just beautiful work. Have a great night." He nearly ran from the place. It was a mistake. Like dropping an envelope when you're picking up the mail.

Tonight, he knows what's coming. He's chosen it. The last thing he needs is to labor against thoughts of Stella standing at the kitchen sink, her knees against his thighs in bed, bows saved and put into a box, Zander with his earbuds on.

Once they unpack, Adrian takes a Cialis and orders himself two vodka martinis from room service. He tells Deborah how happy he is she's come, and he is, too. He's seeing to his own joy. He kisses her, long. She tells him she's happy he's happy, and he downs the first martini almost like a shot, drilling a tiny hole through his gut for ventilation, while Deborah takes her Dewar's with a decaf chaser to the bath. Occasionally he hears the water as she splashes it over herself and the clink of the glass on the tub as he waits, not even picking up his phone, thinking how much he wants her to forget his awkwardness and juvenile jealousy on the plane, but by the time he's halfway though his second drink, she's slipped, nude and scented, under the covers.

"Let me tell you what I see," he says, slurring a little, pulling the sheet from her nakedness.

"What do you see, Doc?" she asks, grinning, sly.

"I am not your doctor," he says, "I am *another* kind of scientist," and flings the sheet the rest of the way off. "Compact, curvaceous frame, wide rib cage, short wingspan. Stunning auburn plumage."

"You scientists *love* the redheads."

"Particularly lush plumage"—he sucks the saliva from his lips—"around the pubis, the biological norm for this particular species."

"Too much? Should I shave a little more?" She swirls a finger in it.

"Lush and dense," he says, rising to his knees and looking

down at her, "and tightly ringed." His teeth feel like they've softened, but this too shall pass.

Deborah slowly opens her knees like a grasshopper and croons, "Mmm . . ."

"Mating behavior evident," he says, his penis finally hardening to the experiment. "A showy display, perhaps somewhat less common in the female . . ."

She rocks from one butt cheek to the other, back and forth, her inner thigh muscles flexing with each movement, her face growing into a mask of only partially feigned impatience. "Just fuck me," she says.

"Ah, she seems to want to form what we call a promiscuous pair bond with the polygynous male," he says, as his head collapses back a little between his own shoulders.

"Okay." She runs her foot along his calf. "Enough."

"How about *the song*?"

She heaves herself back up onto an elbow, lifts her hair at the roots with her fingers and shuffles it. "What?"

"You got a song, don't you, of some kind?" He looks around for his drink, stretches for it on the bedside table, and finishes it.

"I do not."

"Well, maybe you could whistle a tune? Then I'll fuck you." He falls safely overboard into an old familiar mix of glee and self-loathing, pills and alcohol. He licks his lips then wipes the saliva away with his forearm.

There is a moment when all either of them hears is a stranger in the hallway, sliding a keycard into a lock. Then she licks her lips too, a game expression on her face, and starts to blow.

Only a few seconds into an unidentifiable melody, he rocks her over onto her knees and elbows, her forearms lost in the pillows. Balancing precariously on the soft bed, he holds himself in one hand and enters her, his cheeks hot and eyes squeezed shut, thrusting judiciously. Thrusting. Harder. She brings herself to climax with her fingers; he can feel them rhythmic against his balls. She contracts around him again, again, again, and the instant she loosens her grip on the sheets, he ejaculates.

He pauses, dizzy, as his bravado drains away, then pulls gently out like an apology.

He lowers himself back down to the bed, uncertain, offering his shoulder like he does with his wife, but Deborah sits up to cleanse herself sloppily with the errant sheet, throwing her hair back off her neck. So Adrian stands and steps back into his boxers, steadying himself on the desk chair.

"Thank you," he says, oddly, then adds, "Sorry."

She smiles and shakes her head, magnanimously. "It's all good."

Nothing else to say, suddenly; they watch a rerun of *30 Rock*, and Deborah does fall asleep on his shoulder. When the transitional commercials start to blabber, Adrian moves her aside and turns off the lights—the high in a sickening, swooping decline.

He thinks ceaselessly of the past, of his brother and father arguing about primer and sandpaper and Evan stepping into the tray of blue paint, about the time Michaela got into the Thai pepper plant and burned her mouth, about the Ivory-billed Woodpecker he and his mother thought they saw in the Santee Swamp, how the photo she'd taken of the bird was left in the North Carolina house when they fled to Kingston, leaving no evidence for Adrian to examine, to prove or disprove, the crowning moment of his childhood.

Over the course of the next forty minutes, he juggles his

pillows in their stiff cases, takes hurried sips of water, and bull-fights with the too-short bedclothes, until he downs 2 mg of Lunesta and another half a Vicodin to join Deborah in the void.

The morning begins dazedly at 5:30 a.m. when Adrian slips into the bathroom to shower and shave before waking Deborah. He thinks it went pretty well with her last night, everything consid-ered, like the fact that he'd been drinking and taking pills and acted like a complete adolescent sadistic freak—but he's going to focus on his successes, instead of on his thin-limbed children, whom he can't think about at all, not during the light of day, not now that he's done what he's done.

When Deborah gets up, she makes a short braid of her hair and doesn't take a shower, which Adrian decides he will find sexy, that she's going to walk around streaked with fluids the full day, the smells of his own body emanating from her powdery smooth thighs.

They arrive at Bentsen State Park to find the Ruddy Quail-Dove departed.

The wiry park ranger at the scene tells them he's sorry and offers to give them the name of a great breakfast place. As the adrenaline of disappointment surges into Adrian's throat, the ranger raises his index finger and takes a phone call from a local birder, a Pete somebody, who followed the dove when it flew away the night before.

"He says he's looking at it right now," says the ranger, "forest up near the river."

Pete gives the ranger the GPS coordinates, which the ranger in turn gives Adrian, who thumbs madly on his iPhone while sprinting toward the trail leading to the rental car, Deborah trotting along behind him, holding her backpack like an infant in distress.

Adrian knows where he's going. A major migration corridor at the convergence of two major flyways, the Rio Grande is one of the most diverse birding areas in the country, and he's been here a dozen times. They speed southwest out of the park toward the border, as the pulsing blue dot on the iPhone creeps toward the round, red pinhead. They turn down a sandy dirt road and drive until they can't drive anymore, then jog the mile and a half along the muddy river, until they are literally standing on the cross section of the coordinates.

"Where is this guy?" Adrian says, hands above his knees, breathing hard.

Deborah doesn't know, of course, and shakes her head as the sound of a truck motoring away ricochets off the river.

A tickling on his left calf. Adrian yanks up his pant leg to find a small brown tick with its tiny noxious head imbedded in his epidermis.

"Little fucker," he says. He despises all parasites, but especially ticks.

Deborah kneels down beside him to take a look. "Want me to operate on that for you, Doc?"

He chuckles to seem lighthearted, then he carefully pulls it out, crushes it between his thumbnail and forefinger, and ducks under a canopy of trees.

They never find the bird. In midafternoon, Adrian hears a distant *whooo . . . whooo* but sees nothing.

Deborah says, "You heard it. That's gotta be good enough. What's the difference?"

Maybe there isn't one.

When he's dropping Deborah off in Boulder at the end of the long day, Adrian accepts her invitation in for a cup of "Sleepytime tea." He sits at her mini dining table, takes out his laptop, and adds the prized species to his list. No reason to celebrate yet: the late, great Henry Lassiter's year remains a mystery. But whatever Lassiter's final number, Adrian is one bird closer.

*#864 Ruddy Quail-Dove (Geotrygon montana), 11/15/09—
Bentsen State Park, Texas, stateside bank of the Rio Grande.*

Chapter Seven

*M*orning. When he switches off airplane mode, a dozen *ding*s erupt from Adrian's cell, and he leaps to standing from Deborah's futon, penis stuck to his thigh. He rummages through the room for his shirt and jacket. Deborah pushes herself to sitting: "Adrian, hey, what's happening?" while he zips up his pants, jams his feet into his boots, forgoing socks, and hurls himself out her door.

"I'm sorry!"

Sinowitz sets up monitoring while Adrian changes, shamefaced and unwashed. It's the first pre-op evaluation he's ever missed. Since the patient is a kid (Sunshine Bates, a friend of Michaela's with chronic ear infections), Adrian performs a mask induction and keeps her a touch light. There is relatively little pain involved in the placing of a PE tube in an eardrum, and it's worth the insignificant risk to allow for less grogginess during recovery. Her ENT man is Adrian's friend. The operation is performed without incident. A little sevoflurane, a little rectal Tylenol. Ultimately, thankfully, there isn't even any mention of his tardiness, only that Sinowitz says on his way out, "Mandrick. Get some rest."

It's one of those other Colorado days, the ones with spontaneous precipitation in the late afternoon when rain or snow falls steadily and furiously for half an hour. Sometimes there's hail beating the hood of the car like sugar cubes out of a box, littering the drains along downtown streets that empty Boulder of its overflow. Everyone in town knows that in moments it will stop: even in the midst of it, the sky is clearing in patches, and steaming rays of sun filter through branches and into alleyways. Soon sun envelops the valley, and the hurried shower is a wet dream, something spilled in an odd moment of partial consciousness, not lasting quite long enough for comprehension.

Adrian waits at a stoplight on Broadway and Arapahoe. He doesn't know if the kids will be home or whether they're with their grandmother, but there will be dinner to get through with Stella, in any case. She didn't call him when she received his note saying he was going to Texas, not until this morning, clearly worried when he didn't return the night before. He hadn't listened to it.

The rain screeches to a halt and the light turns green. He had sex with another woman. Twice. The birds are dying every day while he's taking out the trash and checking his email. He has the sensation he's pulled the plug on something that's draining away at a rate he can't control, like a bicycle tire you fill with air that hisses out while you fumble with the valve.

Stella sits on the couch reading *The Tibetan Book of the Dead* when Adrian steps into the living room pulling his suitcase. The sun slashes across the floor while the dampness on Mapleton sub-divides into scattered puddles.

"Hi," he says, relieved she's otherwise engaged. "So sorry I had to leave like that. There was a Ruddy Quail-Dove in Texas. It's only been in the US five times before and never in Texas." He leans over to kiss her on the cheek.

She has just been smoking.

"Kids at your mom's?"

She nods. He steps backward into his suitcase, which topples off its wheels to the floor.

"Did you get caught?" she asks.

"What?"

"In the rain."

He stoops to right the bag, pressure gathering in his cheeks. "Yeah, but it was a quick one." He picks up the current *National Geographic*, "Egypt's Animal Mummies," from the seat of the armchair and sits. Tosses the magazine onto the coffee table.

Stella covers her long feet with her pant legs. "Why didn't you call me, Adrian?"

"I left you a note, honey. And I did call you, like, six times, when my flight was delayed, and it kept going straight to voice-mail," he says, feeling dangerous and small.

Stella looks at him with an odd expression, as though someone is nudging her under the table. "So, how was it?"

"I ticked it."

"I mean Sunshine's operation. Wasn't it this morning?"

"Oh! No problems whatsoever."

Stella blinks as Adrian breathes consciously through his nose. "Was Jesse there?" she asks.

"Who?"

"Jesse. Sunshine's mother."

"Yeah. Of course Jesse was there."

"Probably got there really early, knowing her. She's so OCD. It's impossible to imagine her naming a child Sunshine. You know what I mean?"

"Yeah."

"So, did she?"

"What?"

"Did she get there really early?"

"Not that early."

"Did you talk with Sunshine ahead of time?"

"Oh, yeah. I came in early for the patient meeting, just off the plane actually, explained the machines and the mask. She seemed fine. She's pretty grown-up for her age."

Stella stands up and walks to the mantel. She flicks her hand across it as if knocking something off, but nothing's there.

"Why would you lie about something like that? You *missed* the patient meeting. They called here ten times. Are you having a fucking *affair* or something?" Stella asks, almost a joke, neither of them fully believing it as it lands, so clichéd, on the Persian rug between them.

Adrian feels his face fill with blood. He watches Stella watch it fill with blood. The iPhone buzzes in his pocket.

Her eyes dare him to answer it at such a moment.

"Stella, I'm . . . on call," he whispers, extracting the phone from his pocket without taking his eyes from her, nausea bubbling into his esophagus, almost concerned she'll hit him. "This is Doctor Mandrick . . . Oh, Jesus, Evan, I can't—"

Stella waits in suspended animation while Evan Mandrick tells his brother that their mother's neighbor, Willa Hunt, found June dead in her kitchen in Kingston an hour ago in a pool of blood. The paramedics said she had apparently died from a blow to the head. They assumed she fell, with bruises on her shoulder, arm, and rib cage, and a deep gash over her right ear. She had signed on as an organ donor, but because of the pancreatic cancer, her organs were deemed unrecoverable.

I'm sick, she'd been saying. *I'm sick and dying.*

Adrian's side of the conversation tells Stella pretty much what she needs to know, and when it's over, she says, "I'm so sorry. I know you and your mom didn't, you know . . . I'm sorry." She's panting, though, like she's been running.

Adrian glances down between his knees like he's going to cry, but he begins breathing more rapidly every second until he is pale.

Stella hurries out.

When she returns, Adrian's lips are gaping uncontrollably like the mask of tragedy.

"Here," she says. "Take this."

Adrian tears one of Michaela's lunch bags from her hand, thrusts it over his mouth, and breathes in and out of it. There is no other sound in the room but this strange crackling breathing, the bag stretching taut then twisting in on itself as Adrian sucks in his own carbon dioxide. His mother is gone from the world. He hadn't called.

In a few moments, he wads the bag into a rough ball and drops back against the chair. He looks over at Stella and cautiously offers her a clammy, bewildered hand. When she doesn't take it or even look up, he slides it between his thighs.

His mother's death renders them incapable of resuming their roles in the scene they were performing. Stella is unable to weep greedily, as she would have; gloat with moral superiority, as she deserved to; or do him violence, as she surely wanted. Adrian is unable to improve on his lie, make paltry excuses, or admit the error of his ways.

They walk gingerly as if their bones might break, each pouring a glass of water for themselves in the kitchen like they always do, then moving silently about their bedroom, opening and closing doors and drawers. Adrian lies down on his side of the bed with his clothes on, staring at the wall, because he doesn't want to stand and he doesn't want to leave. He watches Stella's eyes as she takes out her earrings and drops them into her jewelry case, hollowed out with shock. And something else: a kind of quiet resolve. He's taken something from her forever, he sees now, and proven something too, just as irrevocably.

He says, "I'll stay in the guest room," sitting up, his arm shaking under his weight. He anticipates what it will be like to walk out into the darkness of the hallway, alone in the house with a ghost.

"I was gonna suggest that." Stella's forehead is in a thick knot, like a much older woman's.

Adrian hesitates, then whispers, "Stella . . ."

Her voice is low and unsteady. "Probably now is a good time."

That night, he dreams of the woodpecker. Adrian is Alexander Wilson, the bird painter, and he has the huge ivorybill attached to his waist by its leg with a telephone cord. They're traveling in a carriage across the small farms and jungled forests of the South looking for a hotel, and as they enter upon a rickety bridge that crosses moving water, a muffled cry rises from below. Adrian (Alexander) yanks back on the reins to stop the horse, planning to search for the sound. But as he starts to climb out of the carriage, the bird begins pecking at his chin and face trying to get free, and when Adrian attempts to unhook the bird—it wasn't *worth* it, he thinks; what was he thinking, he thinks; why would he tie a living creature to his waist; how had he traveled so long without asking this *simple question*—the telephone wire is coiled around the bird's neck and wings, around Adrian's forearms, binding his wrists, choking them both, the bird piercing his eardrums with its wailing. Adrian and the bird fall, in a flailing and constricted mass, to the floor of the bridge, flailing, writhing, trapped together as one being, so that with every panicked movement, the cord gets tighter and more tangled. While from under the bridge, the sound inextricable from the shushing of the moving water, the sustained crying—the voice of his mother, hurt somewhere not so very far away, maybe trapped or wounded. He'll never be able to get to her now.

Chapter Eight

Adrian wakes in exile. The guest room smells like a dryer sheet, and there's a paranormal constriction in the air. A literal ticking clock counts down from the shelf. The whine that lives in his ears is thinner, sharper, unrelenting. He didn't sleep a wink until 2 a.m. and woke again at four. Since, he'd slept fitfully, as though he were waiting through the night in a chair at a foreign airport, with broken dreams he can't recall.

He gazes blankly into the motionless room and flashes on his mother lying dead on the floor of her kitchen. He breathes carefully through his nose, wondering where his pants are, so he can find his wallet, so he can reach into the deepest credit card slot and slide out a Xanax. He turns onto his back, still focused on breathing; then adrenaline erupts into his aorta—sadness for Stella so strong it's like terror, like the night in grad school he fell backward through the opening of the fire escape down a flight of steel stairs. How had Stella felt when consciousness returned to her this morning? He doesn't want to know.

Adrian walks out the guest-room door in his robe and boxers. He forgot his slippers in the master bedroom last night, so he is barefoot. Here is the hall where they tore down the ceiling tiles and put up drywall. Here is the Wallace and Gromit sticker on Michaela's open door. Here is the stairway from which you can see through the front-door window into the sky. Here is the silence of a man walking in a house where he is an intruder.

He pads into the kitchen full of light, surprised to find his family sitting at the farm table eating scrambled eggs, all in one piece.

Michaela pushes out her chair and shuffles over to him, tenderly hugging his arm. "Poor Daddy."

He doesn't know what's happening.

He looks up at Zander, who meets his gaze, closes his eyes briefly, and shakes his head.

He risks a look at Stella.

"I know you wanted to tell them yourself," she says. Her hair is matted, eyes swollen. "But they couldn't understand why everybody was so sad."

"I never got to see Grandma again," Michaela says, as if she may tear up too.

"None of us did, Micki," says Stella. She kisses Zander's cheek as she stands, then goes to take a plate of eggs and potatoes out of the oven with a dish towel. Sets it down at Adrian's place. "You should eat something." She sits back down to finish her eggs, spreads butter on her toast.

Adrian hesitates. Both children are staring at him, so he moves with Michaela to the table, sits, and pulls the robe around his thighs. "Thanks. Thank you."

While the kids wash their faces and brush their teeth, put on shoes and coats, assemble their lunches and backpacks, Adrian showers in the guest-room bath. It feels suddenly questionable to pee in the master bedroom shower while the water runs or to leave his pubic hair on the walls. He does go into the master bedroom to dress. The closet light has been left on and the door left ajar; Stella's clothes from the night before are in a pile on his side of the bed. Her bedside table is in disarray, with a half-empty mug of tea, a dozen balled-up tissues, an empty wineglass fallen on its side. He rights the glass and walks out, back to the living room, to tell the kids goodbye. When he gets there, the dishes are done, and it's quiet.

He looks out the window to find Michaela and Zander already meandering down the sidewalk across the street two blocks away, their bus pulling up beside them, and Stella is opening the door of the Range Rover, her bag slung over one shoulder, winter cap pulled down nearly over her eyes.

Adrian flings open the front door. "Stella!" She doesn't turn around, so he prances out along the damp driveway in his socks. "Stella, hold on a second, okay?"

She's already in the car, sliding her sunglasses on. With Adrian's hand only inches from her door, she drives away.

He watches her taillights snake around the corner, then walks back inside, peels off his socks, and stands weak-kneed in the foyer. He's supposed to be at the hospital in forty-five minutes. If there have ever been grounds for a mental health day, this is it. He imagines taking a couple of Lunesta and going back to bed. But after his fuckup yesterday morning, it's unthinkable to call in sick, especially since he will have to leave tomorrow or the next day for the funeral. He'll drive to the hospital and do his job. He'll call Evan before lunch to make sure he's all right. He'll talk to him about funeral arrangements and purchase both their tickets to Kingston.

He walks to his safe, opens it, and takes out the useful remainder of his stash. He takes a Vicodin and checks his phone. Three texts from Deborah. One, from yesterday morning:

Where did u go in such a HURRY :(

Then yesterday afternoon:

What are you up to tonight . . .

And last night:

Hey! Sup???

Adrian texts back:

Hey. Sorry I've been out of touch. I have to go out of town. :/

That night, Stella orchestrates her silences with the utmost accuracy. When she and Adrian are with the children, she speaks, she touches them, eats, opens and closes the microwave, checks homework, asks questions, even smiles. She seems to watch Adrian but speaks to him only peripherally. When they pass in the hallway or kitchen, she says nothing. He attempts to be present but humble, but he is losing ground every moment. When she's saying good night to the kids, she slips off to bed without him realizing it.

He packs haphazardly for the funeral, which Evan tells him will be facilitated by someone from a Kingston Protestant church, though he's pretty sure his mother never went to church, Protestant or otherwise, a day in her life. After the funeral, they will meet at his mother's house, the same house she's been living in all the years since leaving their father. They will deal with her possessions. They will set up a cleaning service, put the house on the market, and go back to their lives, such as they are.

Adrian sits at his desk, printing out his sky-high ticket from Orbitz and anticipating another dreadful night in the guest room when Stella approaches him from behind. He turns to see her standing with her arms crossed in front of her breasts.

She says, "Don't you even want to talk about it?"

He steels his jaw. He has been craving this, almost. Nothing can be worse than the silence.

"It . . . It was only two times," he begins, standing out of deference and fear. "I didn't—"

"About your mom." She steps back. "Don't you want to talk about your mother. Dying."

He doesn't know what to say. He doesn't understand.

"It must be terribly painful, Adrian. Losing her," she says. Her eyes gloss over with tears. "You've got to *feel* this, you understand me?"

Feel it? He finds himself shaking his head. Why isn't she asking him about Deborah? What kind of bizarre punishment is this? "We weren't close," he says, almost pleading.

"*Adrian . . .*"

"What?"

"She stopped calling, yes, and that was hard for all of us, but what the hell does it take?"

"What do you mean?"

"Look, I get that you don't care about me anymore, that you don't love me, that you . . . found somebody you want to *fuck*—"

"Please—"

"*None* of it surprises me. At all! This conversation isn't going to be about that, not who she is or how old she is or how many times you fucked her in what position when you decided you were ready to ruin *everything*. But your mother just died, Adrian. She died, in her early sixties, and all you can say is, 'We weren't close'? What the fuck is wrong with you?"

He watches her quivering lips, then blurts, "I think she's been trying to call me."

"Recently?"

He nods, searching her eyes, telling the truth.

"And?"

"I didn't pick up, Stella. I didn't know she was sick." The ringing in his ears is so loud, he wonders if she hears it.

"Well, that's heartbreaking," she says. "For you both. I hope you can feel that too." Her head rocks back and forth a little.

"Go with me to the funeral, Stella, please."

She looks him sadly in the eye. "You must be out of your mind."

On a whistling cold day near the Hudson, Adrian and Evan stand at their mother's grave with the group of eight people they met at the small memorial service at First Methodist Church: Bob and Lenora Burcham (who own the stationery store where June bought her paints and brushes and canvases); Willa Hunt (the portly widowed neighbor one house east of June's, who discovered her dead); Drew Simon (June's eighteen-year-old private painting student from a local high school, recently enlisted in the navy); Hillary and Julianne Michaels (two sisters with whom June raised money for a local homeless shelter three years in a row); and the Palladinos (neighbors from across the street whose cat June fed and watered for two weeks every summer while they were on vacation in Santa Fe).

Adrian wondered whether he'd have to face Suzanne, his mother's ex, but Suzanne didn't (or couldn't) come. Maybe no one told her. Maybe she's dead too. She'd sent Adrian cards with a little money tucked inside on his birthday for a decade, then finally stopped a few years after his mother and she broke up. In any case, no one is shoulder to shoulder. This was a small life and it is over. June had no siblings, and her parents are both long gone.

Evan, who isn't much of a speaker, gave the primary eulogy at the church:

"Mom was a great mom when we were kids. She was the kind of person who would give you the clothes off her back, which some people think isn't that great of a trait sometimes, but when you're a kid, it works out pretty good. She found her own way in life, though. After her and my dad got divorced, she started all over again, up here in Kingston with two kids to raise on her own. Some people think she's a pretty good artist, also. I'm proud to say four of her paintings hang on the walls in my house, and when people come in, they'll say, 'I love that painting of the candlesticks on the table' or 'I love that painting of the pelicans.' She did a whole series of pelican paintings, matted three of them, and put them together in one big frame—pelicans in different moods or just from different angles—which is really top-notch, like my mom in general. Truth is, she got kind of quiet these last few years, but that's her prerogative. She earned that right. I guess I don't need to say the obvious, but she went too soon, and me and Adrian are her only kids, and we'll both miss her. When your mom's gone, things will never be the same. But as you also probably know, she had incurable cancer, so hitting her head on the dishwasher was probably a blessing. May she rest in peace, and may the wind be always at her back."

The minister didn't seem to know June, but after Evan spoke, there were a few words from young Drew saying how much June had helped him with his oil painting, and how she'd been supportive of his "plans to enlist and serve our country." This didn't sound like Adrian's mother, this patriotism. Then Drew took a trussed-up cluster of sage from his pocket and lit it. The minister looked panicky. Smoke curled up and away, and nobody knew what to do but watch until Drew walked down the aisle of the church and out.

At the cemetery, Adrian, Evan, Drew, Bob Burcham, James Palladino, and a middle-aged male member of the funeral-home staff carried the coffin to the graveside. There was more disparity in their height than was ideal, and the coffin shifted a little from one side to the other as they walked, the cold air numbing Adrian's ears, his fingers numbing too with the weight of his mother's body and its container. Once they lowered the coffin to the snow-dusted ground and Adrian moved back into the small group, he began to hyperventilate again. He held his breath to retain more carbon dioxide, counting in his head. Pure panic, that's what it was, *feeling it*. As though he had been ambushed, as though a shot had been fired from one dark place into another dark place. The years rose up full between him and his mother. Had he hoped to reunite with her? To confront her? To forgive her? To deliberate her certain denial? He had hoped for all of those things over the years, back when he allowed himself to think of them at all. None would be possible now.

Seven p.m., his mother's house. He sits in the rental car with the motor running and waits for Evan with his head on the steering wheel. Adrian sees his brother infrequently in his adult life. Evan's been married and divorced twice (no children). Always working overtime for his contracting "company," too poor to travel. They've spoken on the odd Christmas or a couple of times when Evan was looking for money. Adrian always sent him what he asked for; it wasn't much in the scheme of things.

The shadowy trees are enormous now, the snowflakes floating through them. Someone's put up a privacy fence on the west side. He scans the dim landscape for some rise or depression a few feet out from the biggest oak where he buried his chemistry set. His favorite gift from June, it had come in an almost indestructible metal box that latched closed, tight as a submarine. Each clinking test tube and chemical held in place with metal clasps, each tightly stopped with a cork. Eyedroppers, tweezers, tongs, burners. So complete. He could open the sides and it would stand on its own, upright, easily accessible. He made healing potions, poisons, immortality serums. Only a year after he received it for his birthday, back in the old house in North Carolina, his father shot it full of holes, target-practicing right into its shining hull. Though it was ruined, Adrian saved the chemistry set carcass, dragging it along when they left Greenville. Originally, he saved it to remind him to guard against his own naïveté. Later, after his father's letter, he couldn't stand the sight of it, so he buried it near the tree a couple of months after his fourteenth birthday.

Unable to sit any longer, he finds his mother's key under the welcome mat, stuck into a fine compost of frozen leaves. He twists open the lock, then walks warily through the front door—not knowing what he'll find.

He flips on the entryway light. The two off-white half walls visible from his vantage point are hung with June's own paintings—watercolor landscapes of forests and meadows, seascapes in oil, domestic still lifes, and birds: more pelicans, a heron eyeing a fisherman's catch, sandpipers chased by a wave.

On another wall, the fireplace wall—he progresses to the living room, squinting, then flips on the lamp by the couch—hang dozens of framed color photographs. Evan and Adrian as teenagers. Stella and Adrian in their early marriage. Zander and Michaela as very young children. June with her grandchildren, each gathered under one arm. Floor to ceiling.

Adrian is stunned. How had June continued to live on as his mother like this, as if they were all still together, their family whole? How is it possible? It's as if a part of him had remained here, though he hadn't known it. As if she had performed some kind of spell, summoning him here daily with his image, and the images of his children, keeping him. Maybe that was why he could never let her go, though he had tried and tried, could never forget, though he was over forty years old. Then in a sudden stab of awareness, Adrian hurtles down the hallway to his mother's room.

It's nearly the same—dresser, vanity, mirror. He rushes to her bed—now with a large Native American dream catcher centered over the headboard, and a plastic hospital bed guard, which he removes and tosses away; he crouches to the floor and threads his arm under the mattress on his mother's side, searching for the letter from his father he hid so many years ago.

He finds nothing. He probably remembers the exact whereabouts wrong, so he moves to the left side of the mattress instead and thrusts his arm under and all around in a fan shape. Shuffles around to the foot, searching under the third corner of the mattress—then to the last—finding nothing. Flashing on all the lights in the room like some drug-addled thief, he pulls open the bedside table drawer, rummaging through pills (taking none), lotions, earplugs, dental floss, more pills, toenail clippers, pens, magnifying glass, bookmark, unopened correspondence from the hospital. He falls to the floor and peers under the bed, picking up lint and threads on his wool jacket, sliding and scooting, breathing bits of down into his nose and mouth, until he relents. The letter is gone.

He walks back down the silent hallway and past the wall of photos, out again to the car, where he continues to wait, confounded, his throat burning, tears shored up against the back of his eyes, unwilling to fall. Had she found the letter? Ten years ago? Two? Last month? When the bed guard was put in. Maybe that was when she called him.

He takes out his phone and presses her voicemail again.

I really need you to come home.

I really need you to come home.

I really need you to come home.

Twenty minutes later, Evan walks right past Adrian's rental car and throws open the front door like he owns the place. Maybe he does now. Adrian gets out of the car and speed-walks in behind him like he used to when they were kids, trying to reach the screen door before it latches closed, and they stand together in their mother's house for the first time in fifteen years.

Evan's eyes are red and puffy from the funeral. His lip hangs low on one side like he's had a stroke, though he hasn't. He smacks Adrian on the shoulder, looks at him a little cross-eyed, embraces him roughly, and says in his ear, "This just fuckin' sucks."

His coat smells like sawdust and the outdoors. Adrian doesn't remember the last time he was embraced by a man.

Adrian says, "You want a scotch?"

"That'd be great, yeah."

The brothers move awkwardly to June's kitchen. Adrian opens three cabinets looking for glasses, then takes out two jelly jars in lieu of something more traditional. He unsheathes the bottle he bought on his way from the airport, and they sit at the table by the window amid the smells—red wine vinegar, old spaghetti sauce, rotting apples. Adrian wants another Klonopin, but he's already had two (one on the way to the airport and one on the way here) plus four Vicodin (two this morning and two at the funeral). He'll take another Klonopin when he goes to bed, with a weak Lunesta chaser.

"What are you up to these days?" he asks, steadying himself as he pours, thinking how he forgot to turn off the lights in the bedroom and left the bed guard in the middle of the floor. Hoping Evan will sleep in there so he won't have to.

"Workin' hard, you know. Trying to keep the business from going under. Nobody's building." Evan takes a long pull of his drink. "I guess you're making a shitload of money."

"Guess so." Adrian doesn't want to tell Evan about his faltering marriage, about Deborah, about his mother's call or the forever-lost note, about anything, if he can avoid it. He's just glad to be sitting down, drinking, so his legs stop buckling.

"You guess so, huh."

Adrian glances past Evan into the living room at one of June's paintings—a gleaming tea tray with an orange cat sitting between two cups and a pot—and the faces of his wife and children staring at him from the walls.

"You gonna be okay about Mom?" Evan asks. "I know how you can be."

"What's that supposed to mean? How can I be?"

"Just . . . weird. Don't let it make you more weird."

"Oh, okay. I'll keep that in mind."

"Probably tripped on those two steps right there on her way from the mudroom. Hit her head on the open dishwasher."

They both watch the dishwasher, imbued, now, with something ominous and strange.

"Pancreatic cancer is caused by mutations to the DNA," Adrian finds himself saying.

"What?"

"If it's not inherited, sometimes it's environmental. Was she a smoker?"

"Was she a smoker? You know Mom wasn't a smoker," Evan says, curling his lip.

"Or heavy drinker?"

"No more than you, my friend."

"Because it's also been linked to herbicides—DDT and more recent ones," Adrian says. "People who work with herbicides and their spouses are at high risk. Remember how Dean used to spread that shit before he started construction? Probably came home with it all over his clothes."

"Adrian, are you serious?" Evan's eyes are wide a moment; he looks like a boy again.

Adrian thinks how Evan has no real family but his mother. He thinks about the power of the assertion of fact. And about herbicide-immune superweeds taking over the countryside. "There's no way of knowing." He drains his glass.

"She never stopped communicating with the guy, you know," says Evan.

"Who, Dean? No way."

"Telling you the truth."

"That's bullshit. Why would they talk to each other?" Adrian feels betrayed but can't say precisely why or by whom.

"She was a lesbian for years and still called him up. You never knew that? Who the hell knows why people do the shit they do." Evan unscrews the bottle, pours himself a little more. "All I know is with the cancer all through her like that, the way she went was a blessing. She didn't have to go through a bunch more medical bullshit for nothing. No offense."

Adrian watches the lights of a car slither up the snowy roadway outside. "How long did she have it?"

"What do you mean?"

Adrian shrugs. Evan peers at him, confused.

"I didn't know," Adrian mumbles into his knuckles, already regretting saying so.

"What are you talking about?" Evan stiffens, glares at him.

"She told me she called you. I tried calling you a bunch of times myself, but I'm used to you never calling me back. She never got you? You never talked to her?"

"Take your foot off the cushion, your boot's filthy," Adrian kicks at Evan's foot.

"She knew for *six months*. Are you out of your fucking mind?" Evan shoves his glass across the table. "She was *dying*. You can't take a break from your perfect little life long enough to call her back?"

"I didn't know she was sick."

Evan stands, knocks back his chair. "That's the *point*. She was closer to you than anybody. You were two fuckin' peas in a pod."

"You have been oblivious since day one," Adrian says, shaking the peas image from his head.

"Oblivious to what?"

"I don't see her anymore, Evan. She never mentioned that? I wonder why."

"What's that supposed to mean?"

"She's not so fucking innocent," Adrian says.

Evan steamrolls over him. "You know what, from what she told me, you got pissy as shit when you were a teenager, like you had to do your own laundry, because she couldn't do it good enough for you, and you never wanted her to come to your shit at school, and when you were in college you always had to go on some vacation with your friends or internship or whatever and never came home, and every time I saw you after that, like that time in Charlottesville, you were way too fuckin' smart for everybody else. Just couldn't be bothered. Now you've got everything you want, a big-ass house and a big-ass paycheck, and you decide your own mother's not even worth a phone call? What part of this is her fault?"

"I don't have to explain myself to you," Adrian says, definitively.

Both their lower lips jut out, middle-aged men in suits in their mother's kitchen.

"Yeah, so, where the hell are Stella and the kids? They got a soccer match or something?"

"Stella and I are in a rough patch. And you can leave my kids out of your sarcastic remarks."

Evan nods, exaggeratedly, paces across the kitchen and back. "You know what, man? It is *your* life."

He opens the dishwasher, looks inside, and slams it closed.

Adrian watches, waiting for him to move again, but he just hunches over a little from the shoulders. Adrian doesn't want to do any harm. He doesn't.

"I didn't mean to say anything against her," he says.

He can't help but wonder (as he has from time to time) if Evan had really escaped a fate similar to his own with their mother, if his childhood had really been as normal and unscathed as it seems. If not, he's certainly put up a good front.

Evan starts away, taking out a pipe and bag of weed from his pants. "You take your bed. I'll take Mom's."

Adrian stands in his old room with two garbage bags from the kitchen in his fist. Evan's room had become his mother's painting studio when he left home, and when Adrian moved out, she combined their things here in a schizophrenic way. There's Tom Wolfe, Jack Kerouac, John Knowles, *Call of the*

Wild, The Shining, Time Enough for Love, Birds of New York State by John Bull, a couple of dozen issues of *The Kingbird* and *National Geographic*, and the red 1977 *Physicians' Desk Reference*—along with Evan's *Rolling Stone, Heavy Metal,* and *Mad* magazines, scattered across the old table Adrian used for a desk. Games rise in zigzagging piles against the far wall: Operation, Life, Monopoly, Clue, Chinese checkers, Twister, Battleship, and Risk.

Adrian's toy motorcycle collection is piled willy-nilly in a cardboard box on a low shelf under the window next to Evan's final shop project, a wooden chess set he never used because he wouldn't (couldn't) play chess. Adrian's amphibian-themed childhood sleeping bag (one of the few items other than clothes and his demolished chemistry set Adrian brought with him when they relocated) is slumped over Evan's first amp in the corner.

Adrian turns back the covers of his old bed and climbs in, the slight grit of the army brown sheets familiar. Startling at the urge to masturbate, he bolts back out of bed and retrieves the laptop from his traveling bag.

He tries to locate himself in the present. In his own life. He balances the computer on his belly, but the room collects around him like a mist as Evan's even snoring rises and falls from their mother's room across the hall.

This is when he would usually call home to talk to Stella—hear her voice at the other end of the world. He could see if she'd answer, but he doesn't want to muscle through the tender possibility of her contacting him first. He shrugs off a momentary prick of desire to call Deborah—though this is surely her territory, dealing with the remains of the newly dead. Maybe he'll never see her again. He doesn't know.

He clicks onto Backyard Birder's chat—just as the lonely man who perches near the water posts—and his throat tightens.

4601 (11/16/09): At about 5:00 a.m. I saw a Wood Stork up on the north side by Yellow River. It is the first time I've seen this bird and I won't soon forget it. It looked downright prehistoric . I looked it up on Wikipedia and I guess I was right because its been around for 10,000s of years All white body, a bald dark grey head and a long dirty yellow bill. At least two maybe three feet tall! From what I gather we get them here but not to often. I had the day off today and I was up there walking around with a thermos of coffee. I couldn't sleep and I guess I wasn't the only one.

"Wood Stork," his mother's breath so close and sharp it almost parted the strands of his hair stiff with salt.

The sun was almost down. They had walked down the wooded path from the simple cabin where they would stay the night, just his mother and him, to sit in the sand by the lagoon. She had been reading a fat paperback book with a picture of a rabbit head on the cover, while Adrian covered her legs with little piles of gray-brown mud.

Now she took his wrist, and Adrian hushed—fingers curling and crusty with muck—because across a shallow pool stood a downy figure nearly as tall as himself.

It had a bark-colored featherless head, as rough and uneven as its body was unflawed and silken white. A weathered bill curved down three times the length of its gnarly skull, with a black scarf tied under its chin like an old woman in the sun. Its legs thin, straight driftwood; its feet a subtle pink; its eyes steadied on the pool it waded in.

"It's fishing," Adrian whispered, bringing his fingers to his mouth in delight.

His mom shook her head and mouthed an abbreviated *shh* and then nodded yes, eyebrows rising.

Breast-high in the water, the Wood Stork squawked and plunged its parted beak into the pool.

Mother and son waited to see what was next—Adrian climbing onto his mom's lap, facing away from her toward the bird, his mother holding him around the waist, her lips pressed into his sun-warmed hair. They waited, giggled, waited, and watched—until the stork's beak clamped fast like a trap as it was yanked from the water.

"It caught something!" squealed Adrian, and the stork's body registered the intrusion with immediate movement.

It hopped, splashing up brackish water, and awkwardly and with effort, lifted into the air.

"Surprise!" June laughed.

His head lying back over his mother's shoulder, Adrian watched the show opening on the stage of the sky. In flight, the bird was something new, as its hidden dark feathers were revealed: a slender white seabird against the backdrop of a bigger, black bird of prey, as if two creatures had merged—with a wingspan five feet across. And under each open wing, Adrian thought he saw a message—lines scratched with black ink across the whitest page.

Adrian's hand hovers over his keyboard, fingers trembling. He hears a metallic *tink* from the darkness of the house. Listens acutely, straightening his spine away from the pine headboard, until he remembers the sound from the pipes behind the toilet.

He focuses back on the post, tears threatening, and clicks comment.

mandrake3: Wood Stork was one of my favorite birds I listed from when I was a kid. I'll never forget it either. Glad you got to see one.

Chapter Nine

Very early the morning of his departure, Adrian returns his rental car and waits at the gate at Newark to jet to morning surgery. Luckily, he gains a couple of hours, and he should be able to make it back by 7:00 Colorado time. He and Evan finished the business of their mother's death without raising their voices again. They gave most of her belongings to Goodwill, took the furniture to the senior center where she volunteered, and shipped her paintings to Evan's address. Adrian sent the photos of himself, Stella, and the kids to the house in Boulder. There was a simple will in which June left all she had to both sons equally, but Adrian told his brother that when the house sold, he should take the profits.

Now, sipping a double espresso, Adrian thinks at least it's all over. He can give himself that much. The freedom to let her die. His mother. He will get through this and start again.

He opens his laptop and stumbles about aimlessly. He enters the Backyard Birder's chat room to see if the man beside the water has posted, and shakes his head, allowing himself a faint smile. He lays his chin gently in his hand.

This is it, he realizes, the one small comfort in his life now—the man's naïveté, his simple joy in the simplest birds.

It's a lifeline. There are no life lists for him (he can barely put a sentence together) but he reminds Adrian of himself years ago, when each bird was a miracle. The purity of discovery and gratitude.

It is as if Adrian's consciousness rises then, up and out, like a plane taking off, climbing through thick cloud cover, and breaking through into the blue sky above it all. Or like the very gannet the man by the water describes.

4601 (11/17/09): Just saw a Northern Gannet flying over the water at the beach. He was a ways out but they're so big you can't mistake there white wings tips that look like they are dipped in crude oil. They kind of look like a sentinel until they surprise you and dive like a B52. Night training last night. I had to be there late. I couldn't even think because of the noise. Same old same old.

Adrian knows the Northern Gannet so well. The scene around him in the airport fades as he hits comment and types his few words of response.

mandrake3: Hey.
Once I saw about five hundred breeding pairs of gannets on a rocky coastline off the Scottish Island of Boreray.

A moment passes, as the sharp intercom alerts of the airport become more distant in Adrian's ears.

4601: Wow. I can't picture that I'll be honest You must be a world traveller?!

mandrake3: Not so much. I haven't been out of the country, other than Canada, in a year and a half. (Short trip to Indonesia just before that . . .) I'm a doc so I usually can't go too far from home.

A longer moment.

4601: What kind of doctor? Surgeon?

mandrake3: Nothing too exciting. Anesthesiologist.

The man goes off-line. That happens with chats, of course, and Adrian has other things to do. He waits a few moments more, sipping coffee with his eyes trained on the computer screen, then allows himself to assume they might resume the conversation later on. He knows they will.

He takes a deep, even breath and clicks onto the rare bird site. Oh-so-rare birds, but not-rare-enough birds, birds he's already seen, birds he's already listed, numbers he's already surpassed—and finds that even *that*, the dynamic tension of the quest for the numbers, is a distant, if sweet-smelling fire far below him now, as he hovers at this new distance, quiet above the landscape of his life. He'll visit it again one day.

Perhaps forty-five minutes later, just as he is about to board, the man reappears and the exchange resumes.

4601: Anesthesiologist huh? At least you can spell it. (Thats better than I could do)

mandrake3: Funny. ☺

Went looking for a Ruddy Quail Dove.

4601: Nice. Doves are a pretty bird.

mandrake3: This one was very rare for the U.S.

4601: Find it?

mandrake3: Yep. Texas, Rio Grande.

4601: You go wherever the birds take you I guess

mandrake3: Pretty much.

4601: Through wind or rain or sleet or hail.

mandrake3: Right! Well, I guess I'd better go now. My plane's boarding.

4601: Hey nature calls anyway. Happy hunting

mandrake3: Thanks. You, too.

Adrian's flight is uneventful, pleasant even, with no turbulence and no delays. When he arrives back in Boulder, he goes straight to the hospital, passing lightly through the cool, nearly empty corridors, with their cleansing, radiating UVC lights and early morning aroma of ammonia and coffee. He's thinking about the kids, about seeing them later, about how strong they are, how adaptable and smart.

A text dings in from Stella:

Hope everything went ok. Thinking of you.

"Stella," Adrian says aloud, stopping in the middle of the hall, and texts back immediately:

Thanks so much for saying so.

He hesitates, then adds:

I've been thinking of you too.

She doesn't reply. When he puts away his phone, though, he tells himself that they will avoid the bitterness and blame that might have come of all this, once the stresses of the last weeks have eased for them both and she's home from Greeley. Though he was hurt (selfishly) when she still planned to attend her friend Matthew's wedding despite everything that happened, perhaps, he now thinks, it's understandable, it's right. He's one of her old college friends, after all, and she's supposed to play the oboe. "Besides," she told Adrian, she "needs time." She needs to "find her footing." But she's "thinking of him," even so.

Trisha Browne lies supine on the table, powder blue on brown, a ringlet of chestnut and gray hair escaping her cap. Here they are, she and Adrian, lashed together by need and demand. They talk casually, Adrian's voice warm and reassuring; hers, understandably concerned. Her eyes close easily from the sedative, capable-looking hands resting by her thighs, the tips of her fingers twitching just slightly, involuntarily, out of her sway, as if hearing the distant strains of a choir.

He unlaces the front of her gown to expose her chest that has been adorned with EKG leads in a kind of constellation. He covers her nose and mouth with the oxygen mask as she continues falling away from herself, then administers a bolus of propofol into the IV bag with the fat syringe that has been prepared for him in advance. At this point, he moves quickly, before the anesthetic disperses through the system into the blood, heart, and lungs to leave her vulnerable. He removes the oxygen mask, then reaches behind her head and extends her neck so her chin touches her chest, and with his other hand, he opens her mouth, carefully inserting the heart-shaped LMA over her tongue into her oropharynx—the natural, defensive reflexes that might push him out already rendered powerless by his drugs.

Next, he breaks physical contact with the patient and turns on the ventilator to administer the inhalational agents. The attending surgeon, Dr. Faust-Lucking, washes up next door. Jenny, the circulating nurse, removes the gown and blankets to scrub and prep the patient, fit her with an Ioban—the plastic-wrap sterile covering that serves as a sort of sheath over the abdomen, through which the surgeon will cut—and drapes her out.

"Did she get preoperative antibiotics?" The surgeon pulls on his gloves, taking in the operating site like a climber sizes up a rock face: total abdominal hysterectomy for uterine carcinoma.

Adrian responds, monitoring his machines, "Nothing was ordered. Want me to give her something?"

"No allergies," affirms Jenny, perusing the patient's chart.

"Gram of Kefzol," requests the surgeon.

Adrian pulls out the bottle from the second drawer of his cart, draws the antibiotic up into a syringe, and injects it into the IV port. "Kefzol," he says, "one gram."

He watches oxygen saturation, heart rate, blood pressure, airway pressure, digital readouts, and waveforms. Strong woman, generally healthy. All is well, he thinks, all will be well.

The surgeon gives his orders to the scrub nurse, centers his scalpel over the abdomen and cuts vertically through the plastic covering and skin, to open her body—

The patient flinches.

"She's light," the surgeon tells Adrian, but of course he can see that, and it isn't unusual for a patient to register an intrusion. Her body felt the cut, though her consciousness had surrendered.

Adrian adds an additional bolus of propofol into the IV to sub-merge her a bit lower, so that in seconds, she will be completely without pain—conscious or otherwise.

"You doing any skiing?" the surgeon asks.

"Hoping to," Adrian answers. "Didn't go once last year, be-lieve it or not." He's really not one for chitchat during surgery, so he leaves it at that.

He turns back to his monitors. The surgeon works, deft and nimble, cutting through subcutaneous fat, fascia, and muscle in under two minutes—then through the peritoneum, the lining of the abdominal cavity, the sac around all the organs, cauterizing the small arteries in his way.

The bowels swept aside, Adrian focuses a moment on the field: a uterus streaked with blood, its cells friable from the can-cer, already being pulled up out of the incision and into the light. Then it's like an air raid.

Four alarms sound at once.

Blood pressure 64/32, airway pressure gauge rising, EKG heart rate 110. Oxygen saturation dropping like a rock.

"Mandrick?" Faust-Lucking wheels toward the monitors.

"Gotta be anaphylactic," spits Adrian. The antibiotic—the patient is deadly allergic.

The scrub nurse's gloves are slick with fluids, holding a retrac-tor and a sponge; the patient's uterus is in the surgeon's hand. "Get Sinowitz," he barks. Jenny lays down her things and vanishes.

Adrian switches off all inhalation agents, puts the patient on 100 percent oxygen, opens up the fluids and squeezes a dose of epinephrine through the IV to boost blood pressure, hoping she hasn't already lost blood supply to vital organs. (Permanent damage is possible even when response time is ideal.) *Steroids,* he thinks, and while the surgeon lowers the uterus back into the body, packing lap sponges into the gaping wound, Adrian administers hydrocortisone.

They wait.

Sinowitz shows up minutes later, pushing open the door with a rush of air, ready to assist.

"He's got it," Faust-Lucking tells him. He means Adrian.

Though the patient's heart rate is still rapid and erratic, her blood pressure is rising steadily. Oxygen saturation improves every moment. Her lips return, a little more as each second passes, to pink from blue. Stabilizing. Everything stabilizing. There will be a tomorrow. The reaction, if not reversed, has been stopped dead in its tracks. Surgery will proceed. Disaster has been averted.

That evening, before he goes home, Adrian decides to check on Trisha Browne. Earlier in the day, he'd been with her a short time in recovery, then given the nurse the go-ahead to move her to a private room. He's never visited a patient postoperatively outside recovery before, but he finds he wants to see her, the proof of her, so he stands silent at the door to her room. She's resting quietly. He leans against the doorjamb and watches her chest go up and down, feeling relieved and at peace like he's watching waves lap at the shore.

She turns to him, eyes in slits, and as he opens his mouth to speak, she slurs, "I remember you."

"Hi, Trisha. It's Dr. Mandrick, your anesthesiologist," he says low, moving to her bedside. "Just wanted to check in, see how you were doing."

"Knew that was you." She smiles a thin smile. "Wanna sit?" she suggests, her eyes closing.

Adrian lowers himself onto the plastic chair beside the bed and she opens her eyes again, pupils reacting slowly to the light.

"They told me 'bout it . . . that terrible allergy you made all right."

"You came through with flying colors."

"'Cause of you," she whispers.

"With a little help from Dr. Faust-Lucking." He smiles. "How're you feeling now?"

She motions weakly for her water. Adrian picks up the cup and helps the straw find her mouth. "Sore pretty much everywhere," she says. Her eyes roll back into her head, so she closes them yet again. Adrian takes the cup away. "Went through menopause for fifteen years. Jus' my luck, minute I get done, they end up taking out the whole damn thing."

"Well," Adrian says, chuckling a little, "surgery went very well. Better be quiet now, though, and keep resting."

"Now they're gonna radiate me, I guess."

"That'll be a piece of cake," Adrian assures her, and stands, just as two twentyish women creep into the room toward Trisha Browne.

"*Mom*," they croon, fatigued, disheveled, picking their way around Adrian, the IV, the monitors, and tray table. They embrace her gingerly, one on each side, and Trisha's face softens all the more.

"There's my girls . . ."

Adrian watches and thinks of his mother, of course. He simply didn't have this, not for the bulk of his life. He didn't have it, that's all. He finds he is glad to be making it possible, though, for them—these young women, Trisha Browne, and the rest. This is how he's made something good of his life.

"This is the doctor," Trisha says. "An'sthesiol'gist. Came to check up on me."

"Oh, thank you, Doctor," says the taller of the two, the one with her hand on her mother's hair. "Thank you so much." Adrian nods, respectfully, then ducks out.

He drives, very slowly, along the nearly leafless streets of Boulder in the warm sanctuary of the Saab. The same attractive women he was so attentive to only days before hold no interest for him as they stand waiting at the flashing corners. The sidewalks and delivery trucks, the cafés and buildings with their tastefully lit entryways, their histories, their architectures—they are nothing more than a muted backdrop. There is only the air, a crystalline mist, shot through with dying sunlight. And, of course, the birds. They stand by, even in the twilight, quiet along fences and rooftops and gutters and electrical lines. Tomorrow they will sing again.

Just as Adrian is pulling up in front of Oma Gertrude's condo, Jeff calls. He thinks he'll let it go to voicemail, then at the last second picks up. Concerned, Jeff asks about the funeral, and Adrian assures him he's all right and everything is done, that he probably needs some normalcy and a few days' rest.

Jeff says, "I'm with you, buddy," and hesitates. "I know it's crazy timing now, but I'm all packed up, if you feel like you still want to go," a barely contained excitement rising in his voice. Adrian had forgotten. The two of them had planned to fly to California together. He says he's sorry but that it's not going to happen, what with everything. Jeff says he gets it, of course, but that if Adrian changes his mind, if he feels it might be a welcome distraction, he'll be ready.

It is an invitation-only gathering of the most elite birders in the country ("plus one," Jeff had joked), mostly in memoriam of the late Henry Lassiter but also to salute the swallows who once returned to San Juan Capistrano in droves but now only trickle in by handfuls to nestle into the eaves of highway underpasses. Adrian could use some champagne and a hot hors d'oeuvre or two, but he really wants to be with Zander and Michaela, to ground himself there.

In moments, he is standing in Oma Gertrude's pristine dining room, still in his coat, waiting for them to bring down their things from upstairs so they can all go home.

"I made knödel," says Oma Gertrude, stacking dirty plates on dirty plates.

"Oh boy, knödel," says Adrian. "Did you guys save any for me?"

"No, I am afraid we did not."

Gertrude shuffles by with the dishes and flashes him that collapsing scowl of hers. Adrian always felt she was waiting for his marriage to falter, suspicious of him, without apparent cause.

Gertrude's been in the US for over forty years but judges all things American as though she's just gotten off the boat from Ellis Island. She had fallen in love with an American soldier stationed in Wiesbaden in her Bavarian hometown of Langensendelbach. She was on her way to pick up wurst from her father's own butcher shop when she saw this man sweating on the side of the road with his bicycle on its side. He respectfully stopped her to ask directions, this American, and not long after, he offered her a ticket out (asked her to marry him), and she took it. She told Adrian once that she was happy to go because she had wanted to wash away all the "sharp smells" of Germany. God knows what that meant. But when they moved to Nellis Air Force Base in the desert near Las Vegas, Gertrude never wanted to leave the house. She had thought America would be fresh and exciting, but it was bleak, uncivilized, and frightening, or so she has maintained ever since. Every day she is shocked anew by the headlines. Every day she is appalled by the fact that no miniature breadboards can be purchased on which to eat the "evening meal." When her husband was taken from her too young, she was unsurprised. America has disappointed her, Stella says. Now surely Stella's told her about Adrian's affair, furthering her argument, proving it.

Though all of this is clear, Adrian just moves aside. He buttons the top button of his coat. His consciousness continues to hover safely above any acute awareness of his own distress, just as his patient hovered above hers earlier in the day.

"Come on, guys! Come say goodbye to Oma, and let's go!" Adrian shouts up the stairwell.

Gertrude brushes by him again and back to the table, which she wipes with a damp cotton rag. There are signs of brown gravy and roasted pork, as well as the potato dumplings. Adrian would usually do most anything for a plate of that food, but the threat of that loss too is manageable.

"The children will stay with me while their mother is gone," Oma declares.

"Uh, thanks, Gertrude," Adrian says, mildly, "but they can stay with me when I'm not at work. Stella and I have it worked out just fine."

"The snow is coming," she asserts, meeting him at the stairs.

Even for her, it seems a non sequitur.

"Hold on, Dad! We're almost done!" Zander shouts from upstairs.

"Just get your stuff and let's get going!"

Adrian moves to mount the stairs, to talk the kids off the old-fashioned typewriter or the game of crazy eights, any one of the things they fall into here that they would never have any interest in at home.

"They stay here," Gertrude says again, and rolls up the dish-rag like a sacred scroll.

"I can't ask you to do that," Adrian says. "It's too much."

"'Too much'? Am I feeble? Am I not calpable? Are my legs broken?"

"I just don't want to burden you, Gertrude. It's not an insult."

Gertrude moves to block him, her stocky body standing in his path like a wide oak daring the weather. "I'll tell you an insult," she says, pointing her finger at him. "Leaving my daughter for another woman. Leaving her children in a broken house. *That* is an insult. *That* is a burden. We are fine without you and your birds."

Adrian takes a deep, conscious breath. He saved someone's life today. He's been free of dreams four nights running. The man beside the water is probably quietly celebrating barn owls. Adrian has nothing to prove to Gertrude and, honestly, no need of her forgiveness.

Just then, both kids blast down the steps with their bags in their hands. Michaela throws hers toward the door and hugs Adrian around the waist. He grasps her head with his hands and holds her tight.

"Hi, sweetheart."

"You okay, Dad?" Zander asks and puts an arm around the two of them. "Did you go to Grandma's funeral?"

"Yeah. I'm okay, buddy," Adrian says, and kisses him on the cheek.

"Sorry you had to go by yourself." Zander looks away, as if a little embarrassed, but this is one of the kindest things anyone's said to Adrian in days.

"Yes. Much sympathy for your loss." Gertrude nods. Perhaps she'd forgotten his mother had just died.

Michaela mounts and remounts the bottom stair. "We were playing Hungry Hungry Hippos!"

"Oh, cool," Adrian says. "Love that game."

They all stand in a short silence.

"I was winning," Michaela adds, peering up at him.

Gertrude stands waiting.

"Well, I was going to take you guys home tonight, but Oma wants you to stay awhile longer. You wanna do that?"

———————

Adrian enters the ballroom of a tidy mansion near the Mission San Juan Capistrano in a navy suit and deep-purple tie, with Jeff trailing him, starry-eyed. A larger-than-life photo of Henry Lassiter is projected on the wall beside the fireplace, and birders—bearded liberals, potbellied conservatives, grad students and professors, bankers, lawyers, East Coast conservationists, Texans, Canadians, Californians, Floridians, and Michiganders—all sit in plush chairs or stand attentive at the drink table, listening to Will Marienthal speak elegantly at the podium.

Adrian slides into an aisle seat, pleasantly high. In pressed khakis and a brown wool jacket, Jeff picks his way past Adrian's knees, looking like a kid who never dresses except for church, and sits next to a young woman with blond hair, natural as a sandbar. Jeff smiles and puts out his hand to her like they're comrades, and they shake in that awkward fashion where there isn't really enough distance between them for the transaction. As usual, Jeff's giddy delight is worth the trip.

Adrian's head swivels easily on his neck, as he looks around for the people he knows (most everyone). There's Shell Eastman on the aisle opposite him, looking down, pursing his lips. Adrian nudges Jeff in the ribs and gestures toward the man, whispering, "Number one," and raising his eyebrows. Jeff smiles conspiratorially and kisses his fingers in a bunch like he's doing a bad impression of a satisfied Italian. Adrian shakes his head, unable to contain a grin.

". . . bridging the gap," says Marienthal, "between 'scientists' and what some of us call 'field ornithologists.' Yet none of that really matters today." He pauses to look out at Lassiter's fan base. "What matters, Henry used to say, is what you seek. What matters . . . is what you find."

And that is it exactly, thinks Adrian. This past spring he traveled to Indigenous Park in Key West to tick a vagrant, shy, and unobtrusive Thick-billed Vireo, bringing his number to 863. It was rumored Lassiter was also on his way that day to list the bird. But Adrian never actually saw him there. Who knows? If it still matters, and maybe it does—of course it does—perhaps Adrian can still overtake him somehow (in the mildest possible sense of the word). The way the horizon overtakes the setting sun. Inevitably. Honestly. Without malice or pride. Maybe he already has.

Marienthal is saying something about "shop talk," his hands gripping the podium. Jeff's mouth is open like that of a boy awaiting his first dance, the light filtering in dusty blocks across the head and shoulders of the audience, the flower arrangements lush, the ice buckets glittering, Marienthal's voice lilting like a song—

". . . as kind a man as you'd ever want to meet." Then he says, "When it comes down to it, I was just lucky to be the guy sharing his canteen." Here he pauses long, and Adrian closes his eyes. Everyone in the room feels it. The reason each of them is here. The gleaming thermos, feet in the muck, the brisk or sweltering or misty day ahead in the wide world of the creatures, just one of a species, surrounded by its fellows. Lucky. "We'll miss you, Hank. God speed."

Jeff firmly grasps the sleeve of Adrian's jacket, and together with the group, they repeat, "God speed."

"Adrian," says Marienthal, shaking his hand by the table of fruit and tiny quiche. "Really generous of you to be here."

"I wouldn't miss it," Adrian says, champagne in hand. "He was a wonderful man."

"Hey," says Jeff, shaking hands with Marienthal. "Jeff Stutsman."

"Great to meet you," the always-gracious Marienthal replies. "Will Marienthal. Did you know Hank, Jeff?"

"Just knew *of* him," Jeff answers, as Eastman appears from behind them.

"He was a no bullshit guy," Eastman says, pulling the knot of his tie away from his throat.

Adrian fills a plate with nothing but watermelon balls, his favorite food to eat when he's feeling the Vicodin: cold, wet, crisp, sweet. "Shell, Jeff Stutsman."

"Jeff, Mandrick," says Eastman.

"So, how's the list, ace? Did you get that Accentor?" Marienthal asks Adrian.

"Oh. *No.* Should have called you back." Adrian smiles. "I saw it, actually, but it was frozen."

"*What?*" says Marienthal, pantomiming a jab to his own heart.

"I *know*, I know. But life is good," says Adrian, giving Jeff a little nod of inclusion.

"Hank had a pretty good year himself," says Eastman. "Hell, I guess I can spill it now, and you know this, Will, but in August, Hank got a call from a friend—"

"Unbelievable story," Marienthal says, popping a rectangle of cantaloupe into his mouth.

Adrian steadies himself against the table, taking in the implications—good year, unbelievable story. "What was it?"

Eastman drops the little bomb. "Eskimo Curlew."

Adrian's consciousness twists upward like the lid of a sardine can, from the base of his skull toward his hairline. "*Come on*," he says.

"Stinebrickner was with him. From Cornell. Made Hank promise not to post it. Said the curlew couldn't risk an onslaught so close to extinction. Swore him to secrecy. It was on private property, and the owner didn't want it either."

"Did he list it?" asks Adrian. His calculations have been nothing but fantasy. He hadn't surpassed Lassiter. God knows what other species Lassiter had ticked this year.

"Well, of course he listed it," says Eastman.

Jeff chimes in, "Of course he listed it!"

Adrian gives Jeff a look, then manages, "Hey, Shell. Hank saw that vireo, right? In Key West, last spring?"

The muted crowd spikes in patches—unrestrained laughter here, animated gesticulating there. A woman's shawl swishes by the drink table, a spray of paper napkins lift, then spread across the floor.

"Nope, he never did. The curlew was the only bird he ticked this year," Eastman says, glancing at Adrian, looking truly puzzled by what he sees: a grown man in a nice suit with his fingers over his mouth like a pinup girl.

The only bird he ticked this year.

Adrian takes in a deep breath, lowers his hand, and shakes his head. "That's a shame," he says. "Not that it matters. Hank's a superstar."

The men make noises of agreement. Jeff nods along with the greatest birders in North America. Adrian means everything he says: Hank was a superstar, not only because of the birds he'd seen but because of who he was—his kindness, his leadership, his contribution to conservation. But none of that negates the additional stunning fact. He and Lassiter are tied; Adrian needs only one more bird.

Eastman finally properly acknowledges Jeff, who's selecting a half-dozen baby quiches from the table. "What do you do, Jeff?" he asks.

"I'm uh," Jeff says, looking up, startled, "working on a book."

"Oh, yeah? Excellent. What about?" asks Eastman, sucking on his bourbon and ice.

"Not sure yet, actually," Jeff says, nonsensically. "It's freelance. *For Dummies.*"

"I was your *wingman*," spits Jeff, happily drunk, his knees nearly up to his chest in a low chair at Hermanos Bar and Grill.

"You weren't my wingman," Adrian retorts, laughing. "A wingman gets you laid!"

"I mean, *straight* man, right? I was your straight man." Then in singsong hip-hop: "Played the fool, you got the four-one-one."

"Close enough!" Adrian laughs, eyes gleaming, raising his Manhattan to Jeff.

"Man, I cannot believe I got to hang with those guys. After all the stories for all the years. It's like being at the Oscars. You guys are celebrities."

"Glad to have you along. I wouldn't have come if it wasn't for you."

"Shouldn't have said I was working on a book," admits Jeff.

"Nah, you are working on a book. You're working on working on a book."

"Yeah. Did it seem like I was lying?"

"Come on, man," Adrian counsels, patting him on the shoulder. "You just got nervous."

Jeff looks at Adrian with an open-mouthed grin. Shakes his head. "*Conversation for Dummies*," he says, "that's what I should write. No, *Dumbass Conversation for Dummies*. I'd be all over that."

They had left the memorial just when the crowd started to wane, then had woven their way out of the mansion and into the little pub on the outskirts of town to resume drinking. "*Brothers*," Adrian had said, when they'd approached the sign.

Now he says it again. "*Hermanos*. You're more my brother than my brother ever was."

At this, Jeff looks him squarely in the eye, then down at his hands open-palmed on the table. "I am honored, my friend. Humbled."

"And toasted." Adrian chuckles and Jeff shakes his head. They both look out into the dim room. The waitress is weighed down with cheap silver and turquoise, unloading her tray at the table across the floor, friendly and unassuming.

"How is your brother?" Jeff asks, clearing his throat.

"Oblivious."

"Really? To what?"

"To the suffering of others. To the possibility he may not have all the four-one-one."

"Right."

"Doesn't matter. Probably won't see him again for another fifteen years."

"Come on. You don't know that."

Adrian nods in agreement, allows the last bit of alcohol and sweetness in his drink to trail along his glass to his lips.

"How's Stell? She still mad about nothing?"

Adrian shifts uncomfortably in his seat. He blinks his eyes, dry and tired now.

"I was seeing someone else. She wasn't mad about nothing."

Jeff is speechless for once. He looks saddened, embarrassed. He makes a little floweret with his lips.

"It was only a couple of times. I'm not proud of it."

Jeff breathes another moment, then says, "Man, I didn't know things were that bad. I mean, I knew you left her at the gas station—"

"*We* left her at the gas station! And I don't fucking want to hear about that."

Jeff lifts his empty hands into the air. "Sorry, man, it was both of us, it totally was." He pauses a moment to recoup their losses. "Where'd you meet this girl?"

"Hospice nurse. I'm still thinking about her. But all I want is for Stell to forgive me, so . . ."

Jeff slowly nods. "So, you're not gonna see her again?"

"I don't know, Jeff. My mother just died. I got through yesterday, and today. You *know*?" He smiles, a little maniacally.

"Fair enough."

Jeff takes out his wallet and makes a move toward his debit card, but Adrian snatches it and tosses it back into his lap.

"Thanks, bro," Jeff says. "Hey, good news tonight, though, right? Only one more bird!"

"One more bird."

Chapter Ten

Zander's Halo game drones its ominous Gregorian chant through the house. The kids started playing right after Adrian brought them home from Gertrude's, after convincing her to allow him one night with his own children, and it's been on pause since he found out they both have tests the next day. The music loops every twenty seconds, always the same, the intense foreboding.

Adrian is making a spice rack for Stella's return.

"All spice racks are too small. Your father was a contractor, wasn't he?" she once said. "Why can't you just build me one?"

Woodworking isn't Adrian's strong suit, and he told her so, but he did finally design something a couple of years back. It took him two nights lying in bed with graph paper and a ruler, and he bought and cut some beautiful cherrywood, then never finished it. He'd glimpsed it stacked along a shelf in the garage when they came in this evening. Now it's all laid out on a tarp on the kitchen table. He'll put it together, give it a natural stain, and hang it before she gets back. It feels overly important, like if it doesn't happen now, it never will.

Meanwhile, through the double doors to the living room, Zander holds Michaela's spelling sheet in his hand.

"How do you spell *kneel*? Hurry up."

Michaela lies along the back of the couch. "*N-E—*"

"No," Zander clips.

Michaela lifts her head and frowns at him in consternation, begins again. "*N-E—*"

Adrian can see them, working together in a pool of yellow light. It's a little eerie to be back home with them again, everything uncertain and in pieces.

"No, Michaela!" Zander raises his voice. "That's not right. This is the screwy one, remember? *Kneel.*"

Michaela slides down off the couch and picks up her recorder. She blows two notes and looks soberly at Zander. "Okay. *N . . .*"

"*No!*" Zander shouts.

"Then what is it?" Michaela stands, legs slightly spread, arms in a gesture of disbelieving indignation.

"*K*, Michaela! *Kneel* starts with *K-N*!"

"Well, what do you think I've been saying all this time!"

"*N*! You've been saying *N*!" Zander shouts again.

Michaela looks at him, stunned. "Oh, I meant *K*. Now, what was the word?"

Zander slaps the paper down and storms into the kitchen. "Dad! Can you help her with her idiotic spelling words?"

"Hold this a sec," Adrian tells Zander. "Just hold these together so I can get the vise on here."

Zander sighs dramatically but holds the pieces. "She's driving me friggin' nuts."

"Come on, Zander, my man. Help me out. Just quiz her. She's got a test tomorrow. And turn off that music."

"Dad! *I've* got a test tomorrow! And it's a lot harder than that crap. You've got to help *me* study. If I get one more failing grade in history, I fail for the whole nine weeks."

"Well, whose fault is that?"

"What's that supposed to mean? It's not my fault I'm failing history!" Zander picks up a bottle of glue and slams it back down on the table.

"Whose fault is it, then?" Adrian chuckles, wryly. "Now settle down."

"*Daddy!*" Michaela yells. "*My nose is bleeding!*"

Adrian leaves the glue to dry, tension building along his shoulder blades, and strides into the living room with Zander tailing him like a mad dog. "That's just great, Dad! Mom says if I do my best, that's all I can do. And you make me feel like a retard!"

"Zander. Language."

"*Dad! My nose!*" says Michaela, her fingers full of blood.

"Hop up off the couch, honey."

She stands, and he presses her head back along the crook of his arm, then produces a handkerchief from his pocket to pinch over the bridge of her nose.

"Now you hold it," he says. "I'm making something for Mom. If you get your studying done, you can help, okay? Come on, guys. Everything's cool." Everything's cool, and everything's cool.

"*Dad*," Zander pesters, "what about my test?"—gathering his history book and notebook from the coffee table and holding them up as evidence.

"I don't know what to tell you, Zander. Study. Don't study. It's not the end of the fucking world." Things are getting away from him.

"What? You've got to help me," says Zander, thrusting the books into his father's chest.

"No, Zander, I'm not your mom, I don't do everything *for* you."

"Oh, okay, great!" Zander flings the spiral notebook out into the room, which opens a moment as it flies and lands splayed out on the floor.

"*Oh, okay, great!*" Adrian apes, grabbing the history book. He flings it too, to show the boy how ridiculous he looked, but it's heavy. It doesn't travel as far as he might have imagined, just skids on the entry table, scattering the coffee mug of pens, the brass Tibetan bell, and the framed photographs of them all at the sunny Denver zoo, at Longs Peak, of Gertrude in the sunny front yard. Glass shatters into thin shards along the wooden floor.

Zander and Michaela go silent.

Adrian's face is only inches from Michaela's; it's as if she's trying not to breathe, as if she's trying to make herself invisible.

"It's okay, honey," Adrian coaxes her, his voice calm as he can make it. His knees are weak under him. "Hey, Zander? You know I didn't mean to do that."

Zander nods haltingly, then clambers up the stairs by twos.

Adrian eases the handkerchief from Michaela's hands—her nose and mouth a sticky mess. "Come on, Micki," he says. "Let's get you cleaned up. Does that sound good?"

She looks at him like he's a stranger but lets him lead her toward the bathroom.

When Adrian catches a glimpse of his face in the mirror, he doesn't recognize himself either.

Michaela dabs at her nose with the heel of her hand. She says, "We're going to Oma's house again tomorrow, though, right?" timid as a lamb.

Later that night, blood caked in Michaela's nostrils and tears dried into pale blots on Zander's pillow, the snow begins to fall. Adrian has just taken a Klonopin and three of his last four Vicodin and passes through the living room like a wandering spirit. He kneels to pick up Zander's history book, extracting it like a dead thing from the litter of glass. "Goddamn it."

He should clean up this mess, for all of their sakes. But later, before he goes to bed.

He sits heavily on the couch with the book in his lap, staring vacantly at its cover: *The History of Our Nation*. Regret fills his stomach like a cold, weak tea. He opens the book, thumbs through discovery and expansion and agriculture and government, until he comes upon a section marked with a turned-down page with its title highlighted in yellow. He's pretty sure children don't own their textbooks anymore and wonders whether he'll be charged for Zander's impropriety. He takes in the title of the chapter: "Chief Niwot and the Sand Creek Massacre."

Every Boulderite knows about the legendary Arapaho chief who came across the first gold prospectors arriving in Boulder Canyon in the mid-1800s. When the travelers attempted to dazzle Niwot's hunting party with whiskey and gunpowder, Niwot refused it all, uttering the words that became known as "Niwot's Curse":

Seeing the beauty of this valley, your people will be compelled to stay, but their staying will be the beauty's undoing.

What a radical concept this would have been in the Americas: that such a thing, the very world, could be undone.

On November 29, 1864, the book says, five days after the newly proclaimed "Thanksgiving," Colorado territorial governor John Evans ordered a group of two hundred peaceful Arapaho and Cheyenne, Chief Niwot among them, to camp near Fort Lyon along Sand Creek near Boulder Valley, while his cavalry searched for hostile Indians in the vicinity.

Chief Niwot quieted his people's fears of betrayal, telling them that nonresistance was the only way to coexist. Still, he flew an American flag outside the encampment so no mistakes could be made, nothing forgotten or misunderstood.

Just before dawn the next morning, frustrated in their impotent search, seven hundred US Cavalrymen rode thundering into the dim camp.

Nausea swirls in Adrian now, his drugs betraying him. He sees crows, cormorants, mergansers, and finches lift high over Sand Creek like a drove of locusts. He sees scalps stuffed into saddlebags, borne away on the heaving haunches of horses. He sees tiny severed fingers lying in the dry leaves, skulls emptied of their brains. He sees the earth—cool like a mother's hand on the fevered forehead of its people—befouled by the great lie of domination, told over and over again. Adrian is losing his mind.

Chief Niwot disappeared, the book says. This in a text box at the bottom of the page:

Chief Niwot's image continued to appear in photographs of the time, fueling rumors of his survival. One report claimed that, each year, a week after Thanksgiving, the regal chief could be seen dancing atop a mountain overlooking what became known as Left Hand Canyon dressed in a loin cloth and red feather head dress, the white bill of a woodpecker swinging from his neck.

Adrian lies back on the couch. The Sand Creek Massacre. Maybe this is what Zander was trying to study. He wanted your help, you *dick*.

He takes out his phone, looking for a missed text from Stella to find nothing, then lays his head onto the wide, cool pages of the book. Broken glass glitters on the floor across the room, his eyes growing heavy. He feels feverish almost. Two minutes pass. Then five. The clock ticks upstairs. He thinks again about the woman's life he saved only two days before and about the clouds of peace he sprays, every day, over the ailing world, making feasible what had once been impossible. Not that long ago, the sick and wounded had to bite on leather straps, suffer through bloodlettings or muted hammers to the skull. Pain was pain, and when mistakes were made in their rudimentary surgeries, the consequences were brutal. All Adrian's ever wanted is to make life less brutal.

He picks up his phone again, studies his grimy fingerprints on the screen, and texts Deborah:

It was actually recently discovered that birds were on the Earth
even before dinosaurs dont know why I didn't say that before

He frowns at his own text, but in a matter of seconds, she responds:

Haha. Thanks for clearing that up! :-) Are you back? Are you ok?

There she is. He swallows and thumbs:

Whats the most important thing about dying?

He stares at the screen. The message says "delivered." There is no response. He shouldn't take drugs, read about genocide, and text. Then she says—

For the one dying or the people left behind?

Good question, Adrian thinks. He considers an answer, then types, simply:

Either.

He pictures her, not sexy or teasing, not even in his office, perching friendly on his desk, but as hospice nurse, in her capacity as midwife for the dying, standing in the dim light of any bedside, with anyone, appliances humming monotone in the kitchen, bathroom smelling of sickness and talcum powder, sheets thrown aside and breath rasping. What's the most important thing about dying? She responds:

That it's permanent.

Back in the hospital the next morning, Adrian is walking from the men's room by the cafeteria to his office when the first dull pain arises under his ribs.

A few minutes later, he's walking down the corridor from the reception area on his way to Sinowitz's office with several files under his arm, and he drops unexpectedly down onto both knees in response to a very sharp pain in his lower right abdomen. Files scatter.

"Dr. Mandrick?" A woman from the lab scurries up to him and is herself on her knees in a matter of seconds. "Are you okay?"

"I just dropped these papers and I'm . . . you know, picking them up." He tucks papers back into folders, masking the pain in his side with haste.

"I thought you were hurt or something. The way you just . . ."

Adrian stands by the sheer force of his will, and the woman stands with him.

"Scared me for a minute there. Sorry," she says.

Adrian attempts a smile of curt gratitude, but nothing comes of it, so he turns away from her, leading with his shoulders, saying, "No problem," whispering, *"Fuck."* It could be appendicitis, he thinks, or very severe gas. He's been eating haphazardly all week—grabbing take-out Indian, fish and chips, even Wendy's. He turns the corner of the corridor toward preop, and the pain shoots out and strikes at him again, harder still—a black, gut-wrenching wallop that collapses him into halves like a switchblade. He's got to get out of the hospital before someone else sees him looking like an ailing patient loose in the halls.

The pain subsides enough that he risks standing upright, then shuffles the next two doors to Sinowitz's office, sticks his head in, says to the nurse, "Hey, could you tell Mike I can't meet with him this afternoon? Emergency with my son."

Before she can ask questions, Adrian is making for the back entrance door, where he stands for several seconds to ward off another threatening stab, then scoots out to the Saab. The sky is still spitting snow. Secure in his car, he pokes and prods at his lower abdomen, feeling for the tenderness that would signal appendicitis. Perhaps there's a little something, he thinks, but the pain seems too sporadic.

He makes it safely home and collapses against the kitchen counter, keys and phone still in his hand. Then he exchanges his work clothes for the silk drawstring pants Stella bought him and a long-sleeved tee shirt printed with the Lunesta butterfly, and walks gingerly to his office, where he hopes to catch up on paperwork while monitoring his situation. Sure enough, an hour passes without incident, and he begins to wonder if he overreacted or whether it was, perhaps unsurprisingly, a psychosomatic response.

As he's checking the balance on his Apple Store account for the MacBook he's paying off for Zander though, he begins to discern the indisputable symptoms of a fever—a descendant, dense fog of chills and aching. He remains at his desk, warily shuffling Amex bills, FedEx receipts, ABA life list printouts, and his auto insurance policy that needs updating now that he's bought . . . He has to lie down.

He makes his way, disoriented, to his bedroom, thinks to take a Vicodin, but remembers he took his last one that morning. He'd meant to squeeze a pill from a couple patient orders today, knowing he could get away with justifying the absence of just those two, if asked, but he hadn't gotten around to it before he fell ill. Now, he has no recourse. No recourse but the bed, which, though unmade and cluttered with newspapers and books, is a distinct comfort, as he settles into the cool sheets still smelling like his marriage.

———

Waking in near darkness, still in his clothes, not a light on in the house, Adrian thinks he's missed work before he remembers having fallen onto his knees in the hospital hallway that afternoon. Oh, he is blazing. He's always believed in burning through a fever, and he doesn't want to relent, but now he's not sure. If it were appendicitis, it would mean a rupture (even an anesthesiologist knows this much), but since the pain in his side is all but nonexistent now, he rules it out entirely.

He craves vitaminwater—his lips cracked and crusted, eyes shrinking painfully even from the subtle sunlight now spilling at the horizon, with only the trees moving outside and snow falling steadily. It is morning, he thinks, not night. Was Stella here?

The bedroom door . . . jimmies itself loose from its hinges and stands blankly.

"Stella?" Adrian calls feebly. The door begins moving, shifting quietly through the room like a giant domino. Adrian's mouth hangs, in foggy anticipation of Stella's entrance. "Could you bring me a vitaminwater?"

Stella doesn't emerge, but a succession of sweet, sharp chirps swings percussively through the still air. Adrian knows the bird—not the Brown-capped Rosy Finch but the common House Finch. A female. It has been here all along, but the chirping is soon eclipsed by a low rumbling pulse rising in volume, both rough and silky, echoing, repeating as the snow continues to build a low wall between him and the outside world, and time passes as it does only in sickness—slowly, unevenly, with a texture thick and dense and then obliterated.

He *knocks, knocks, knocks*, until Ellen Rason opens the door a sliver and says, "Come in, come in." He's been running, and there is snow everywhere, sparkling, swirling from the street into the air. He enters the house and she tells him, "Sit down, sit down, what is it?" *Hurry*, he says, *I have to use your phone,* but when she shows him where it is, he can't remember what he wanted to call about. He just wants to be near her. She says, "How about a Dr Pepper?" And he drinks and she drinks. They laugh about how his pants are tucked into his socks, and the movie, *Arthur*—how, when Arthur says he's going to take a bath, Hobson says, "I'll alert the media." Then when Ellen says, "Be right back, I've got to let the dog out," Adrian says, "I'll alert the media!" She laughs and gathers her hair in her hand, and he takes her other hand in his. She's a little surprised, but not that surprised. He's young, but not that young.

He walks home. Through the snow. Across a wide valley to a ski lift with skeletal chairs that rise up the mountain, one following the other, and trees covered in frost. He doesn't want to stop here; he has to get to the heart of it. So he keeps walking, until he can't see any more lights and there is a darkness many people never see. Only an owl speaks to him here, unburdened with humanity, as Adrian lies back in the powdery snow as if it's his own bed. That's what he loves. That the earth is a bed he can lie down on when he needs to, his entire body held. He will go somewhere warm next, he thinks, and then he's on his front lawn where the crows are a tattered cap on the head of the big oak.

He finds his mom inside, cooking spaghetti with canned mushrooms on the stove, which he likes, and garlic bread, which he loves, and when he goes to his room, he sits Indian style on his actual human bed made in a factory. He has Ellen Rason's number. There is nothing on his bedside table but his globe, which shows him all the places he can go and will go, so he drags the phone into the hall closet and crawls over the boots and under the clothes to call Ellen, dialing the numbers already etched in his brain, cradling the phone, which rings like a tiny bell.

"Hello?"

Adrian startles awake, his head reeling.

Blinking back to the room, he drags his hand across the bed-side table for his cell, furiously scratching his itching calf, wondering what the hell could have bit him this time of year?

On the phone is a voicemail from Zander. "Hi, Dad. Just wondering where you are over here. Did you forget about us, or what? Isn't the snow great?"

No, not forgotten, Adrian thinks, never for a moment forgotten.

And a new email. Amazing, his phone is so bright and so colorfully lit, when he can hardly raise his head. It's got a little atomic stamp on the back. The inventiveness of man, it says. Atoms for Peach. No, peace. Atoms for Peace. The screen blinks, "low battery, 5% remaining." Adrian barely touches it, the email loads—a missive from someone he knows but doesn't know, someone who watches birds and can't sleep. As he attempts to focus his eyes to read, dizziness descends, but he reads anyway, this message in a bottle.

4601 (11/21/09): Hey I'm just writing this to you doc so there won't be a tidal wave. Only you. You won't believe me but this is what happened. This morning about 11:30 a.m. I saw a Ivorybilled Woodpecker!! You heard me right. I was taking down old nesting boxes for the Red cockededs and after I was done I drove east past the swamp to find a place by the river to eat. There it was. A male. Perched in a narly old cypress and me watching it. I see pileated woodpeckers every day. Thats not what this was. I scared it (didn't mean to!) and it took off so I saw it in flight to. It headed into the swamp where I couldn't go unless I wanted to get real wet. Couldn't anyway cause I had to work. But its here And its real.

Adrian's torso sways ever so subtly from the waist like a sapling in a light wind. Stunned, confused, he rereads the message, something about his mother and the bird—but not. He struggles to comprehend the implications of its contents, twinkling at some distant point where he can't quite reach them, until tiny stars begin to explode around his peripheral vision like Elmer Fudd's at the bottom of a dry ravine.

Smelling the sickening sizzle of his gray matter, like burning sage, he flings off his blankets and stands, then eases his way directly to the floor.

After a long moment, he pushes himself onto all fours, without quite remembering why, and crawls over cherry planking, the Tibetan rug, the bathroom threshold, and the cold hand-painted ceramic tile, to find . . . what? Vitamins. In the small dark room where the toilet is.

No, he thinks, vitamin . . . *water,* knees splaying beneath him, mouth hanging open, but there is no vitaminwater in the bathroom.

Just coherent enough to remember he'll soon be nothing more than a piece of toast, he struggles to stand again, heart pounding anew, finds the thermometer, pushes the speculum into his ear canal, and waits like a defendant for the determination of the jury. In spite of his agitation, he starts to fall asleep again, nodding though he's standing, dreaming though awake: a griffin—lion's body, eagle's head and wings—is the crossing guard, showing him the way, holding fluorescent orange sticks which go *beep, beep, beep—*

105.4 degrees.

105.4 degrees.

Where is his Vicodin now? Adrian flings open the medicine

cabinet: Stella's homeopathic treatments—chamomilla, arnica, bel-
ladonna, pulsatilla, aconite, gelsemium, hypericum; Stella's herbs—
echinacea, goldenseal, mullein oil, skullcap, St. John's wort, Rescue
Remedy—there's lavender massage oil, vitamin E oil, Pepto-Bismol,
Children's Tylenol, Q-tips, lip balm, moisturizer, tampons . . . How
is this possible? Purposelessly sweeping his hand through the bottles,
blood pushing into his carotid arteries—911, he thinks, *911*, then
mistily takes in the orange-and-white label on the bottle of Children's
Liquid Tylenol rocking under the toilet.

He lunges for it, chucks the eyedropper top at the shower
door, and drinks, before lurching back through the bedroom—
doorway to dresser, dresser to chair, chair to bedpost. The room
whirls unpredictably as he reaches the bed, and he retches onto
his sheets, while the screen of his iPhone twirls its white flag of
surrender on the bedside table, its charger forgotten in Adrian's
bag in the back seat of the Saab.

He can only throw the comforter over the shivering bile, re-
mount, and fall back. His wrists, his palms, under his tee shirt . . .
all spotted red. That beautiful auburn-headed midwife has
infected him with something, and he searches inside his pockmarked golf ball of a brain for her name, her name, how can he
not remember her name? The one with the small apartment by
the mall. The one who ran out of gas. The one on the banks of
the Rio Gr—

The *tick*.

An oil slick of understanding glides toward him. It's something
to do with the tick. A little courier from the trenches, leaving a
tiny message in his skin. And it's *Deborah*. The hospice nurse.

He looks out the window. He wouldn't make it ten feet in that
snow. He squints at the 500,000-watt Colorado sun ascending

into the sky, just as the House Finch lights on the feeder Michaela put up last spring.

"Oh, lord . . . ," Adrian whispers, reverently.

The bird pokes, full of blind hope, into the crevices in the wood in search of a seed, snow dripping through glinting cracks onto her dreary brown back. The common little House Finch. So drab but for her bruise of a head.

Adrian lays his own head in his hand, breath puffing from his nose warming his palm, watching this shivering paper bag–colored bird on stick legs with an armored mouth and wings ribbed like the most fragile fan. She looks right at him through the frosted glass. He'd like to hold out a millet spray for her, but he doesn't even have a glass of water for himself, let alone food for birds. There's nothing in the feeder, of course, this little convenience store that had been constructed in a moment of expansion, then abandoned, just when she needed it most.

Chapter Eleven

Rocky Mountain spotted fever is rare, even rarer in November, even in Texas. Though men contract the disease more frequently than women, the vast majority of cases are children, most of them under nine years of age. Also, not every type of tick carries the *Rickettsia rickettsii* bacteria, not all the Rocky Mountain wood ticks and American dog ticks that can carry it do, and only a small percentage of the ticks that actually are carrying it at any given time are pathogenic. Nevertheless, Adrian had contracted it.

"I could have died," he kept saying, which is true. In fact, if Gertrude and the kids hadn't found him lying, unconscious, in his bed, had he not been given massive doses of doxycycline, rehydrated, and hospitalized within five days of the onset of symptoms, his chance of dying would have tripled. As would the likelihood of coma or neurological damage or blindness or deafness. Adrian was lucky. Lucky to be alive.

He lay in bed at the hospital for days as the initial battle was waged in his body—sleeping, losing weight, sipping Gatorade, and thinking of all that had happened to him. In the midst of recovering from the fever itself, he suffered from withdrawal—sweating, sound and light sensitivity, diarrhea, anxiety.

They actually gave him Vicodin for the body aches and headache caused by the fever, but it was only 5 mg / 300 mg three times a day, just enough to tease him but nowhere near enough to get him where he needed to go.

During the first forty-eight hours, he succumbed to superstitious panic: he was being punished (for adultery, for drug abuse, for lying)—that's why he was in this pain and everything had spiraled out of control. Soon after, he decided against the idea, once he got some of his wits about him again. Life isn't that simple, he knows, or that elegant. (Science is elegant, yes. Nature is elegant.) But he doesn't believe in God or the devil, and the concept of karma is complicated and incomprehensible, so he finally let all that go.

One night after the nurse had made her final rounds, though, when there was nothing but a series of lights blinking out his own heartbeat in the darkness, he thought, what about *curses?* Was he cursed? Well, he doesn't believe in curses, either, of course he doesn't. Believing in curses, personal curses, is like believing in Santa Claus—an external, intelligent force singles you out and delivers something to your home, tailor-made for you. Life doesn't discriminate like that. But neither does life behave the way it had lately—following him like a rabid dog into every shadowy corner—*as far as he knows.* Maybe it would be just as foolhardy to believe there is nothing to be gleaned from all this. You can't lose your mother, the well-being of your marriage, and fall deathly ill all in a month's time, without taking stock, without acknowledging that *something* is going on. Not paying attention to a streak like that is what lands you at the bottom of a well, clawing at the walls, screaming the famous last words, "I didn't *know*!"

He hadn't been attentive, that's what it was. He had been arrogant. He hadn't listened hard enough, watched closely enough, heeded enough of the signs. There are temptations in this world, and there are signposts. This, he does believe. The trick is to distinguish between the two. He hadn't been careful about that. He had been lost and forgotten to study the map. As the crisp sunny days yawned before him (he couldn't get outside, so was judiciously forced to turn inward), he asked himself, as honestly as he could, in spite of the withdrawal symptoms and the weakness: What should he do now? The answer had to be both intuitive and proactive.

He would stay off the pills. He would be a better father. And he would be like a yogi, listening for the perfect hum of the universe, attentive to the signs.

On the fourth day of his hospital stay, when he's moments from being released, Stella comes and sits at his bedside. She's home from Greeley. Adrian had already called Jeff to pick him up, but perhaps, unbeknownst to him, a happier arrangement had been made on his behalf.

Stella's hair seems different—sparklier and fuller—but she doesn't take off her coat, and her eyes are rimmed in red. This is what Adrian notices, but he can't know at first glance whether it's the result of grief or anger or regret or sentiment or gratitude— the swelling of her lids, the matting of her lashes, her chafed nostrils, the blotchy discoloration on the smooth grade above her upper lip. It's possible she's been crying from concern about his well-being, from coming so close to losing him, from the humbling force of some kind of epiphany, the kind that he thinks maybe he's had himself. But it could be something else.

"Are you better?" she asks.

"Stell," he smiles. "A lot better than I was, yeah. I guess I could have died. It's . . . unbelievable."

She nods.

"For now, I just want to thank you for coming. And for your text," he says softly. "It means a lot to me. I know we still have a lot to talk about. We just have to wait for Ricci to sign something, then we can get out of here."

Stella stands up and closes the door, then comes back to sit down. Maybe she doesn't want to wait.

"I asked the kids about the breakage," she says.

"What breakage?"

"The breakage you didn't clean up. From your episode."

"Oh." Not a good sign. "No, that was . . . I don't know what they told you . . ." She just keeps looking at him, so he keeps going, faster now. "Look, I'm sorry. I should never have lost my temper like that. You know how much I—"

"You've been through a lot, between your mom and this . . . sickness. But I don't want you to come home, Adrian. Obviously, you're too stressed to be with the kids right now. You won't have any trouble finding an apartment, and I get that you still need bed rest, but you can afford to hire someone to help out."

"Stella. Stella, hold on. Can I just say something? You're right. I was incredibly stressed. And beside myself. I know what I did was . . . unforgivable. I know what that means to you, to both of us—"

She looks down at her thighs. "I think I might want a divorce."

He shakes his head. "You don't mean that."

She raises her eyebrows as if he's thrown a cloth napkin into a plate full of gravy.

"I'm sorry," he says, quickly, knowing he's said the wrong thing, that already, he's not really listening.

She chuckles ruefully. "I don't care what you think. I just want you out before the kids get home from school. I don't want them going through the drama of you tramping through the house with suitcases. I spoke to Jeff. He says you can stay with him until you figure out something else."

Okay, these were the signs so far. By the time Adrian arrives at Jeff's condo with his things, Jeff has set up a little nest for him in his guest room that doubles as an office. The bedside lamp has been left on (though it isn't dark yet), a tan wool blanket lies folded on the foot of a tidy daybed, an eight-pack of vitaminwater, called Revive, nestles on ice in an open cooler so Adrian won't have to get up.

It's a kind gesture, and it isn't a terrible place to recover, just odd. In front of the room's one window, a kitchen table has been set up as a desk, and there is an old leather armchair with only one arm onto which Jeff tends to throw things he doesn't know what else to do with, including a bowl of poker chips, a tiny watering can, unopened boxes of ant traps, the third season of *The Sopranos*, and homemade CDs with titles like "R&B from Mom!" and "Happy Car Songs." The rest of the room is nearly overwhelmed with stacks of books, and though the initial appearance of these books is impressive, upon closer inspection it becomes evident that each of them is written for "Dummies" or "Idiots."

Adrian climbs wearily, dizzily, into the little bed to find *Bird*

Watching for Dummies tucked under his pillow, which he slides soberly under the bed, thinking about what Zander and Michaela might have told Stella. He had been deathly ill and had obviously been unprepared for her to come home. It was like being caught with his pants around his ankles, or zigzagging naked and ignorant across the mall with a pumpkin on his head. If he'd had his wits about him, if he hadn't been dying of infection, the bathroom wouldn't have looked like a cyclone hit it, and he would have cleaned the mess from the broken frames in the living room. But the fact is he had lost his temper and thrown something in the presence of his children. He had behaved like a bully. He'd frightened them both. And whatever Stella might think, he would be the last one to forgive himself for that.

Now he's stuck in this room for idiots. Okay.

He plugs in his phone, which had died and lay unnoticed when he was taken to the hospital. He waits for the fat battery icon to go from red to green. Once it does, he finds among his missed calls six from Zander, one from Stella (yesterday), two calls from Jeff, five from the hospital, a call from Deborah, texts from Zander, Deborah, and Jeff, and three from the Rare Bird Alert site (all birds he's already seen).

He plugs in his laptop—that revelatory music swelling, always unanticipated, from the hidden speakers—and checks his email: a half dozen from Boulder Community Health Administrative Desk, something from the American Society of Anesthesiologists, a couple from the American Birding Association, one from some site selling pirated Levitra with the subject line "The big DICK she always wanted," another selling Ambien—and a private message from a Backyard Birder chat-room member.

The man beside the water. Adrian is pleased and intrigued, but it looks like it's already been opened.

4601 (11/23/09): Hey, I'm just writing this to you doc so there won't be a tidal wave. Only you. You won't believe me but this is what happened. This morning about 11:30 a.m. I saw a Ivorybilled Wood-pecker!! You heard me right . . .

Adrian had thought it was *a dream*—the woodpecker that invaded his painkiller-induced euphoria in the hospital bed when he was laced up with IVs and monitors. He thought it was some festering from the wound of his mother's death, a memory sketched into shaky relief by grief and narcotics, echoing from the cypress swamp in South Carolina where he had paddled a little closer to the bird. Yet here it is, now, the words on the screen bold as a Rorschach.

For one moment—unsteady as he is—Adrian allows himself a furtive glance down that path, the path away from regret, self-recrimination, and loss and toward some red, black, and white pinnacle looming large in the branches of a pine. But this bird that requires acre upon acre of vast virgin forest in order to survive, this Ghost Bird, is the most implausible, the most hotly disputed, the most elusive creature of all. The man beside the water might as well have reported spotting a yeti.

The facts (and facts are essential) are these. *Campephilus principalis* used to range all across the southeastern US and up the Mississippi and Ohio Rivers. By the 1930s, with most of the hardwoods in the US already destroyed, there were only about twenty ivorybills left, mostly in a rare old-growth forest called the Singer Tract in Louisiana, which the Chicago Mill and Lumber Company decided to shear off at the ankles. Preservationists offered them serious cash to leave the birds alone, but they clear-cut it anyway. A couple of years later, one last female was sighted, alone in the forest, surrounded by wreckage. By 1944 she was gone too.

There have been hundreds of reported "encounters" with the ivorybill since, every one disputed. There were vocal recordings in Texas, a sighting of a subspecies in Cuba, countless grainy photos taken from difficult angles impossible to authenticate, expert sightings *unconfirmed* in Louisiana and Alabama. People have been accused of mounting stuffed specimens to trees and photographing them as living birds. They've been accused of mistaking gunshot echoes and "duck wingtip collisions" for the ivorybill's tree knock. They've been accused of sentimentality, deceit, pride, and naïveté.

In 1994 the bird was labeled "extinct" by an international conservation organization, though it was later reverted to "critically endangered" based on the never-ending reports of sightings. One, in the Pearl River region of southeastern Louisiana in 2002, led to a thirty-day hunt by hotshot ornithologists *certain* they'd heard the putative double knock, *convinced* they'd found evidence of possible ivorybill activity in the trees. Finally the swamps spit them out and wouldn't let them through.

In 2005, scientists from Cornell, some of the foremost experts in the world, announced that one of their number had seen a male Ivory-billed Woodpecker on a kayaking trip in Big Woods, Arkansas, and during the next fourteen months, they undertook a secret search and believed they'd spotted the bird over and over again, so they bought adjacent land to add to the habitat, made a video recording of a bird they claimed was, indeed, an Ivory-billed Woodpecker, and revealed their findings to the world. Not long after the article, sound, and video were published, heated debates over their authenticity erupted like poison ivy. There was no *definitive proof*. They kept searching, from 2005 to 2009, to confirm their original claims, installed an arsenal of robotic video cameras in the Big Woods to watch for any evidence of an ivorybill, and people were kept out to give the bird a chance to show itself. Finally, they offered a fifty-thousand-dollar reward to anyone who could lead a project biologist to the bird. What have they found since? Nothing.

It's like the late, great Henry Lassiter always said: "Bird sightings are like police lineups. People see what they want to see."

This is surely his first true test, Adrian thinks. This insanity. This trillion-to-one wet dream. Adrian has a life to live. He has a marriage to excavate from rubble and two children who probably won't look him in the eye. He exes out of his browser. He powers down. He unplugs.

The next morning, it's Thanksgiving, as bleak a Thursday as Adrian has seen in years. The sky is uncharacteristically gray, and when he places his feet onto the floor, he knows there is nothing—no family, no work, no birds. No morning cinnamon rolls. No apples and onions cooking in butter scenting every corner of the house. No oyster stuffing. No house.

Jeff had to go in early to A Good Sport to get ready for Black Friday. He's left a box of Honey Nut Cheerios and a half-blackened banana out on the kitchen counter, with a note that says, "Keep your strength up. Happy Thanksgiving!"

Adrian's muscles ache. Anxiety is mounting under his breastbone and a dull haze hovers over his brain. The drugs, all his drugs, have leaked their way out of his body and left a gaping hole that he's rattling around in.

Sheepishly, he eases Jeff's medicine cabinet door open to see if there is anything he can borrow, only to help him taper off, but as he suspected, there's nothing. Only an empty tube of testosterone gel, a gooey bottle of Rogaine, scattered Bengay pain relief patches, and a Speed Stick deodorant with no lid. Good, then. This affirms his decision to stop with the pills. Adrian sticks two of the Bengay patches to his shoulders, dresses, and wanders outside.

He will rebuild his strength. He'll walk to the mall, and once he's there, he'll turn around and walk back. Each day, he'll walk a little more, until he starts driving up Canyon to take his walks in the brisk air of the foothills. This afternoon, he'll call Zander and Michaela. Maybe he can meet them for a hot chocolate somewhere and they can talk. They must be worried, as much as they're confused and upset. He only hopes Stella hasn't enough ill will to malign him to them. Surely they haven't come to that. At her core, Adrian tries to believe, she is more hurt than angry. At her core, he hopes, she remembers who he is.

Boulder, May 2001, around 8 p.m. Zander was five and had just been put to bed by a woman Adrian hardly knew—Barbara, the nurse midwife, maybe fifty years old, sinewy as a marathon runner, frizzy gray-and-black hair—while Adrian stayed with Stella in the bedroom. He held her, standing, as she hung her body on him like a soaking wet coat, minute to minute, contraction after contraction, her mouth open against his neck and hands gripping his sweatshirt for more than an hour, when his arms started to shake. The midwife moved to them to say it was time to check the baby's heartbeat, and Adrian looked helplessly around the room, then headed to the kitchen. The house was so thick with pain, no one remembered to turn on the lights though the sun had nearly set.

Stella, a *doctor's wife*, had convinced Adrian that she wanted nothing to do with a hospital (or even the birthing center where she'd given birth to Zander) and absolutely no drugs during the birth; she would deliver naturally at home.

"Why," he had asked her, "would you *choose* pain?"

She found the question insulting, it seemed, but he meant it sincerely. He had felt reckless when the subject came up around his associates at work, as if he were a suicide bomber indoctrinated by an enemy side. When he thought about it, though he'd attended dozens of C-sections and given probably a hundred epidurals, he realized he'd never even seen an unmedicated childbirth.

Now he was desperate for action and nauseous with worry, and though Stella wasn't the least bit interested in the laboring tub they'd rented at the full package price of three hundred dollars, by God, Adrian would fill it. And heat it. Just in case. He also had an epidural kit in his back pocket, just in case. A vial of morphine, also, just in case. Keys, just in case. Portable oxygen in the car. And some local anesthetic *just in case* the midwife had to do stitches (though, the vagina is so pummeled and numb by that point, even some OBs forgo anesthetic and stitch at will). The Klonopin was for Adrian (all he was taking at the time).

Two long hours later, Stella decided to make the journey from their bedroom to the laboring tub. It took a full half hour to work her down the stairs; Adrian and Barbara half-carried her a few steps until she would sink to the floor during a contraction, when they would wait until she was ready to walk. Once she was in the warm water, they both knew there was no hope of moving her again. Within half an hour, she was "in transition." Adrian muttered a few words to the midwife, suggesting that none of them had prepared for a water birth, but he was powerless. All he could do was bring ice chips to lay gently on Stella's tongue like communion wafers.

He knew very well what was going on—her cervix was opening to its full dilation, ten centimeters, the size of a bagel (from the size of a lentil), when the baby's head would start to urge through. Then the shoulders.

She was making a sort of screeching moan along with each contraction now, and Adrian squatted alongside the tub, taking her hand when she'd let him, letting it go when she pulled away.

Barbara spoke in soothing, firm tones between contractions. "Stay with it, now, Stella. Don't forget to *breathe*."

"Where's my . . . ? Where's Adrian?" Stella called.

"I'm right here, Stell, honey," he said. He was just outside the tub, laying a careful arm around her upper back.

"I can't *feel* you," she cried, and began to wail with the next swell of torment, hair spiraling from her bun, eyes squeezed shut, face and chest mottled red.

As Barbara looked on, Adrian lifted his sweatshirt over his head, took off his socks, and unzipped his jeans. As they fell to his feet, the vials, syringes, and keys in his pockets clinked against the tile floor.

He knelt to Stella, leveling her chin in his hands, peering into her eyes. "Want me to come in there with you?"

Stella gazed at him blearily, then sobbed, "*Yes.* Come in. Just don't touch me, okay?"

He stepped into the deep water and lowered himself down.

Stella collapsed onto his chest, her face contorting, and bellowed into his ear. "Oh, *God*."

He held her like that until she spasmed away from him again. She would lean onto the inflated rim of the tub, panting and breathing, then she would rock back into the center, growling deeply, utterly inside herself and the terrible limitations, the terrible limitless power of her body.

Before half an hour had passed, she began to bear down.

The midwife pierced the water with her flashlight, latex gloves on her hands, saying, "Good. Now, slow it down. Give it its time."

Adrian wiped her brow with the washcloth Barbara had given him, as Stella drew in and out of the relentless ebb and flow of it. He spoke steadily to her, watched her, begged her, "Breathe, Stella, and wait for the baby. I'm right here with you."

When Stella's sounds began to catch in her own throat, Barbara told her, "Do what you need to do, darlin'," handing Adrian the flashlight, her hands poised in the water.

Adrian illuminated the darkness between Stella's legs—as she pushed, then panted as though she would hyperventilate, then strained and pushed—and there was a sudden matted swelling.

"It's *coming*," Adrian said, flashlight in one hand, the other floating in the water, feet propped against the sides of the tub as if he, too, were pushing. Stella bore down and bore down, until the whole sphere of the head thrust forward.

Adrian watched as the midwife unwound the umbilical cord from the baby's throat, deftly and quietly, as if attending to a garden on a summer afternoon, and when Stella pushed again, howling, Michaela was free, floating under the water amid a gush of blood and fluid.

Adrian gasped and lifted her up and out—onto her mother's heaving chest. The baby was covered in the emollient vernix caseosa, eyes puffy and nearly closed, hands opening and closing, taking sharp gulps of air. Adrian slid around the side of the tub to get behind Stella, to hold her as she came back to herself, and she lay against him, caressing Michaela, crooning, "*Baby*. It's our *baby*."

It is quarter to nine when Adrian lowers himself into a chair at the Trident Café, legs shaking and nose dripping, tamping down his thoughts but trying not to extinguish them completely. This is one of the hardest things about living—keeping thoughts alive without letting them overwhelm you; keeping thoughts at bay without letting them slip away. He honestly doesn't know how people do it.

When the barista asks for his order, he startles at the realization that he hasn't got his wallet, not only because he feels naked and unsafe without it, but because he knows now that he left the house thoughtlessly, like a sleepwalker, though he was trying to do something right.

"Can I just get a glass of water?" he asks, and when she's gone, he closes his eyes and realizes he hasn't brought his laptop or his phone either, and suddenly he can't imagine what he will do without them. Then the café door opens and the chilly air washes in, and Adrian looks up to see Deborah, standing alone, looking at him without malice.

He palms the table for support and smiles feebly.

How is she here? Had he called her, somewhere in his somnambulistic, withdrawal-addled stupor? Temptation or signpost?

She hurries over in her peacoat and scarf, shaking her head, and reaches down to hug him robustly. "We were all so worried,

Adrian. You look so *good*. What are you doing up and around?"
Then she sits down without asking.

"I forgot my wallet," he says.

"Oh," she says, and grins tenderly, if tentatively. "Well, do
you need to borrow some money?"

"No, no," he says. With no Xanax or Vicodin, the anxiety is
palpable, and he tries to remember how he had once calmed himself before any of it. How he had been a child in a canoe, floating
downriver. He didn't call Deborah, he realizes, just came at the
same time they had met here before, when he pushed his knee
between her thighs at the table.

She takes his hand.

"I can't stay," he says, "I'm working out." He eases his hand
out from under hers, just as he has done pulling a tooth from
under Michaela's pillow while she was sleeping.

"Do you want to come over later? I heard you were . . . living
with a friend. Should I make you some turkey soup?"

Adrian can't figure out how she knows he's staying with Jeff,
but there it is. Her eyes are gleaming. He breathes in through his
nose, straightens in his seat. A child, in a canoe, floating downriver.

"No," he says. "No, I'm . . . Can't do that. Anymore."

Chapter Twelve

Once back at Jeff's, winded and chilled, Adrian searches frantically around the house for his phone, before finding it between his bed and table. When he checks his messages, he finds nothing from Stella and the kids, just a private message from the man beside the water.

4601 (11/26/09): Hey Haven't heard back from you? Thinking of notifying those follks at Cornel. I don't want this guy to get away from us. I guess it has to be validated someway. You probly don't need the money but $50000 is a hell of alot to somebody like me. (Not that thats what its about)

Adrian stares at the screen a moment. Somebody's been doing some research, but, he reminds himself, this is really no concern of his.

He retrieves a Revive from his watery cooler. Sits on the couch. Drinks. Looks around the silent room. Jeff's TV blinks: 12:00, 12:00, 12:00, 12:00—

After a short nap, Adrian calls Stella to set up time with the kids. Stella answers almost right away, and when she does, Adrian hears the clattering of pots and pans. He can almost smell the giblets simmering away with celery and onions on their way to becoming gravy. He can almost see the pies sitting out on the sideboard, sugar crystals sparkling atop the apple and the even slick of the pumpkin to be topped with whipped cream. Stella says, "No problem," but that he should have the kids home by four, so they can "get ready for dinner."

Once showered and shaven, he drives to the house, texts Zander to say he's arrived, then waits outside. After a couple of long minutes, the kids slink out to the Saab with their heads down, wearing jackets Adrian's never seen before. In as animated a manner as possible, he hops out to greet them and let them in the back, but Zander shuffles around to Stella's spot in the front passenger's seat. Before Adrian can think about the proper new order of things, Michaela slides into the back, says, "Oh, okay," and slams the door.

Soon, they're drinking white hot chocolates at Starbucks, Michaela swinging her legs under the table without saying a word and Zander gazing, glassy-eyed, at the hipsters working the bar, his eyebrows lifted slightly in wry, exaggerated boredom.

"Well, I'm feeling a lot better, you guys," Adrian tells them with a measured grin. "So, don't worry about me."

A gaping silence ensues while the children maintain their previous postures and expressions almost perfectly.

Adrian tries again. "I'll bet you're looking forward to a great dinner, though, huh?"

Michaela says, "I am, at least." She glances furtively over at Zander, who frowns back at her as some kind of signal.

Adrian looks questioningly at the boy. "How about you, buddy?"

"No, yeah," Zander mumbles and looks down at the crumpled paper napkin on the table.

Adrian has perhaps never felt more sorry than this.

He pulls himself in closer to the table, takes Michaela's hand and kisses it. "Been missing you two."

"Mom says you're 'too sick' to come home right now." Zander still won't look at him.

Adrian doesn't know how to respond. He doesn't know what excuse he expected Stella would give, but he wasn't prepared for this one. "Well, I guess I could have died, so . . . I've been pretty sick."

Zander crosses his arms suddenly, thrusts out his pelvis, and shoves his legs out beneath the table, sending the chair scooting. "We *know* what's going on, Dad."

Michaela looks worried and watches Zander to see if he'll make any more sudden movements.

Zander says, "You and Mom are fighting."

Adrian wishes for words to fix this, even to address it. He says, "It's going to be okay," but of course, he doesn't know that. He's still waiting for signs.

"Hey, you know what, though?" he says. "I have a surprise for you."

When he pulls the Saab along the field in front of the old shell of a house, though both kids wear their doubting smirks and grip their empty Starbucks cups, once they follow Adrian's pointed index finger, all seems redeemed.

"Oh, my God! Daddy!" Michaela shrieks.

Zander's already thrown off his seat belt and is yanking at the door handle, as a small palomino horse steps from just inside the missing front door to the breezy field, its ears back and head high.

"Hold on a minute," cautions Adrian. "We've got to be very stealthy. Hang on!"

They come together in a little pod. Adrian gathers Michaela under his arm, ruffles Zander's hair.

"All right. Now, don't scare them, okay? Be very quiet and very slow. Be 'one with the field,' " he whispers, grinning.

Michaela whispers back, "One for the field."

"Okay?" he asks Zander, and the boy smiles and nods.

They begin their surreptitious trek toward the old house, the three of them, all breathing high in their chests, cheeks flushed, eyes trained on the palomino. Though the horse is acutely aware of them, it sets off no alarms, and to Adrian's surprise, they make their way across without incident, stepping cautiously around piles of manure and the occasional hole, elbowing each other in the ribs. When, in the doorway, a second horse, a paint, pushes from inside the house past the first, shoulders and rumps colliding, they both squeeze out like fish from a bottleneck into the open pasture, and the children laugh out loud.

"Look," Adrian whispers, pointing at the front windows.

The kids gasp. A horse is clearly visible in the living room, and another darker horse withdraws from it as they're watching, deeper into the house in a quiet sweep of movement.

Adrian can hear Stella's voice in his head in teasing disbelief, "*In* the house?" she'd say. "You guys are making this up!"

"Can we go in?" Zander pleads.

"Please, Daddy?" says Michaela, pulling at the arm of Adrian's jacket.

Adrian wonders why he didn't anticipate this moment. Of course they want to go inside. Hadn't *he*? Wild horses are wild, but when he was here last, the one he encountered was gentle enough.

He plants his hands on his hips a moment as if considering, then turns his back to Michaela and lowers himself to a squat, winded but so happy. "Hop on," he says. "And hold on tight in case we have to run."

"Yes!" hisses Zander.

"No talking," warns Adrian. "Stay right by me." And they enter the place like those with missing pieces entering the palace of Oz.

Once inside, two horses loom, breaths barely visible in the air—one peering out the window toward the sky, one looking dead-ended at an interior wall, no food or water around, only mud and clots of grasses and manure. Michaela's legs squeeze Adrian's waist as she holds tight to his neck. Zander is making his silent, wide-mouthed expression of amazement.

From elsewhere in the house, they hear a brief, impatient snorting.

Zander pulls at Adrian's arm and gestures toward the sound, mouthing, "Let's *do* this!"

Intent on avoiding the kitchen this time, with its land mine of scattered shot, Adrian leads them instead toward a dim hallway. They venture in slow motion through the living room, each passing a hand along the crumbling plaster wall with its two ancient electrical outlets and one discolored well where a switch used to be. The place has been stripped clean. No curtain rod dangling above the window, not even a charred stick of kindling in the fireplace. Only the two mute beasts standing large. Adrian considers touching one on its hindquarters, because he's seen people do it, to calm a horse when approaching. He thinks better of it, but he and the kids pass so close they can see the horses' wide, damp nostrils and the yellow white of their eyes.

When they make the turn into the hallway, the broad rump of a bay mare materializes in the space before them.

Michaela gasps, Adrian backs into Zander, and they all fall back against the wall.

The mare's head and upper torso were concealed beyond a doorjamb opening into another room. Now she yanks back in surprise, scraping her muzzle against the splintered frame, and trots out the way they came in. Her escaping footfalls soften once they hit the ground outside, then come immediately back around toward their side of the house.

Zander is grinning, breathing hard, until he glances into the room the mare had been blocking and his mouth falls open. "Dad."

Adrian rounds the corner to peer into the small bedroom. Nearly at his feet there lies a tiny dead horse.

"Jesus!" Adrian gasps.

When Michaela squeals, the horses in the living room spook and run.

Adrian lowers her to the floor, takes her head in his hands. "It's okay, honey. Don't worry."

"What *happened* to it?" Zander asks, jittery with adrenaline, his hands around his throat.

"You guys go back outside," Adrian says. "I'll be right there."

Michaela allows herself to be taken under Zander's arm. "Is it dead?"

The foal is covered in a hardened coat of birth slickness, seasoned now into a grossly pockmarked glaze. The curve of the neck, the peaked ears, the wide forehead, everything is in miniature, so that Adrian almost expects to find the coiling tail of a seahorse at its end, but there are the spindle legs, tucked under it, never opened, its visible eye closed. Out in the pasture, the bay mare paces back and forth like someone trying to make up her mind before knocking.

Adrian forces himself to look again at the decomposing foal, then scans the hopeless room. What can he possibly do here? If he could find a spade, he'd bury the animal, but there's nothing. He could cover it, but there's no tarp, no trash bag he can empty, no scrap of plywood.

He should just attend to the kids, he thinks, get them out of here—but the mare still stands breathing, twitching, and staring through the window.

Adrian sighs deeply, then shrugs off his jacket, folding it shoulder to shoulder and laying it along the windowsill. He calls out, "Be right there!" and unbuttons and peels off his shirt, the late November air amassing in layers around his arms, his chest, his stomach, then pulls off the pristine undershirt he considers one of the last remnants of polite society.

Squatting unsteadily, he lays his tee shirt over the torso of the liver-red foal and around its stunted ridge of a mane, pressing the cotton with his palms like a bandage and swiping at his nose with his knuckles. He knows a fool's errand when he sees one, and this is it, but maybe it will quell some of the stench; maybe it will obscure or confuse the visual impact of the thing on its grieving mother.

They drive back to town in silence. This obviously wasn't what Adrian had in mind. They'd been having so much fun too.

When they get to the house, he says, "Happy Thanksgiving, guys. Call me later?"

They look at him, as if confused. Michaela gives him a quick peck on the cheek and says, "Oma's bringing hazelnut cake!"

Adrian looks to Zander, who says, "We'll try. You call us," and stalks back toward the house.

At seven that night, Adrian has a light dinner at Jeff's kitchen island—kale and potato soup with good bread from Alfalfa's—reconsidering his position. He clearly isn't paying the right kind of attention. He'd been so pleased to be with Zander and Michaela, and they'd been happy too, then they were rewarded for their efforts with this macabre thing. He shouldn't have taken them there. He wants to be with them, but he doesn't really know how. He needs help. He needs a sign.

Jeff watches the Broncos stampede the Giants from the couch, eating three fried eggs, raisin toast, and cheap pumpkin pie from King Soopers.

"Hey," he shouts, "you should come in here! I've got an extra cap if you want to put one on."

Adrian tells him he's got to rest and catch up on a little reading, and that's just what he does. Then once Jeff's fallen asleep in front of the TV, he steals out to the parking area and drives home again.

He's brought a few things with him, like an extra shirt and underwear, his bag with his laptop, and his antibiotics, in case he were to end up staying, though he isn't counting on it, of course. He's done nothing to earn it. He knows that. He hasn't been listening.

He's not really sure what he's doing, so he idles near the mailbox, not entering the driveway that leads to the house, just trying to catch sight of someone he loves walking through an illuminated room on Thanksgiving night.

All is still.

There is his house, sitting in a champagne pool of light, the little aspen to the left of the front door perfectly shaped, the careful grouping of waxflower bushes to the right stiff and bare, the shape of the stairway, just visible through the frosty front door window, leading up to the bedrooms. It's as though he's viewing an exhibit in a museum on a subject he's always been interested in but knows nothing about firsthand.

If he's honest, he wants Stella to see him waiting at the curb. He wants her to crack open the door and wave him inside, fill him in on what he's missed, tell him what to do next. Maybe he should knock on the door.

He decides that if a light in the house goes on or off while he's sitting here, he'll do it, he'll knock. He'll wait for a sign.

After a few minutes, he eats a stiff granola bar he finds in the bottom of his bag; then he cleans the dashboard with the Armor All wipes he keeps in the pouch behind the passenger-side seat.

Finally he takes out his laptop and plugs it into the lighter, connects to his home Wi-Fi, and logs on to Backyard Birder, to the posts and messages from the man beside the water.

Just out of curiosity, because there's really nothing else to do, he copies and pastes all the man's communications to a new document. He studies their preternatural glow—curious, naturally curious, about where he's been writing from.

The first post is from November first, late Halloween night after the pumpkin runners mowed down his family. The man reported a Northern Cardinal, but a cardinal could be seen anywhere in the eastern and southern US.

Later in this same post: "We're getting a new batch of boys from Georgia" and "The north field is like grand central station." Very odd. Maybe the juxtaposition of the arrival of "boys" with a "field" indicates involvement in a sport. A coach at a university maybe? Unlikely, since it's the wrong time of year for new recruits, and anyway, it tells him nothing about the location.

Adrian glances down the street as a van rolls right through the stop sign. He gives it two clipped honks of his horn. Once it's gone, he looks up to see whether Stella heard him, and with no change in the house, he scrolls to the November second post.

Here, the man reported having seen an American Kestrel, which is so common and widespread, it's no use at all. He did say the weather "got so cold I put on a jacket," which likely implies a warm climate in which a jacket is usually unnecessary in November. So, likely *south*eastern US, and if there were an ivorybill still extant, there's no other place it would be. Then: "the new guys are breaking down getting their hands burned and black." No idea. Auto mechanics? Welders? Coal miners? Blacksmiths?

Michaela's light is still off, and Zander's is still on. It's an odd light, actually, as if he's replaced his usual bedside bulb with one of those colored "party" bulbs. A shadow of movement cuts across the room. Adrian squints up at the hazy window, then realizes he has his binocular and takes it out, just as Zander moves into full view.

Adrian's heart contracts at the simple sight of his son in his room, his head with that new-penny sheen, wearing the light-blue tee shirt he likes to sleep in. He's got something in one hand, a notebook or magazine, and a can of something in the other, probably those health-food sodas that Stella buys as a compromise, the tangerine that Zander prefers. He arcs it across the room, out of sight, then slings the magazine too, like a Frisbee, and moves away again. He's angry, Adrian thinks, or he's just a boy aiming for a basket.

Adrian taps the command button to light up the next entry: A Great Blue Heron "fishing on the SR sound." A coastal location, yes, but something else—one of the "new boys" was "impressed by *the reservation.*" He hadn't noticed that before.

Intrigued, Adrian Googles "American Indian Reservation" and "American southeast." He finds the Poarch band of Creek Indians (the Muskogee), which looks to be on and near the coast in Alabama; the Chitimacha tribe in Louisiana; the Miccosukee tribe in Miami; and the Seminoles, in a few coastal areas of southern Florida.

When he backspaces to add in "coastal," he clicks on the wrong option in the dropdown menu and a list of North American tribes appears:

A'ananin (Aane), Abenaki (Abnaki, Abanaki, Abenaqui), Absaalooke (Absaroke), Achumawi (Achomawi), Acjachemen, Acoma, Agua Caliente, Adai, Ahtna (Atna), Ajachemen, Akimel O'odham, Akwaala (Akwala), Alabama-Coushatta, Aleut, Alutiiq, Algonquians (Algonkians), Algonquin (Algonkin), Alliklik, Alnobak (Alnôbak, Alnombak), Alsea (Älsé, Alseya), Andaste, Anishinaabe (Anishinabemowin, Anishnabay), Aniyunwiya, Antoniaño, Apache, Apalachee, Applegate, Apsaalooke (Apsaroke), Arapaho (Arapahoe), Arawak, Arikara, Assiniboine, Atakapa, Atikamekw, Atsina, Atsugewi (Atsuke), Araucano (Araucanian), Avoyel (Avoyelles), Ayisiyiniwok, Aymara, Aʒtec, Babine, Bannock, Barbareño, Bari, Bear River, Beaver Bella, Bella, Bella Coola,

Beothuks (Betoukuag), Bidai, Biloxi, Black Carib, Blackfoot (Blackfeet), Blood Indians, Bora, Caddo (Caddoe), Cahita, Cahto, Cahuilla, Calapooya (Calapuya, Calapooia), Calusa, (Caloosa) Carib, Carquin, Carrier, Caska, Catawba, Cathlamet, Cayuga, Cayuse, Celilo, Central Pomo, Chahta, Chalaque, Chappaquiddick (Chappaquiddic, Chappiquidic), Chawchila (Chawchilla), Chehalis, Chela, Chemehuevi, Cheraw, Chero-enhaka (Cheroenkhaka, Cherokhaka), Cherokee, Chetco, Chey-enne (Cheyanne), Chickamaugan, Chickasaw, Chilcotin, Chilula-Wilkut, Chimariko, Chinook, Chipewyan (Chipe-wyin), Chippewa, Chitimacha (Chitamacha), Chocheno, Choc-taw, Cholon, Chontal de Tabasco (Chontal Maya), Choynimni (Choinimni), Chukchansi, Chumash, Clackamas (Clackama), Clallam, Clatskanie, (Clatskanai), Clatsop, Cmique, Coastal, Cochimi, Cochiti, Cocopa (Cocopah), Coeur d'Alene, Cofan, Columbia (Columbian), Colville, Comanche, Comcaac, Comox, Conestoga, Coos (Coosan), Copper River Athabaskan, Coquille, Cora, Coso, Costanoan, Coushatta, Cowichan, Cowlitz, Cree, Creek, Croatan (Croatoan), Crow, Cruzeño, Cuna, Cucupa (Cucapa), Cupeño (Cupa), Cupik (Cu'pik, Cuit), Dakelh, Dakota, Dakubetede, Dawson, Deg Xinag (Deg Hit'an), Delaware, Dena'ina (Denaina), Dene, Dene Suline (Denesu-line), Dene Tha, Diegueno, Dine (Dineh), Dogrib, Dohema (Dohma), Dumna, Dunne-za (Dane-zaa, Dunneza), Eastern Inland Cree, Eastern Pomo, Eel River Athabascan, Eenou (Eeyou), Eskimo, Esselen, Etchemin (Etchimin), Euchee, Eudeve (Endeve), Excelen, Eyak, Fernandeno (Fernandeño), Flathead Salish, Fox, Gabrielino (Gabrieleño), Gae, Gaigwu, Galibi, Galice, Garifuna, Gashowu, Gitxsan (Gitksan), Gos-iute (Goshute), Gros Ventre, Guarani, Guarijio (Guarijío),

Gulf, Gwich'in (Gwichin, Gwitchin), Haida, Haisla, Halkomelem (Halqomeylem), Hän (Han Hwech'in), Hanis, Hare, Hatteras, Haudenosaunee, Havasupai, Hawaiian, Heiltsuk, Heve, Hiaki, Hichiti (Hitchiti), Hidatsa, Hocak (Ho-Chunk, Hochunk), Holikachuk, Homalco, Hoopa, Hopi, Hopland Pomo, Hualapai, Huelel, Huichol, Huichun, Hupa, Huron, Illini (Illiniwek, Illinois), Inca, Ineseño (Ineẓeño), Ingalik (Ingalit), Innoko, Innu, Inuktitut (Inupiat, Inupiaq, Inupiatun), Iowa-Oto (Ioway), Iroquois Confederacy, Ishak, Isleño, Isleta, Itza Maya (Itẓah), Iviatim, Iynu, James Bay Cree, Jemeẓ, Juaneno (Juaneño), Juichun, Kabinapek, Kainai (Kainaiwa), Kalapuya (Kalapuyan, Kalapooya), Kalina (Kaliña), Kanenavish, Kanien 'kehaka (Kanienkehaka), Kalispel, Kansa (Kanẓa, Kanẓe), Karankawa, Karkin, Karok (Karuk), Kashaya, Kaska, Kaskaskia, Kathlamet, Kato, Kaw, Kenaitẓe (Kenai), Keres (Keresan), Kichai, Kickapoo (Kikapu), Kiliwa (Kiliwi), Kiowa, Kiowa Apache, Kitanemuk, Kitsai, Klahoose, Klallam, Klamath-Modoc, Klatskanie (Klatskanai), Klatsop, Klickitat, Koasati, Kolchan, Konkow (Konkau), Konomihu, Kootenai (Ktunaxa, Kutenai), Koso, Koyukon, Kuitsh, Kulanapo (Kulanapan, Kulanapa), Kumeyaay (Kumiai), Kuna, Kupa, Kusan, Kuskokwim, Kutchin (Kootchin), Kwaiailk, Kwakiutl (Kwakwala), Kwalhioqua, Kwantlen, Kwapa (Kwapaw), Kwinault (Kwinayl), Laguna, Lakhota (Lakota), Lakmiak (Lakmayut), Lassik, Laurentian (Lawrencian), Lecesem, Lenape (Lenni Lenape), Lillooet, Lipan Apache, Listiguj (Listuguj), Lnuk (L'nuk, L'nu'k, Lnu), Lokono, Loucheux (Loucheaux), Loup, Lower Chehalis, Lower Coquille, Lower Cowlitz, Lower Tanana, Lower Umpqua, Luckiamute (Lukiamute), Luiseño, Lumbee, Lummi, Lushootseed,

Lutuamian, Macushi (Macusi), Mahican, Maidu, Maina
(Mayna), Makah, Makushi, Maliseet (Maliceet, Malisit,
Malisset), Mandan, Mapuche (Mapudungun, Mapudugan),
Maricopa, Massachusett (Massachusetts), Massasoit (Massas-
soit, Mashpee), Mattabesic, Mattole, Maumee, Matlatzinca,
Mayan, Mayo, Mengwe, Menominee (Menomini), Mescalero-
Chiricahua, Meskwaki (Mesquakie), Metis Creole, Miami-
Illinois, Miccosukee, Michif, Micmac (Mi'gmaq), Migueleño,
Mikasuki, Mi'kmaq (Mikmawisimk), Mingo, Minqua, Minsi,
Minto, Miskito (Mosquito), Missouria, Miwok (Miwuk),
Mixe, Mixtec (Mixteco, Mixteca), Modoc, Mohave, Mohawk,
Mohegan, Mohican, Mojave, Molale (Molalla, Molala), Mo-
nache (Mono), Montagnais, Montauk, Moosehide, Mult-
nomah, Munsee (Munsie, Muncey, Muncie), Muskogee
(Muscogee, Mvskoke), Musqueam, Mutsun, Nabesna,
Nadot'en (Natoot'en, Natut'en), Nahane (Nahani, Nahanne),
Nahuat, Nahuatl, Nakoda (Nakota), Nambe, Nanticoke, Nan-
tucket, Narragansett, Naskapi, Nass-Gitxsan, Natchez, Natick,
Naugutuck, Navajo (Navaho), Nawat, Nayhiyuwayin, Nde,
Nee-me-poo, Nehiyaw (Nehiyawok), Netela, New Blackfoot,
Newe, Nez Perce, Niantic, Nicola, Niitsipussin (Niitsitapi),
Nimiipuu (Nimi'ipu), Nipmuc, Nisenan (Nishinam), Nisga'a
(Nisgaa, Nishga), Nlaka'pamux (Nlakapamux), Nomlaki,
Nooksack (Nooksak), Nootka (Nutka), Nootsak, Northeastern
Pomo, Northern Carrier, Northern Cheyenne, Nottoway, Nuu-chaa-
nulth (Nuuchahnulth), Nuxalk, Obispeño, Ocuilteco, Odawa
Ofo, Ogahpah (Ogaxpa), Ohlone, Ojibwa (Ojibway, Ojibwe,
Ojibwemowin), Oji-Cree, Okanagan (Okanogan), Okwanuchu,
Old Blackfoot, Omaha-Ponca, Oneida, Onondaga, O'ob,
No'ok, O'odham (Oodham), Opata, Osage, Otchipwe,

Otoe, Ottawa, Pai, Paipai, Paiute, Palaihnihan (Palaihnih, Palahinihan), Palewyami, Palouse, Pamlico, Panamint, Papago-Pima, Pascua Yaqui, Passamaquoddy, Patuxet, Patwin, Paugussett (Paugusset), Pawnee, Peigan, Pend d'Oreill, Penobscot (Pentagoet), Pentlatch (Pentlach), Peoria, Pequot, Picuris, Piegan (Piikani), Pima, Pima Bajo, Pipil, Pit River, Pojoaque, Pomo (Pomoan), Ponca, Poospatuck (Poosepatuk, Poospatuk, Poosepatuck), Popoluca (Popoloca), Potawatomi (Pottawatomie, Potawatomie), Powhatan, Pueblo, Puget Sound Salish, Purisimeño, Putún, Quapaw (Quapa), Quechan, Quechua, Quilcene, Quileute, Quinault, Quinnipiac (Quinnipiack), Quiripi, Raramuri, Red Indians, Restigouche, Rumsen, Runasimi, Saanich, Sac, Sahaptin, Salhulhtxw, Salinan, Salish, Samish, Sandia, Sanish (Sahnish), San Felipe, San Ildefonso, San Juan, Sanpoil, Santa Ana, Santa Clara, Santiam, Santo Domingo, Saponi, Sarcee (Sarsi), Sastean (Sasta), Satsop, Savannah, Sauk, Saulteaux, Schaghticoke (Scaticook), Sechelt, Secwepemc (Secwepmectsin), Sekani, Selkirk, Seminoles, Seneca, Seri, Serrano, Seshelt, Severn, Ojibwe Shanel, Shasta (Shastan), Shawnee (Shawano), Shinnecock, Shoshone (Shoshoni), Shuar, Shuswap, Siksika (Siksikawa), Siletz, Similkameen, Sinkiuse (Sincayuse), Sinkyone, Sioux, Siuslaw, Skagit, Skicin, S'Klallam, Skokomish, Skraeling, Skwamish, Slavey (Slave, Slavi), Sliammon (Sliamon), Sm'algyax, Snichim, Snohomish, Songish, Sooke, Souriquois (Sourquois), Southeastern Pomo, Southern Paiute, Spokane (Spokan), Squamish, Stadaconan, St'at'imcets (St'at'imc), Stockbridge, Sto:lo, Stoney, Straits, Sugpiaq, Suquamish, Susquehannock, Suwal, Swampy Cree, Swinomish, Tabasco

Chontal, Tachi (Tache), Taensa, Tahltan, Tagish, Tahcully, Taino, Takelma (Takilma), Takla, Taltushtuntude, Tamyen, Tanacross, Tanaina, Tanana, Tano, Taos, Tarahumara, Tataviam, Tauira (Tawira), Teguime, Tehachapi, Ten'a, Tenino, Tepehuano (Tepecano), Tequistlateco (Tequistlatec), Tesuque, Tetes-de-Boules, Tewa, Thompson, Tigua, Tillamook, Timbisha (Timbasha), Timucua, Tinde, Tinneh, Tiwa, Tjekan, Tlahuica (Tlahura), Tlatskanie (Tlatskanai), Tlatsop, Tlicho Dinne, Tlingit, Tohono O'odham, Tolowa, Tongva, Tonkawa, Towa, Tsalagi (Tsa-la-gi), Tsattine, Tsekani (Tsek'ehne), Tsetsehestahese, Tsetsaut, Tsilhqot'in (Tzilkotin), Tsimshian (Tsimpshian), Tsitsistas, Tsooke, Tsoyaha, Tsuu T'ina (Tsuutina), Tualatin, Tubar (Tubare), Tubatulabal, Takudh, Tulalip, Tumpisa (Tümbisha, Tumbisha), Tunica, Tupi, Tuscarora, Tutchone, Tutelo, Tututni, Tuwa'duqutsid, Twana, Twatwa (Twightwee), Uchi (Uche, Uchee), Ukiah (Ukian, Uki, Ukia), Ukomnom, Umatilla, Unami, Unangan (Unangax), Unkechaug (Unquachog), Upper Chehalis, Upper Chinook, Upper Cowlitz, Upper Tanana, Upper Umpqua, Ute, Ventureño, Virginian Algonkin, Wailaki (Wailakki), Wailatpu (Waylatpu), Walapai, Walla Walla, Wampano, Wampanoag, Wanapam, Wanki (Wangki), Wappinger, Wappo, Warijio (Warihio, Warijío), Warm Springs, Wasco-Wishram, Washo (Washoe), Wazhazhe, Wea, Wenatchi (Wenatchee), Wendat, Weott, Western Pomo, Whilkut, White Clay People, Wichita (Witchita), Wikchamni, Willapa (Willopah), Winnebago, Wintu (Wintun), Wishram, Witsuwit'en (Witsuwiten), Wiyot (Wi'yot, Wishosk), Wolastoqewi (Wolastoqiyik), Wyandot (Wyandotte), Yakama (Yakima), Yanesha,

Yaquina (Yakonan, Yakon), Yavapai, Yawelmani, Yaqui,
Yinka Dene, Yneseño (Yneẕeño), Yocot'an, Yokaia (Yakaya),
Yokuts (Yokut, Yokutsan), Yoncalla (Yonkalla), Yowlumni,
Ysleño, Ysleta del Sur, Yucatec Maya (Yucateco, Yucatan),
Yuchi (Yuchee), Yuki (Yukian), Yuma, Yupik (Yu'pik,
Yuit), Yurok (Yu'rok), Zapotec, Zia, Zimshian, Zoque, Zuni

Stunning. Unimaginable.

Adrian tries to take in this list, the incomprehensible depth and breadth of it. Where are they?

He scans the list for familiar names, only finds a fraction he knows: Algonquin, Apache, Arapaho, Catawba (his maternal grandfather's tribe), Cherokee, Cheyenne, Chinook, Crow, Delaware, Hopi, Iroquois, Mohican, Nez Perce, Pueblo, Seminole, Ute, Wichita, Zuni.

His breathing becomes shallow and rapid, and he gulps down air to compensate when his heart skips a beat. If he keeps this up, he'll have to go into the house for one of Michaela's lunch bags. He lays back his head.

Your staying will be the beauty's undoing.

He glances again at the list, then clicks off it. Urgently now. Back to his document, scrolling down to the man's November eighteenth Wood Stork posting "by Yellow River."

He Googles "Yellow River," and he finds one in Georgia, noncoastal, emptying into a lake. Then a *coastal* Yellow River in Florida and Alabama that drains into Blackwater Bay in the Panhandle, only an hour from the Poarch Indian Reservation in Southern Alabama. Yes. He may be getting warm.

Finally, the man reported the Ivory-billed Woodpecker perching on a cypress. Said he was taking down nesting boxes for Red-cockadeds before driving to the swamp . . . This is *key*.

Red-cockadeds only nest in living longleaf pines infected with a particular fungus. The trees are only susceptible to this fungus when they're between eighty to a hundred and twenty years old. The "red-heart disease" that results from the fungus's interaction with the old trees softens their inner heartwood and only *then* can cockadeds build nest cavities. If the trees aren't old growth, you won't find Red-cockadeds. The Ivory-billed Woodpecker *also* happened to thrive in this type of terrain—hardwood swamp with lots of dead and decaying old-growth trees, and the two birds were sometime companions for centuries, until one of them went missing.

When Adrian checks the National Resources Conservation Report on the Poarch Indian Reservation to search for longleaf pine, he does find some, but it's new growth only. Then he types "Florida Panhandle," "reservation," and "longleaf" into the Google search bar.

In addition to the price of beachfront hotel reservations and reservation-only horseback riding, several links appear in which *reservation* refers to, of all things, a military installation. *Of course.* The man's references to night training, the boys arriving from Georgia, the hands of the men, burned and black—Eglin Air Force Base. Its 463,000 acres happen to contain the largest remaining old-growth longleaf pine forest in existence.

Back at Backyard Birder's chat, this in a private message—

4601 (11/26/09): Hey Doc.
Wanted to tell you something. Morning before I saw the bird I woke up with my buddy Trammel pressing a Miller lite up against my

cheek telling me wake up I need to help him get a family of possums out from under his porch.

His whole house was trashed with our weapons of mass destruction (not actually) but we did have a long night. I didn't want to shoot any possums which he calls alien rat bastards and not many people do like possums. but he says I owe him since he paid for the booze ect. Anywy he sets me up in a lawn chair and hands me his rifle and hes got a length of PVC he shakes around under the porch and we do the dirty work. Spare you the details. When I'm getting ready to take my last shot I look up and see this brown sparrow staring down at me from a limb. Staring at me Doc like what the fuck are you doing. What the fuck are you doing. I stand up and chuck Trammels gun at the ground and walk out. Him sayingk what the fuck to??

Its my lunch that afternoon I'm taking a slug of mountain dew when I see him. The huge woodpecker on a tree in front of a crack in the clouds. This bird has the power of rightiousness. You should come see it. Might never have another change.

Adrian glances up one last time at the place where his family is sleeping. The lights in the house remain consistent. Outside, all is pristine Colorado darkness now.

"I've had *lots* of great relationships since *my* divorce," Jeff says, as he peppers his matzo ball. "I went to Junior's in Brooklyn once. Their matzo balls were much smaller. I like 'em big like this." He'd brought home some soup from the deli.

"Yeah, these are good," Adrian says, but he's listening for the *ding* of his cell phone in the pocket of his robe—waiting for a reply, an address, GPS coordinates.

Twenty-four hours have passed since Adrian messaged the man beside the water asking for his exact location, but no reply. No word on the Ivory-billed Woodpecker either, no earth-shattering sightings posted on any of the websites, no urgent phone calls or messages from his birding colleagues. (If the bird exists, at least the man has kept his word about exclusivity.) Adrian is about to tell Jeff everything, show him everything, ask him to come on what may be the greatest adventure of his life. "I'm not divorced, by the way," he begins, "but listen—"

Jeff barrels forward. "You know the woman I'm seeing now, with the New Age record company? Incredible girl, but—we're being straight with each other, right?"

"Uh . . . I assume so." Impatient, Adrian rhythmically ladles the rich chicken broth into his mouth.

"You know when you go house hunting?" Jeff says.

"Jeff—"

"You notice how when you first see a house, you block your mind to all the faults it's got? You're in a bubble, kind of. A self-imposed real-estate bubble. You don't even *want* to see the real house. You just want to see what's great about it. Then you and your wife or whoever start thinking where the dresser is gonna go in the bedroom, what wall your favorite painting'll hang on, where you'll plant the garden. You've got yourselves moved in already, before you even make an offer. Before you walk back out to your car. You just want to make it to closing before the lights go on. Well, that happens to be bullshit. Gets you in a dump truck of trouble down the line."

Adrian takes out his phone, glances at the screen, and lays it on the table.

"See, I *know* about that," Jeff continues. "What I do is, I wait. Doesn't matter if the house goes while I'm waiting. If it does, it's not meant to be. I wait until I feel the bubble go 'pop,' *then* I go back, see? I look at the peeling paint around the heating ducts, I look at the furnace real close, I look at the ceiling stains and the water pressure and the foundation and the zoning. See what I'm saying? I let the bubble break open and spill its guts before I make my move. Most people *want* the bubble. I don't want it. I'm on to it."

"So . . . what are you saying?"

"I'm talking about women, I'm talking about a lot of things. I'm not looking to fool myself, is what I'm saying. Been there, done that. Doesn't mean I'm not having a good time."

"Well, there's a difference between a bubble of illusion and a bubble of . . . possibility," Adrian says, out on an unfamiliar limb.

"Ha ha," Jeff chuckles with condescension. "You ever notice how when you look through a bubble, everything's distorted?" he continues, holding possibly the best metaphor of his life in his mouth like a cat with a canary.

"Yeah, whatever. What about your potential book deal, huh? You're picturing yourself on the back jacket, signing your autograph? Isn't that a bubble?"

"That's entrepreneurship."

There is a short silence between them as they scrape their spoons along the bottoms of their bowls and Adrian watches Jeff out of the corner of his eye.

Though Jeff is the man he considers his dearest friend, if he's attentive to signs, and he is now, Adrian is convinced in this moment that Jeff is somehow standing in his way, waiting with a sharp pin around the corner of his future, a future that requires an almost spiritual suspension of disbelief, that requires complete surrender to the unknown.

"Yeah, well, thanks for the soup," Adrian says, standing. "Have a good night."

He will journey to find the bird alone.

Adrian pulls himself out of bed the next morning full of an energy that belies his muddled condition. He packs the essentials into his dry pack (which he leaves half-empty to accommodate what will be his new prescriptions). He hoped to hear from the man beside the water before he took off, but birds don't wait, and neither can he.

He takes his binocular in its case; the digital video camera—essential; he borrows Jeff's backcountry backpack from his basement; he borrows his camo chest waders and boots from the coat closet. He's going to have to get wet.

When he's packed, he pens a note on one of Jeff's index cards and props it against his outdated Dell desktop, saying, "Have to leave for a few days. Not to worry, all is well!"

Then he calls home, hoping it will go to voicemail, but Stella picks up.

"Hey. What's this about your taking the kids into a house full of wild horses?"

"Hey," Adrian says, startled. "No, they were really gentle."

"Mm-hm. What's up?" She never says that. She hates that expression.

"Just," he hesitates, then continues, measured, "I'm going out of town for a few days. I didn't want you or the kids to worry if—"

"I thought you were recuperating."

There is a short silence when only his breath, still a little thick with the vapors of infection, is audible.

"Okay, then," she says. "I'll let them know."

She hangs up.

Who can blame her? How can he possibly expect her to understand? He might never have another change.

Within minutes, Adrian's driving to CVS to fill his brother's prescriptions: Xanax, Lunesta, Vicodin, some Adderall, and of course, he'll bring along the antibiotics he's been taking for the infection. Then on to Eastern Mountain Sports (avoiding Jeff at A Good Sport) where he will fill the gaps in supplies—first aid kit, new knife, insect repellent, water purifier.

By two in the afternoon, he's flying high over the clouds toward Tallahassee.

Chapter Thirteen

Highway 20 past Dismal Creek. Adrian drives mile after mile on roads so straight he takes his hands off the wheel. He's been taking Adderall to get through the travel day, and he's buzzing. He's driving to drive, sucking in the dense air of the Panhandle, the eerie darkness of the roads. Dreaming of the bird.

Still wired, he turns into Ebro Greyhound Park past ranch houses so small you want to call them something else, patchy yards cluttered or bare. Jeff's called or texted eight times in seven hours, and when Adrian pulls into the parking lot, he hammers one back, saying Jeff's clogging up his phone and to "please leave me the hell alone. ☺"

The murmuring dog track is teeming with suspects. Adrian loiters along the wall, watching tellers shuffle bills—eight dollars, twenty dollars, three hundred. Only when the bell *rings* do they glance up to watch disappointment wash over the horde like baptism.

Adrian picks up a racing form to check out the dogs: Blue Bayou, Wayward Son, Jenny's Best Hope, Wilmington Willy. He won't bet. He's not looking for that kind of sign. But he ambles outside all the way down by the fence, standing in the surreal light, when the mechanical rabbit, Rocky, is released, and the lean, muscular dogs shoot after it, lapping up the track.

He finds himself searching for the man beside the water, watching for a particular gait or tone of voice, a cigar, and he walks among the customers, along the fence line, along rows between bleachers in the stands, into the men's room, at the food stand. He imagines zeroing in on a stranger, saying, "Are you the one who saw the bird?" and the look on the man's face when he knows he's been found.

He weaves onto side roads and sandy drives off Highway 20 on his way to the hotel, tired now but too excited to sleep. He's got to see the water. He follows a sign toward a place called Historic Freeport—down a county highway through the town, out the other end—and nearly slams into five gargantuan circular white tanks (he can't fathom how big—50 feet in diameter, maybe 500,000 gallons each?).

Murphy Oil Terminal.

A ghostly compound surrounded by chain-link and sky-high gates above disco ball waves. GPS calls the water it borders La-Grange Bayou, which flows to Choctawhatchee Bay, then on to the Gulf. Adrian's the only human in sight. There's only a high, tight electrical hum and the smell of oil.

Adrian gets out of the car to stand on the gravel shoulder. It feels illegal, hidden—both his presence and the operation itself. He can just see a flat-bottomed oil barge approaching some quarter mile away, parting the dark water to push wide into the port. He remembers now: Murphy Oil—the million-gallon spill from their Louisiana refinery, the one that ruined Katrina's floodwaters and slicked the neighborhoods with poison. Now they're drilling deeper, penetrating the sandy bottom of the Gulf and the cold shelf of the Arctic, with only the seabirds to make report.

Spooked, Adrian gets back in the car. He idles a minute until the insects begin singing again, then drives away. He will search for the small thing that matters, and follow the sound of what's lost.

Not an hour later, he's gathering himself in earnest for the quest—sitting at the table by the air conditioner at the Niceville Hampton in Bluewater Bay, heartbeat rapid but steady, feet flat on the floor, surrounded by pamphlets on white-sand beaches, the armament museum, and the Indian burial grounds.

Google-Earthing Eglin Air Force Base on his computer, he zooms in from the top of the world to the Yellow River that worms along forests and unmarked military buildings, then slides into Choctawhatchee Bay to the south. He pulls out, and it's a whole country—then a whole continent—the earth itself.

Zooming in again to Florida, the Panhandle, Eglin, he flies like the most omniscient bird over the satellite-induced landscape of the base, taking in the tops of thousands upon thousands of longleaf pines. On the periphery, pods of military housing dot the streets, like streets in any town where people work as accountants or sell computers or patch drywall instead of sharpening and lubricating the churning blades of war and defense. He's lived his whole life without ever having set foot on a military base. He reads about drone strikes on the *New York Times* website, debates with Jeff about the quest for oil that drives US foreign policy, and laments with Stella the debt accrued, both fiscal and moral, under various administrations. But he's never known anyone, personally, who fought in the desert wars, and the prospect of venturing into this alien world of soldiers and their families makes him feel both anxious and captivated.

It's the way he felt when he rode behind his father on the back of his motorcycle as a child. Dean's ribs were thick under Adrian's fingers, and the road was hot beneath them. The powerful machine roared between Adrian's legs, guided by the reckless man who'd been designated by some crazy mechanism his de facto protector.

He must sleep. He swallows his pills with bottled water, plugs in his phone and two extra battery packs to charge, and makes his last plea of the night to the man beside the water.

mandrake3 (11/27/09): Please tell me exactly where you saw the bird. I'm here now! I'm assuming I follow the Yellow River? Then what? GPS? Call or text me day or night. 303-749-6202.

Adrian phones the base early the next morning, having received no call or text and slept fitfully from joint pain, anticipation, and Adderall. He wheedles his way through the Eglin AFB operator and various stiff-lipped receptionists, who will tell him nothing—nothing about the birds. When he tries to negotiate using his ornithological credentials, they pass him along to other phones in other offices where he has to leave messages. Finally, from a woman in Natural Resources that he impresses with his knowledge of longleaf habitat, he learns the base is the largest refuge in the world for Red-cockaded Woodpeckers as well as an important refuge for the Piping Plover, the Pine Barrens tree frog, the Okaloosa darter, and the leatherback sea turtle.

He'd simply never thought of it before. In a country swelling with strip malls and housing developments, spread with corn fields to feed the beef cows and supply corn syrup for nearly every product in the grocery stores, with highways and factories and airports and high-rises blotting out the habitats of the jackrabbits, the bobcats, the spotted owls, the wolves, and the buffalo—one of the main sources of land left undisturbed are the protected parcels owned and operated by the US military. Bases like Fort Campbell, Camp Pendleton, Fort Bragg, Fort Hood, Eglin, and the naval stations in Norfolk, Jacksonville, and South Carolina. These are the sanctuaries for the endangered and the weary—in all, 24 million acres of land.

The irony of this fact is not lost on Adrian, and as it begins to form a hazy shape in his head, with the phone between his shoulder and his ear, he parts his hair with both hands and asks, "How do they survive in the midst of the blasting and the detonating?"

Here the woman hesitates, perhaps insulted, perhaps irritated, so he barrels on to the crux of the matter—civilian access to the base. How can he get in?

Eglin AFB Environmental Public Affairs is the place where Adrian finally finds an answer to his question. There, an energetic male voice virtually ringing with understated authority tells Adrian he's welcome on the base, and that for ten dollars he can purchase an outdoor recreation permit to bike, hike, or canoe through a number of areas on the "reservation." In order to receive the permit, he'll have to get a bit of education at a place called Jackson Guard, where he'll sit through a quick video. Since Eglin's primary mission is the development and testing of munitions for the Air Force, they need to maintain a tremendous amount of buffer space for safety, the man explains. There are areas that are off-limits to civilians at all times, of course, and certain areas that are often open but that, on any given day, are off-limits for certain periods, due to testing or training ops. Today, for example, and for the next nine days, road 4D is closed, as are the southern Yellow River and East Bay access roads through the base. Jackson Guard will provide a map along with a complete list of off-limits areas at the training session.

Adrian snags his zippered bag of medication from his bedside table. He swallows his antibiotic, a Vicodin, and an Adderall. Maybe he didn't fully take in the information about the closings. Maybe he's feeling invincible, or maybe he's just counting on his luck. But he's already shoving his swamp clothes into his pack and jimmying his feet into Jeff's boots. He's packing up the Deep Woods Off and stuffing electrolyte Jelly Bellys into his pockets.

By the time Adrian buys food, rents the kayak, loads it onto his car, and gets to Jackson Guard, it's 10:00 a.m. He attends the recreational-permit video session, where he learns that the Eglin Natural Resources Branch is locally referred to as Jackson Guard from the days when Andrew Jackson, not yet president, had kept prisoners there during the Seminole Indian Wars. Within the next few years, Jackson would become commander in chief and formally set into motion the Indian Removal Act, when a hundred thousand American Indians would traverse one thousand miles west on foot along the Trail of Tears, some in chains, and many dying on the journey.

Adrian doesn't hear about that part at Jackson Guard, only that during the late thirties and early forties, as the United States prepared for World War II, the Pentagon began buying up enormous parcels of relatively unspoiled land—forests and swamps and deserts and coastline—for military reservations. Some 40 million of those acres were Native American lands. While the rest of the country spent decades getting clear-cut, plowed over, and developed to the gills, the relative tranquility of Department of Defense lands gradually became home to four hundred threatened or endangered species. Piping Plovers fluttered over warning signage into airfields; flatwoods salamanders scurried unfettered through barbed-wire fences into munitions training ops; black bears ambled over demarcations printed onto a map.

When environmentalists thought of those animals caught in military crossfire, blasted in a hail of gunpowder and experimental Agent Orange, they demanded their protection, and like anyone under the legislative gun, the armed forces were "happy to compromise." Soldiers redirected their tanks from the turtles' nests and drilled nesting cavities into ancient trees. They got out of their jeeps to lift rare snakes out of harm's way. They moved only quietly and at night near the nests of bald eagles, planted only native trees and flowers. Eglin Air Force Base alone planted over two million longleaf pine trees on its reservation in one year, by hand. In a four-year period, the four branches of the military spent over $300 million to protect species designated endangered. Adrian listens to this part of the video with genuine interest. He doesn't know what to make of it—this paradoxical tale of perpetrators and saviors.

Finally, he learns he has to watch for UXOs, unexploded ordnance, basically anything metal on the ground or in the brush or trees from the size of a bullet to the size of a barrel, that may, in fact, be "live." No one has yet been killed on an innocent hike on Eglin, but the military has to spend a great deal of time picking up the lead from the ground, both live and spent—hundreds of tons a year, in fact—to keep things tidy.

Adrian tells the attendants at Jackson Guard he plans to hang out on the banks of the Yellow River, maybe do a bit of hiking, float around a little in the boat. He tells them he wants to watch the Gulf sturgeon jump, take some photos. All this to get a detailed map of the place. When he asks about the swamp, the woman at the desk says she has no knowledge of one and points out the same closed access roads the man mentioned on the phone.

Leaning against the hood of his car, holding the precious four-foot-wide map like a soldier's letter from home, Adrian searches for but doesn't find any swamp area specifically designated as such. In general, the map isn't nearly as detailed as he'd hoped, though a hell of a lot bigger. His early morning research did, however, confirm an area off the Yellow River referred to as Boiling Creek Swamp—this from an Eglin environmental report on the endangered Okaloosa darter from 2005 and confirmed in other documents easily accessible on the Internet, mostly internal Eglin reports.

There were also several links to articles on the four Army Ranger students who died of hypothermia in the Boiling Creek Swamp on Eglin during a training exercise in 1995. It seems, over the years, twenty-two such students have died on their way to becoming the Army's most "elite warriors," trained to fight in all climates. But somewhere in this same Boiling Creek Swamp is where the man beside the water saw the bird near a cypress. Adrian suspects the swamp doesn't show up on the map because it's located in some hidden part of a wide swath marked through with red. Red, the woman told him, means "no public access." When Adrian asked how the river could snake so near to the red spaces, the woman said that, of course, Eglin did not own the river, but that if a person "so much as *touched* the left bank" where Eglin's restricted property began, he or she would have to be DoD (Department of Defense) or go against the law. "Not even all DoD have access over there." She seemed suspicious of Adrian with his disconcerting combination of Boulder smugness and bags under his eyes, but he didn't take it personally, and gave her a jaunty smile on his way out the door.

Past the town of Crestview, 87 South takes Adrian to a left turn at a dirt road marked clearly on the map. He motors down, idles—squints through the trees, the vines, the birds flitting from branch to branch, the hovering and zigzagging insects—and he can just make out the water up ahead, flat and brown.

He continues along the river for about five miles, as the woman at Jackson Guard told him to do, and pulls his sun-warmed Subaru Forester off to the right at the approach of a cleared, sandy river-access point, just as she suggested: "easy to find, easy to load in." Once he's got his (Jeff's) sleeping bag and backpack down at the shore, he eases the aging red kayak from his roof. It's the most effort he's made since his illness, and he's breathing hard when he drags it along the sand.

The kayak sloshes, half in and half out of the water, Adrian's boots submerging a few inches with a gurgle. Though alert to the potential presence of alligators and snakes, he fears them not, having encountered copperheads, cottonmouths, rattlesnakes, a seven-foot alligator, and numerous crocs over the years. (He's no pussy, contrary to what his father always said.) The water is surprisingly clear, reflecting the weaker November sun, so he can see the foggy toes of his shoes on the river bottom. He balances his weight evenly on his hands, his arms shaking a little, either side of the kayak. Then he lowers his butt into the boat, followed by each of his dripping legs, and pushes himself away from the bank, paddling soft into deeper water.

Now he is quiet. The ragged sadness on Stella's face, Zander's thundering footfalls as he mounts the steps fade, June's pathetic funeral fades, Adrian's future, his past, his illness, and even the ivorybill fall away when the tea-colored water, the light cool wind, and the sounds of the natural world fill his head with safety and goodness.

He paddles and watches. For a while, that's all. He is utterly focused on the task at hand. In the course of a few bends in the river, an old bridge rises before him—skeletal, wooden, and black—nothing left of it but vertical beams with an occasional support beam crossing on the diagonal. The river is wider here, maybe a hundred feet across, more ruffled by the breeze, and the trees give way farther from the shoreline to grasses, then sand.

He allows himself to simply float along the current, occasionally checking the bars on his cell: coverage is sketchy, in and out. He's glad to be alone. If Jeff were here, he'd be talking. For Jeff, nature is a social backdrop, an excuse for conversation and companion-ship. The alligator Adrian spots now, for example, off the left bank, just up ahead under the exposed roots of a scrub pine, will not be commented on aloud. If Jeff were here, it would be a whole story. The alligator is utterly still . . . utterly still . . . then submerged.

Adrian rechecks for a text or call from the man: there is

nothing. So he glides downriver eating trail mix, baby carrots, and dried trout from his pack. The banks pass steadily by—everything punctuated by saw palmetto—as he moves farther from civilization, where the ivorybill prefers it. The water, he finds, is moving at a faster pace than he anticipated, and he wonders at the prospect of eventually paddling against it.

As he is skimming through a patch of wide floating leaves, he's able to log on to the Backyard Birder's chat room, and shockingly, he finds a message, right there, posted and buried at three o'clock this morning:

4601 (11/28/09): Hey! Bud lite can hangng from a tree at boiling creek downstream past old brige

Adrian is shot through with promise, his heart speeding, his paddle slipping toward the water before he catches it.

He replies:

mandrake3: Then into the swamp, right? Will you meet me there??

Though the message was sent hours ago, Adrian immediately scans the trees near the water for a shiny metal can. Probably some fisherman's trick, he thinks—marking the best spot for bass. Or maybe the man put it there himself to mark where he'd seen the bird. Or it just marks the mouth of the creek. Adrian desperately hopes he hasn't already missed it, but he's next to certain the bird will be deeper downriver than this.

Nevertheless, while his peripheral vision is alive to the potential glint of aluminum, he now sweeps the ever-changing canopy for the bold colors of the bird: if in flight, its open wings would exhibit a brilliant-white trailing edge, not black as in the smaller Pileated Woodpecker so commonly confused for the ivorybill. If the ivorybill were perching, an ample white patch would be present where the wings lie on top of its back. The pileated shows no such patch, with only the smallest sliver of visible white. There are other differences to do with the overall size, the bill, the face: the pileated has an all-red crest, but the ivorybill has a red crest with a black forehead, etc. He knows what he's looking for.

What he does observe as he paddles along, watching, waiting: a Swallow-tailed Kite swooping high over the river, forked tail fluttering; a late-season Belted Kingfisher conspicuously eyeing Adrian without moving from its branch; a pair of egrets startling and flying away in unison; and a doe. All this in the course of an hour and a half as the river narrows, crumbling stumps and fallen logs multiplying along its banks.

Chapter Fourteen

Eight kilometers later, a Coors Light can winks in the sun. The man had said Bud, but close enough. Though he's heard nothing back, Adrian sends another text saying he's found the can and would love to meet him, if he could just text him back and let him know if he's on his way, or at least that he's getting his messages. Even if, in the worst-case scenario, the man hasn't seen the bird again, Adrian will help him find it.

He feels fine about waiting here a while longer, though, since the river remains one of the best places to see the woodpecker, and he engages in a series of exhausting figure eights down river and back, rounding again and again past the hanging weathered can, hoping to hear back. Though his repetitive maneuvering only amounts to perhaps fifty feet, one way, paddling upstream is, just as he imagined it might be, nearly impossible. He distracts himself from the aching in his arms and back and the dizziness that's begun to swoop like a swallow over his frontal lobe by thinking of his future, once he finds the bird—if he finds the bird.

In reports dated 2005 and 2006, an Auburn University and University of Windsor team claimed the ivorybill had surfaced in the Florida Panhandle. They boasted hundreds of recorded sounds and visual foraging and nesting evidence in the lower

Choctawhatchee River, very close to where Adrian floats right now. Since there were no photographs or video recordings and no DNA (feathers, etc.), the Florida Ornithological Society refused to change the bird's current designation: extinct. The Panhandle researchers continued posting web updates of reported sightings in the region up until only three or four months ago, when they finally stated that the sightings had diminished to such a degree that there was "no way to know whether the birds [were] in different areas in the Choctawhatchee Basin, different forests in the region, or dead," and signed off.

What if Adrian were to find the bird? There would, of course, be a media bonanza. When it was believed the bird was sighted in Arkansas, it was like Michael Jackson dying. Movies and documentaries were made, books were written, songs were sung, television shows referred to the bird in their narratives, and newspapers and journals throughout the world splashed the bird's image across their pages. The town nearest to where the bird had supposedly been sighted, Brinkley, became a thriving tourist attraction, where they'd cut people's hair to resemble the head of an ivorybill, with a little red Mohawk up the center and black-and-white-dyed stripes along the sides. Stores all across the territory displayed ivorybill figurines, decals, drawings, key chains. The state of Arkansas even created a license plate engraved with the ivorybill's image. If Adrian were to find the bird, his name would be known throughout the world, no question. He'd be asked to conduct lecture tours, to appear on talk shows. He'd write articles for ornithological journals. He'd be loved (and envied). If there happened to be a mate as well, the bird might live on to reproduce, and with very special care from the experts, the species might be reestablished. There would be hope again.

In spite of his fantasies about seeing his name in lights, Adrian can't paddle any longer. So he drifts over to the left bank to hold on to a branch protruding from a fallen tree while the water flows past. The dizziness brings him back to the misery of his sickness, how he yearned for Stella, how the tiny colt had died before it was born, how he watched Zander toss the can through his binocular while he waited, idling, against the curb.

Just as his thoughts become almost unbearably maudlin, out of the corner of his eye, Adrian catches a glimpse of a *large, mostly white-winged bird* above the trees flying toward the swamp—in a microsecond of protracted time—its wings beating rhythmically, flying straight and true, then gone.

He bolts to standing like a man making an ovation, nearly losing his footing before he grabs at another branch, higher out of the water, to anchor himself. Scanning the canopy, his eyes try to part the trees from the vines, the leaves from the branches, but he can't see anything else. There did appear to be some darkness on its wings, which is promising, he can't be sure if on the leading edge or the trailing edge, it certainly could have been a pileated, or even perhaps a duck, but yes, this could have been the bird.

The phone dings, suddenly, and Adrian jerks it out of his pocket, still standing, still swaying:

4601 (11/28/09): I fell off the wagon Doc that night with Trammel. That's what I did. Fourteen years. Easy as falling off a log.

Years ago I burned a bush I wanted to get rid of by sprinkling it with gundpower and shooting it with a flaming arrow. Which messed up the right side of my side of my face and chest and arm when I went to throw some lighter fluid on it to get it going again. Another time I drove my car into a creek and couldn't get back out. Trashed the jeep

which I still owed a bunch of money on it I had to pay off for a car I
couldn't even drive. Another time I rode all night with a paper bag
between my legs on some batshit crazy revenge trip.

   I don't want to go back there man. You don't wan tto see me.

Adrian takes in the message like a bitter tonic. Hopelessness
builds in his mouth like saliva, then drips from the corners of
his lips to his chin. He's poking about on a "reservation" three-
quarters the size of Rhode Island with no signposts and no guide.
He writes:

mandrake3: We all make mistakes.

   I'm here. At Eglin. In the middle of the swamp. Can you give me
   a hand?

Gaping at the screen, Adrian hopes the man will write back
on the spot. The air around him is a quiet buzz. The sweet bay
trees have formed a thicket on the edge of the water alongside
titi, tupelo, and gum trees—each with their sturdy, shiny leaves
like rain jackets, unencumbered by the dampness all around
them. The light bark skirts of the cypress trees fall stiff over the
water—reflected there with the sturdy trunks of the spruce pines.

In another hour, he's pulling the kayak through the silty water,
decay circling around his chest, wading through what can only
be Boiling Creek Swamp in the direction of the forest, somewhere in the red section of the map. As he inches along, the
cypresses begin to look like Ents, the walking trees from *The
Lord of the Rings*, whose brave brothers helped save the realm

from the curse of greed that rang from every mountaintop. This all-consuming hunger was what elves, humans, and dwarves alike had come to believe would rule their destiny. Adrian can't remember how the trilogy ended, just that he watched it or the sequel at least twice with Zander and they were long damned movies.

The water is cold, maybe sixty degrees, and it is dark here as though it were dusk, when in fact it's just late, late in the day, and swamps are dark places. Adrian knows he needs to keep moving and get out of the water as quickly as he can, but the swamp floor is now even, now a hole, now falling like a ski slope. He struggles to keep his head up and keep hold of the boat, threading it like a needle through cypress knees, fallen oak, and pine trees and dense reeds. He's now certain, much as he doesn't want to face it, that he can't paddle back up river against the current. He had planned to camp for the night, of course, but even tomorrow, or the next day, he won't be able to do it. As insects nibble at his face, he shakes his head in and out of the water, in and out of the water, and he decides it doesn't matter how he'll get back.

Then as the dampness clears from his ears, echoing from the forest, tapping against his eardrum—

The famous *double knock*.

Was it? The ivorybill hammering twice into a tree.

He stops, still, the water continuing on, and waits to hear it again, the *batop*.

Something swirls by him on his right, touching his elbow. A snake, maybe, but already gone. He has to move.

He continues his slow, watery trek, yearning for a bit of dry land and enough physical stability to take a pill or two, to ease the anxiety that mounts as he considers finally finding the pathetic man, or not finding him—as he considers actually seeing the ivorybill, or never seeing it.

"Please, be the bird," he whispers into the cold lip of the swamp. "Please."

Two hours later, Adrian is mired in shit-brown muck. The sucking sounds as he lifts his boots then sets them down again are flat obscene, and he sloshes forward, portaging the kayak on his left shoulder, backpack perched on the other like Quasimodo's hump, edging toward the idea of higher ground. He considers abandoning the boat, but if he travels far from it, he's afraid he won't be able to find it again. He knows from experience with this type of terrain that without a boat, his exploration will be short-lived, that water is the only thing that guarantees movement. But his shoulder burns from the weight of the thing, and there is still no confirmation from the man beside the water.

When he finally makes his way out of the muck, his feet are like freshly poured cement blocks, and though the transition out feels like a victory, conditions are hardly improved. The jungle is such a tangle, the vines and bushes and palmettos so thick a mass, that he could no longer carry the boat if he tried. The itch and sickening dampness of the waders where the swamp water entered at his chest and seeped down over his body makes his bladder feel full and chilled. He lowers the kayak to the ground and unbuckles his waders, resting his hand against a pine for balance, and edges them down and off. When he pulls back his hand from the tree, it's black with soot. The place is charred from the swamp up.

Free of the waders, Adrian lays them in a semilight spot and sits inside the grounded kayak with a nice view downriver. Even with Adrian's weight, the boat suspends nearly a foot off the ground over a complex network of brush, so that he looks like a sailor navigating a gnarled green and brown sea, his breathing labored and raspy, all the while looking around as if for a storm, but he's scanning the air for the bird. He takes a Vicodin, finally. He listens like the bobcat, the bear, the swamp deer, and the alligators crouched around him in the deepening dusk. Still only for a moment, the gnats, flies, and mosquitoes find his hands, his face, his neck again, and he wonders if there are ticks here this time of year—then quickly dismisses the whole line of thinking as unproductive and, really, the least of his worries. Listening for the double knock and peering through his binocular, his cigarette-pack-sized video camera in its waterproof case at the ready in his pocket, he will wait for the bird that will make sense of it all, even the pieces he left behind from blasting through the wrong doors.

She'd been looking at the journal where he keeps all the birds, drinking his wine, reading his entries, smelling of tart sweat and freesia.

"This is just amazing," she said, her thumb running along its cracking edge, as if along his own spine. "And here I thought we were equals earlier today."

"Just wanted to show you," Adrian said, sheepish as an altar boy, knowing that she now knew everything there was to love about him, and that maybe it wouldn't be enough to hold her. He took it from her hands and set it on the coffee table to put a stop to the longing, to the tensing in his groin and the slacking in his mouth. Then he bit his lower lip and nodded, senseless.

Her green eyes liquid, she said, "I have something I want to show you too," and took his hand.

They lay naked under the ceiling fan in his sparsely furnished bedroom, and he thought of nothing else. He pressed his mouth into the crease of Stella's arm, the opposite side of her elbow, and the pulse in the veins lacing through her skin resonated in his lips. He found her left breast by way of that arm, approaching it from the side, feeling its weight as he lifted it with his face before her nipple fell into his open mouth like a berry. The fan paddled, paddled, paddled above them, the air flicking over their exotic, common bodies. Her thighs opening under him.

In what seemed like the boldest of gestures but was, really, momentarily unintentional, the tip of him came to rest against the rim of her, that warm, stretched soft-skinned arrow thick as a sapling suddenly straining against—then penetrating—her outer folds, her inner folds, the soundless, lightless, boundless, hot squeeze. She swelled and enveloped him. He pressed forward, and out, forward, and out.

"That's enough," he whispered wet at her temple. "We probably shouldn't . . . Isn't that enough?"

Adrian jerks himself awake.

The temperature has dropped: the air is maybe fifty degrees now. He's clutching a life vest to his chest in the dark. He closes his eyes again, cramped in a kayak over a tangle of jungle, to allow the perfect ache of the past to sustain him a little longer. That first night with the woman he knew would be his wife, though he was ablaze with passion, some effortless but overwhelming gratitude overtook him, allowing him to pause, and that moment, that feeling, was stronger than even desire. It's the deepest pleasure he's ever known—that pausing, that restraint in the midst of everything he had ever wanted.

Adrian wills his eyes to open, tosses the life jacket aside, and fishes out his phone to check for messages. He's got to get to higher ground, to a soft needle bed under some longleaf pines or the protection of a live oak grove, to put on some warm, dry clothes, spread out his sleeping bag to dream again. He wonders what he's done. Legs cramped, hungry, feverish, damp.

At least the camo waders are a bit drier. He pulls them on to avoid having to carry them. Abandons the boat. Finds his flashlight. Shoulders his pack. Sends his GPS coordinates out to the man beside the water, and slogs his way through the jungle. In a particularly dark patch, he fords a spider web so strong, the force of it slows him down. The forest is too dim to make much out now, so he trains his light on the web, to find a black-and-yellow arachnid big as a half-dollar scrambling away, leaving only a decomposing green-bean-sized lizard hanging by one arm.

Farther on he trudges into nothingness. A quarter mile later, his light skims a patch of waist-high grasses, and something flickers back at him. When he approaches and threads his fingers down to the grass roots, he pulls up a bullet casing. He drops it quick, like a fool, then says aloud, "What can it do to me now?" no one to hear him. He's weaving his way through an arsenal, built over native bones that are scattered underground.

Blood roars in his head as he reaches to the ground to pick up the casing again, and he walks on, holding it tight in his palm, looking only for an open space out of the mud, with darkness nearly full upon him and fever building behind his eyes.

Finally he spies a clearing up ahead where the muddy earth is patted down to a sheen, protected on three sides by thick grass and short leafy bushes as if made for him. He moves nearer—as the brush shuffles with an agitated grunting—and two wild boars charge out of the bushes, their razor-sharp tusks gleaming in the moonlight and one of their long snouts bloody red. They see him there and stand stock-still too, then just as quickly trot away.

Startled into a wave of nausea, Adrian warily approaches the clearing the pigs had rooted out for themselves. He flashes his light at the underbrush to be sure there are no more, but finds, on the ground under the sheared-off branches only just broken, oil paints freshly squeezed onto his mother's palette. *No*, a fallen Wood Duck, nothing left but the feathers—blue and scarlet, black and white, green and gore.

He presses himself back to standing, throat closing, aimlessly circles the clearing, counting steps, then leans against a sooty pine. He shakes hornets of sleep from his head, as his mother sings a lullaby: "Been a busy day . . . with some heavy seas . . . but you've done your best . . . sleepy boy . . ."

From the north, a flash and muted *BOOM*. Just what he needs, a storm. Just what he needs, more water to contend with. "Keep moving," he whispers, so he pushes off again from the tree, aiming his flashlight back out into the jungle, walking, always walking, toward something, never resting. The light reflects back at him again from the distance. Another piece of forgotten ammunition, he thinks, but as he moves toward it through the tangle, he sees, to his utter amazement, the beer can, hanging eerily from the tree. He's somehow back to where he was.

Some twenty feet nearer, something uncoils thickly from the darkness. Some beast being birthed from the ground.

Chapter Fifteen

Y ou lost?" the shadowy figure murmurs, almost inaudibly.

Adrian gasps, starts to bolt, then blinks. "*Jesus.* Is that . . . Is that you?"

It rises, stiffly, heavily, and says, "Can't see you too good."

Adrian laughs, instantly giddy. "Can't see you too good, either." He teeters on unsteady legs, staring out into the dark.

"I . . . got a tarp down over here," the figure mumbles, and sinks again. A dim lantern is shakily lit.

Adrian makes his way, stunned with relief, to what looks to him like a sturdy skiff in a black sea.

"We can rest here a minute," the man says.

Adrian lowers himself, grateful, onto the camouflaged tarp, letting his pack fall away from him. "*Wow.* Jesus Christ."

The man shakes his head over and again, as if he too has just emerged from the belly of the swamp. He looks maybe sixty-five in this light, gnarly and gray. Nauseous, sore, waders slippery with muck, Adrian's head reels.

"You haven't got any other gear?"

"I, uh . . . left it a ways back," Adrian says, and he knows that sounds idiotic, but he doesn't want to explain it all, because, well, it is idiotic.

He puts out his hand, "I'm Adrian. I don't know your name, but glad you changed your mind."

The man doesn't reciprocate the gesture, probably doesn't see it. "Rick," he says.

Adrian tries to settle his breathing. He feels like a kid, up way too late, fragile and saved.

"This where you saw it?" he asks.

"What's that?"

"The ivorybill."

The man glances at Adrian, then motions with his hand. "Down the swamp that way. There's no marker, so I thought, tell him the beer can."

"Good idea," Adrian chuckles. He feels as though he's going to cry. Above them are stars he hadn't noticed until this moment. Everything seems possible now. "Thanks for . . . coming out."

When they are quiet, the night sounds swell. Half a million dark acres breathe.

"Been watching you for a year," the man says.

Adrian looks over at him, mouth slightly ajar.

"On the Internet. Read your article about thrushes. Kept seeing your name."

"Oh, well, thank you. I'm always glad if I can . . ." He suddenly doesn't know what he was going to say. "Thanks."

Adrian's been watching him too, truth be told.

"Sorry about those fucked-up messages. I took the rest of the Jack Daniel's and poured it out in the sand. Took my lighter to it and made a nice little blue fire."

Adrian nods broadly, his head still throbbing, still reeling. He can smell the alcohol coming off this guy in waves. He looks like he's been through a firefight, his bulky shoulders pulling him forward, rutted scarring down his cheek, his ear, and his neck.

"We can pitch a tent," the man by the water nods, looking straight ahead.

"Sounds great," Adrian agrees. There's nothing they can do in the dark.

The man unzips a pack Adrian can barely see, produces a thermos. Shakily, deliberately, he unscrews the cup and pours something into it. "So, you're a doc."

"I am, yes," replies Adrian, hoping he's getting some of whatever's hot.

"Kids, you said." Rick passes him the cup, holding it near the ground, like it's heavy.

"Thank you." Adrian drinks—cold, black coffee. "Yeah, Zander's thirteen, Michaela's eight." He swishes it around in his mouth, tannic and sour. "How about you?"

Rick slurps out of the mouth of the thermos. "I had a family." He moves to stop the coffee spilling down his chin. "But I lost it . . ."

"Sorry to hear that," Adrian says.

"To alcohol and ignorance."

AA guy, thinks Adrian, probably a vet. They dominate Boulder's parks every summer, a look in their eyes like they're peering out from a long distance.

"I started going job to job, couldn't keep a place, spent any money I made on booze. Finally couldn't eat at all, even mac and cheese and ribs."

The man is visibly trembling. Probably wants a drink right now.

"First they said irritable bowel, then they said pancreatitis. Said I had to stop drinking or I'd be dead in a year."

Another *BOOM* rumbles in the distance, but neither mentions it. Why are there stars if a storm is so near?

"Sounds like you're back on track now though," offers Adrian.

"I was planting trees at a maximum security prison in Jersey. Next thing I know I'm in the hospital throwing up blood." He takes a drink of his coffee and spits it out. "Last time I saw either of my kids."

Rough, Adrian thinks. He hopes this isn't going to be the longest night of his life.

Rick slaps at the side of his neck, sits up a little straighter, sharply inhales. "You get along good with your son?"

"I love my kids," Adrian replies. Zander stands on the bench at the Pearl Street Mall, shouting his name into the crowd. Michaela's nose is bloodied. He presses his forearms into his knees to take the weight off his back.

"You see the bird today?" he asks. That's why he's here.

"Week after I got out of the hospital," Rick continues, unimpeded, "I got a DUI and landed in rehab at the YMCA. Figured twelve steps was better than puking up my own stomach lining."

Adrian takes a laborious breath. "Well, good for you, man."

"I admitted I was powerless. Then I made a 'searching and fearless moral inventory.' Got a job in a auto-glass factory, working six days a week, going to meetings at night. Next thing I know I'm up against step five. 'Admit the exact nature of your wrongs.' So I told my sponsor a lot of ugly shit. Couldn't tell it all, though. Didn't feel like I could anyway."

"Right," Adrian says, wondering what the man left out. Probably something from the war. Some dead comrade, some unforgivable mistake.

A tiny light some distance away swells and disappears like a firefly.

"Step eight," says Rick. "'Make a list of all the people you harmed.'"

The smell of the swamp rises on a light wind so the forest creaks. "No easy matter," says Adrian. He knows it isn't.

Rick says, "That shit will . . . bring you to your knees."

The silence between them expands again. Adrian's eyes feel like burned-out buildings.

He reaches toward his bag for a Xanax, but when he glances at Rick, the man's lips are peeled back in a grimace from some kind of pain, so Adrian draws back his hand. His gut contracts. *Powerless*, he thinks. He is powerless.

Rick drains the rest of the coffee out onto the ground. "You gotta make *amends* with the people on that list," he says. "Except when it would cause them more harm than good. You understand that?"

"Uh . . . yeah," Adrian answers, "I think I can imagine how telling somebody the truth might hurt them worse than leaving it alone." He's spent his whole life that way. He holds out his empty cup to Rick, but he doesn't take it, just rubs, up and down, up and down, along the length of his left arm.

"I didn't know the difference between making amends and harming somebody. Didn't see how I ever would."

Making amends. Adrian moves the words around in his head, wondering if they will ever settle into an order he can comprehend, wondering if they are possible. "Did you make amends?"

"Drank another seven months and ended up back in the hospital."

"Seriously? I'm sorry, man." The tiny light reappears, less tiny now, in the trees. "Do you see that?"

"Had to quit all over again."

Adrian watches the light.

"One night there was a rainstorm. I was listening to the radio and eating chicken rice soup, about to turn fifty years old, and I call my ex-wife on the phone and . . . and I tell her I'm sorry for all the things I did. I name some of those things but I don't name the rest."

He's leaving things out again. Napalm or desertion, a maimed civilian child.

"She forgave me though. Said she did anyway. I was a drunk, you know, the whole time I was married. Nobody had to tell me that. I know what I was."

Know thyself, thought Adrian. Do no harm.

"It's what I did to my son," the man says. He wags his head, disagreeing with someone Adrian can't see. "What I did to my boy, that was the worst of it."

It was what he did to his son.

"That's the thing I could never say." The now-zigzagging light is gaining.

"What was it?" Adrian asks. "What was the thing you did?" He listens to the man's anxious breathing.

"I took his mother out from under him."

The storm rumbles from inside the trees. Raps on the insides of their trunks.

The words are a hoarse, jagged rush—"Anything I tried to do for her, he jammed himself in between us. Smart as a whip, loyal as a Boy Scout. Made me look about as crass and meaningless as a pornographic fucking postcard. I called him a 'momma's boy.' One time I called him her whore." He tries to swallow. "When they left me, I couldn't take it. So I came after."

"Oh, Jesus," Adrian whispers.

He didn't recognize him. Didn't recognize the voice, now gravelly and broken. The face, scarred by fire and hidden in the gloom.

Adrian ekes out, "What are you trying to do?"

His father is hunched so near he can hear the fabric of his jacket as he shifts. The cavalry is coming.

"I found you," Dean says low. "Like you did me." He cradles a loose fist in his hand, like it's injured. "Online."

Adrian is a child again, everything rushing in without his consent. His feet are strangely light against the ground, like he needs to run.

"I'm working, not drinking. I look in on you. Read what you say. Sometimes I make a post if I know you're on, so maybe you see it." He smiles, but starts to shake like a washing machine on its last legs. "Then June dies . . ."

Adrian strains to conjure the cyber trail of the last weeks in his head. He can't make sense of it. Hadn't he been the one to establish communication—in Kingston, after the funeral? "Did you . . . Did you even see those birds?"

"*Yeah*," Dean answers, kneading his fist. Then he mutters, rasping, into his sleeve, "most of them. But I remembered that Wood Stork you saw with June. And, you know, the woodpecker."

Adrian closes his eyes in the dark.

Dean nearly whispers, so Adrian hardly hears. "I had to get you here."

"*Why?*"

Dean pivots on his hip, heavy boots pulling at the tarp. "You looked at me like I was some kind of a monster." He shrugs, his face coiling against a buried sob, only the unscarred parts of it moving, cracking into fissures when he squints over at Adrian, like he did on the icy driveway, a briefcase in his hand and no jacket, boring a hole through Adrian's chin.

"She never did anything to me, did she?"

Adrian waits. The forest waits.

"No," his father says, tears thick in his eyes. "No, she did not."

The constant, maddening static goes suddenly silent.

Adrian is almost entirely unaware of Dean, as a chorus of emotion swells in his chest, the harmonic convergence of which can only be described as joy. His mother. His only mother, come back to him. Then, so fast on its heels, like a computer program searching for a virus, his brain begins checking and rechecking a lifetime of compromises—hurried breakfasts, nonexistent good nights, the absent summers of his adolescence, the abbreviated visits of his early adulthood, the chaperoned outings with his children, the dwindling phone calls, the empty years, the funeral—shot through with the poisonous sludge of a lie.

Dean chokes out, "I was . . . twisted up with what I couldn't have."

To locate all the sullied memories, Adrian thinks, to burn them clean and release them, whole, back into the world, would take up every hour he has left. It isn't even the same world anymore.

Dean struggles to stand, legs spread wide to steady himself. He looks out into the forest, his breathing ever more labored, and he lumbers away. "I'm sorry," he says, as if to someone in the darkness ahead of him. "Adrian, I'm sorry." And he's out of sight.

Adrian shouts, "Where are you going?" but the approaching light has arrived.

It flashes once, accompanied by one perfect gunshot—a long whistling, a *BOOM,* and a prolonged flash like the atom bomb.

Stunned, half-blind, alarm clock in his ears, Adrian can just see Dean drop to his knee with one hand over his heart. Both his palms hit the ground.

Adrian runs into the black woods toward his father, but his boot wedges between stump and scrub oak and, as he tumbles forward, he hears his anklebone snap. He screeches, goes down with the pain.

A flare slithers up beyond the longleaf pines—lights the oil barges on the Sound, Adrian's wrenched leg, a dozen soldiers in dark clumps, Dean crumpling to the ground, rolling onto his back, mouth agape.

Someone far off screams, *"What the fuck?"*

Adrian drags himself toward Dean, ankle searing, heaving over branches and thorny brush, through weeds and briars, along slicks of mud. A globe of light lands on his hands, sweeps into his eyes, then crisscrosses its way to Dean. There is the scratch of walkie-talkies and something progressing clumsily through the jungle.

When Adrian finds his father—the pain in his ankle rushing his foot, his calf, his knee—he collapses again, panting and gasping, inches from Dean's rutted face. He smells the coffee and alcohol, fear and fatigue on his breath. He recognizes him now. He's the one who lurks, desperate and weary, beside the water, who searches for birds and can't sleep, with heavy-knuckled hands, dark-tufted eyebrows, a face like a forest leveled and burned. Afflicted with lies. Breathing one minute, extinguished the next.

An approaching soldier shouts something in their direction, but Adrian knows what to do. Bracing himself with his uninjured leg, he unzips his father's jacket. He places the heel of his left hand on Dean's chest and covers it with his right, touching him for the first time in twenty-five years. He thrusts down, hard, the weight of his whole body behind it. Then again, and again, he thrusts, counting in his head—his raw palpitating pain beneath him, bound to him—as the lumpy, lifeless form rebounds.

As soldiers gather around, a racket of walkie-talkies in the trees, Adrian lifts the heavy head. He inclines the salt-and-pepper chin toward the sky, pinches closed the nostrils, and covers the mouth with his own to make a seal. He delivers one powerful breath into the idling lungs—tilts the head, lifts the chin—delivers another . . . Then compresses the chest again, four, five, six—counting—fifteen, sixteen, seventeen, eighteen . . . his own spittle a slick film across his father's cheeks as he counts in grunts and the leaves and sticks crackle and break.

On the twenty-sixth thrust of the twelfth cycle, a helicopter lands, but Adrian continues to thrust in the awful wind of it—twenty-seven, twenty-eight, twenty-nine, thirty, a rib fracturing under the heel of his hand—and breathes once, and once again, into the old man's lungs, until Dean is lifted out from under him, placed on a gurney, and carried away.

At Eglin Air Force Base Hospital, Dean is rushed to the OR, and Adrian's broken ankle is verified. It's the fibula this time, but they can see from the X-ray the ankle had never healed properly from his injury as a child. Once he's fitted with a CAM walker boot, given metal crutches, and written prescriptions, they tell him he should come back in a few days for a cast, once the swelling has had a chance to run its course.

"I understand you saved your father's life," the nurse says, a gray knot spilling from the back of her head.

"What?" Adrian asks. He can't hear anything. His ears are worthless now.

She hands him a plastic Eglin Hospital bag, raising her voice. "Here are your father's soiled clothes."

"I'm from out of town," he mumbles, but he takes the bag as the nurse picks up her clipboard.

"Do you want to stay here at the hospital while your dad's in the OR, or do you have somebody who can pick you up, maybe get you a shower and fresh clothes?"

He stares into the graphic on the biohazard bin, at the three black, partially closed circles converging on a center circle, pulsing with the afterimage of the grenade simulator. "Why don't you lie down and be still?" the nurse says, and helps him to the white paper pillow. "I'll be right back."

He's in the bathroom with his mother, four or five years old. She's wet and soapy. She pulls him into her body, while he wails at the blood dripping from his finger. From the knife. The knife he'd been using to carve a potato into a swan.

Adrian's breaths come in gasps, but she is so beautiful, his savior, as she finds a washcloth underneath the sink and wraps it around his hand, saying, "Okay, sweetheart, breathe. I've got you."

From down the hallway, his father's voice calls, "June?"

She shouts, "We'll be out in a sec," shower water cascading behind her.

"What's going on in there?"

Dean rounds the corner to find Adrian dripping wet and

red-faced, one hand resting on his mother's naked shoulder, water dripping from her nipples to his bare feet.

"Adrian's—" June begins.

"Sonofabitch!" Pushing her aside, Dean grabs Adrian, slipping and squealing by the collar.

"What're you doing?" June calls out, grasping a towel to her torso.

"You're a boy, you understand me?" Dean shakes him so hard his teeth clack together. "Your mother's naked!" he bellows. He shoves Adrian out of the bathroom at the shoulder blades, repeating, "You understand? Answer me!"

June whimpers, "Dean."

Adrian urinates into his pants, nodding his head as a dark stain blooms along his leg.

Dean watches, catching a glimpse of his own eyes in the foggy mirror, and turns away from himself with an expression of revulsion, as June finally calls out, "He's hurt! Can't you see that?"

Lying on the hospital cot, his mouth in a crusted dry O, Adrian stares up at the ceiling until the images have cleared. The memory that had merged with his father's lie. The blameless thing in the bathroom. His mother's nakedness. The humiliation and the fear.

He turns onto his side. He can see his face in the mirror over the sink, full of what he's done, like his father's face had been, even then, all those years ago. He takes in the creases of his brow, his cracked lips, his ruddy cheeks, his hair, matted with dirt and sweat. He looks around the examination room, where symptoms and causes are revealed.

Raising himself up on his elbow, he opens the bag of Dean's clothes: heavy muddied pants, wet socks, a dull-white tee shirt, and a work shirt. They've obviously kept the jacket and boots on the off chance he will survive.

He takes out the shirt printed with "Eglin AFB" and finds something stiff in the pocket. It is a plain white envelope with his name printed on it, written in his father's hand.

Chapter Sixteen

Adrian's plane doesn't take off until late afternoon, so he sits alone on a bench at the boardwalk overlooking the Gulf. His ankle is counting out his pulse in swollen beats. He's decided to feel it.

As he sat in the waiting room the day before, while Dean was under the knife, a trim older woman showed up with a tanned complexion, long shorts, and running shoes that squeaked when she walked. She said she wanted to introduce herself. Her name was Marilyn Whitehead, she said, and she was a friend of his father's. She was very concerned about Dean but said he'd been wanting to talk with Adrian for a long time, and she hoped it went well. She looked as though she'd been crying.

Adrian moved a box of tissues someone had left on the chair next to his, and she sat down. They sat together like that for some time, watching a set of twin toddlers tear up magazines.

Adrian couldn't help himself and asked, "Are you two . . . together?"

"We're old enough to know we're lucky," she said, "to have someone appear out of nowhere to care whether you come or go, to have someone to eat a meal with or call you on the phone when you're not even expecting it."

"Are you married?" he asked, thinking how he couldn't picture any of it, this tidy, sane woman choosing his father.

"One time over dinner, he asked me if I would, and I told him, 'I never want to be your wife.' I cried with happiness, like I never had at my own wedding." She looked over toward the double doors to the OR.

Adrian found himself awkwardly nodding as though he understood, wanting to take her hand in his.

"That way," she said, "there's never a day after which, like the people in the church, you're 'saved,' not the kind where you believe redemption is guaranteed."

Now Adrian waits for afternoon. Dean is in intensive care, stable. The breeze off the Gulf is a little crisp, the sky sleepy. A congregation of white ibises strolls along the shoreline. Fearless, gregarious birds, with their long red bills. If they could talk to Adrian, they would. Tell him a joke. Keep walking.

"Would any of you be willing to trade seats with our Dr. Mandrick? He's got a leg injury and needs a little extra room," the flight attendant says with a malevolent smirk, then looks from one passenger to the next as if hypnotizing them into cooperation.

"I thought you had to be able to help people get out if you were sitting here. He can't even walk," says the woman in 14B with the triple wedding band and the Staten Island accent.

"Sometimes we have to make an exception."

Adrian doesn't speak for himself. He knows he's the last person in the world who should be taking up a seat in an exit row.

The earnest young man in 14D asks, "Where's his seat?"

"Six F, window seat, first class." The flight attendant's impatient now. He has people to strap in, overhead compartments to close, seat backs and tray tables to bring to their full upright and locked positions.

"I'll do it," the boy says. He gathers his things from under his feet while the flight attendant takes Adrian's crutches from him to an invisible closet up near the cockpit.

Adrian edges his way in, everyone shrinking into their seats as he passes as though he's carrying a virus. This must be what it is like to get old, he thinks, gratefully lowering himself into the seat. Taking up valuable space with your infirmity, praying for the compassion of others more vigorous. Now he can stretch out his leg, anyway.

He lays his head back and tries to relax. Everything is smooth, not quite audible, warmer than is comfortable, then cooler and staler, intimate, anonymous, and within minutes, they are off. The Panhandle grows more distant by the millisecond, its shimmering arteries and scrubby banks and roadways. As the plane lifts into the clouds, Adrian gets a glimpse of the watery disc of the Gulf; then it's gone, and he is groundless, drifting, his head tipping forward, jerking back, listing to the side.

The dunes of the Midwest are a wasteland of crumbling roads. A woman Adrian doesn't know sits in a canoe with no water under it, far out in the distance where the desert meets the insomniac eye of the sun and the dust twists into funnel clouds. Where are the children? They're lost, where the sun pricks harsh like needles and the wind blows with no seeds in its fingers. There isn't so much as a dragonfly or lizard under this sun. How could he have left this to chance?

He and his mother lift broken trees from across the jungle

path, searching under road signs and car tires and dried pitcher plants. She has on her cuffed brown shorts and a dark-blue bandana. This is back when there were children. They dip into a corridor of trees and it gets dark. A firework explodes in the sky and there are drones along the hillside, all lined up for dinner like hungry men at a soup kitchen. When the next firework goes off, it's just them again, his mother and him, searching under welcome mats, searching under hubcaps, searching under kneecaps and the lids of biohazard bins.

"Sir?" she says, pushing aside the broken pieces of cloudy brown glass. "Would you like something to drink?"

The flight attendant's cart has passed Adrian's row and the man sitting next to him is pouring Beefeater into what looks like tonic or club soda in a plastic cup.

Adrian wipes his mouth on the back of his wrist and sits up a little taller in his seat. He has the envelope from his father in his hand. He looks out the window. They're following the dusk across the country.

He presses on the bubble light over his head so it shines on the white chalky paper. He slides his index finger under the flap.

Inside the envelope is a folded piece of old, blank stationery. Inside the piece of stationery is a single photograph of him as a child.

He is standing half-submerged in swamp water, looking over at the crossed arms of a cypress. His face is stretched wide with an open-mouthed smile as he points with his whole hand, like a magician toward a rabbit. Atop a low branch, in stark blue-black, white, and a powdering of red is an Ivory-billed Woodpecker.

The bird's head and upper body are slightly blurred. It's in the very moment of taking off from the tree. One of its wings is just out from its side, the other is almost fully extended, the ebony plumage on the leading edge of the open wing followed by a long, wide, white trailing edge at the back. Adrian remembers now clearly how it poked its beak in and out of the cavity it was perched before, looking for beetle grubs, and how its head bopped back and forth on its long neck just before it flew away from the old tree. This exuberant bird.

He really did see it. Warmth suffuses him from his head to his chest, through his groin, all the way down his legs to his ankles as though someone has taken a deep ladle and doused him with the warm water of the Gulf.

Adrian can imagine his mother in a bent-knee stance to center her weight and steady the canoe. He can see her forearms opening out from the camera she holds to one eye. She's who Adrian's smiling at.

The cab driver opens the door to Adrian's bedroom at Jeff's, having insisted on helping him in with his things. He lays them on the floor by the bed, and Adrian thanks him again and gives him another twenty.

"Can you let yourself out?" Adrian says, aware he's never said those stilted words aloud before. Who knew he would find an occasion for them?

"Absolutely," the man says, already gone, nothing left of him but his cigarette smell.

Adrian sits on the bed and unzips his suitcase. He lost all his original pills in the jungle along with the backpack, but he's got his anti-inflammatory, a new antibiotic, and the pain meds (Percocet) he's been keeping himself from taking. Thankfully, his video camera was in his pocket, so he's got that, but there's nothing on it—not a single pixel of footage. He pulls a bulky, misshapen trash bag out of his suitcase and extracts the waders and boots. Then he remounts his crutches, carries his filthy gear to the bathroom tub, turns on the hot water, and lets it run.

The map of Eglin made it home too, in the chest pocket of his waders. He spreads it out on the daybed, all 123,000 square miles of it. He sees the river, of course, and the light-red areas ("closed to public access because of active military testing, training, and/ or unexploded ordnance contamination") and the dark-red areas ("Department of Defense personnel only"). Even now, he can't figure out exactly where he'd been.

Chapter Seventeen

E xtinction is a black-and-white equation. No amount of financial wizardry, artistic genius, media glitz, religious feeling, or political heft can influence it once it's reached critical mass: it is where math and science have the final word. It could be said that evolutionary history is unforgiving. Utterly dependent on its habitat, a species cannot continue without it. If that habitat is sufficiently degraded, overtaken by an invasive species, or altered by climate or other environmental changes of note, the species must either adapt to these changing conditions (i.e., by changing as well) or locate and adapt to a new habitat. If it is incapable of making these changes, the species in question will become extinct.

These are the cold, hard facts with which Adrian is familiar. Changing is always difficult. Sometimes it's too late.

Adrian sits in his car at the end of the driveway. The bristling cold is seeping in through the seams, and his seat is pushed all the way back to make room for his ankle. His toes are blue.

He can see Stella standing in front of the window washing dishes, in the same way one can see a face card turned at an angle in someone else's hand. Every now and then she seems to be looking his way, but maybe it's only a trick of light on the glass. One can never assume. He's mistaken love for torment, based entirely on faulty perception. He's capable of any number of other misinterpretations: familiarity for frustration, numbness for painlessness, blame for responsibility, melancholy for regret.

He starts the car and pulls slowly forward, closer to the window, and she disappears. He climbs, stiff and aching, out of the car and limps on his crutches to the front door. He pulls open the screen door, then quietly knocks. There's no need to herald his presence. If she doesn't want to answer, no amount of hammering will convince her. He's not in the mood to hammer anyway.

He waits. Thinks maybe he hears footsteps. Then nothing.

He can imagine Zander sleeping upstairs, all his covers tossed off, his body in the shape of someone falling face down toward the earth. Michaela, bundled in down and quilts, pillows stacked high behind her, her head resting in front of them on the bare sheet with a bit of spittle gathered at the crook of her mouth, breath even as a timekeeper.

There is a terrible pain in his ankle. His bone is broken. He repeats it in his mind, to help him remember the truth. *My bone is broken. My bone is broken.* If he doesn't remember it, he'll fall back into illusion. How can he hope to get well, if he doesn't acknowledge that something is wrong?

The door squeaks open and she is there, as if backlit by firelight. He can't quite see whether she looks broken too. He doesn't speak right away. She looks down at his ankle, then quickly back to his face.

"Hi," he says.

"Hello. How are you?" not quite like a stranger, but nearly.

"I would like to do something brave," he says.

Her eyes narrow. "What?"

"I'd like to do something brave and selfless," he repeats. "But in the absence of that, I'd like you to have this."

He takes the book from under his arm, the one with all the tattered pages and a continent full of birds. He holds it out to her.

"Why?" Does she shrug? "Why do you want to give it to me?"

"For safekeeping," he says.

There is a sound from upstairs. Maybe one of the kids hears his voice or is on the way to the bathroom. Maybe it's just the furnace lurching on.

"Are you going somewhere?" she asks, rubbing the ball of her foot into the floor like she's putting out a cigarette.

"No. I just want to turn this over . . . to you."

She hesitantly takes the book from him.

"I would happily do something harder," he says, "if I only knew what." He's grateful she's taken it. He didn't know if she would.

She studies him, as if trying to decipher a message. She looks down at the pages and solemnly flips through them with her thumb. The cold is filling the house as they stand at the open door.

She finds a photo, plucks it up, and holds it out toward the light. "Is this you?"

Adrian nods. It's the one his mother took.

"I didn't know you kept any pictures from when you were little."

"That's a woodpecker."

"I can see," she says, like someone who thinks there are more birds like it somewhere.

Adrian thinks he'll say, "Well, I'd better let you get to bed," but instead he gestures to the photo. "Those birds are all gone," his eyes suddenly brimming. "Every single one of them."

He hasn't cried since Michaela was born.

"They're so much more fragile than anybody thought," he says. "The birds. You think, because they can fly, they can do anything, survive anything."

Stella nods, her eyes still narrowed, the book's weight in her hands.

His crutches don't allow him to cover his face, and Adrian weeps.

Stella touches him on the hand. She holds the photo out toward him. "Why don't you take this back, okay?"

He nods and takes it from her, gratefully, sliding it into his coat pocket. "Thank you." He hadn't meant to give that away. If she ever lets him into the house again, he's going to tell her that. He'll tell her everything.

Stella looks suddenly behind her as if she's heard something. A light goes on in the upstairs hallway.

Adrian finds the light with his eyes, then says, "I should let you get to bed."

In another moment, she's closed the door, and he's crunching over the frozen grass, poking perfect holes in the thin covering of ice with his crutches.

He just wants another chance. To nurture and protect his own two children, to keep them safe in his own home, sleeping in the room down the hall until they are grown.

As he backs out onto the cold street, he doesn't think of blame or guilt—either his or his father's. Only that what's been soiled must be cleansed, so that his children may thrive. Only this rings clear to him in the dry air. The simplest of creatures hears it too. He just wants another chance.

Epilogue

Adrian enters the hall alone. It's a small theater, all made of light-colored wood—the floors, the walls, everything new and airy—perhaps large enough to seat a hundred and fifty people. Adrian finds an aisle seat only one row from the back where he can quietly observe, relatively unobserved. He doesn't want to make a show of his presence. He just wants to be here. People mill about in the direction of their seats with their scents and their markings and their calls, ignoring each other's presence or quietly saying, "Where were *you* last week? We missed you," or "Is David here yet?" A great number of them are between forty and sixty years old, fit, and understatedly stylish, either well-to-do or artistic or both, the sort of people who don't hide their gray hair. The rest are students from the university, in groups of two or three mostly, talking into each other's ears like children at their parents' party. Zander and Michaela are sitting with friends of Stella's in the third row just right of center, the best seats in the house.

One chair and one stool stand on the stage, filling two of three neat pools of light. Adrian watches as a radiant young black woman all in black steals onto the stage with three bottles of Fiji water gathered in her hands and places one in each pool of light, then slips off again the other side. Behind him and through a glass window, a middle-aged man and a slim boy sit sealed off at a light board, headphones around their necks, laughing uproariously about something no one can hear.

Two months ago, British Petroleum spilled 210 million gallons of oil into the Gulf. Last week, Adrian flew in and had dinner with his father, whose heart is stronger now. He invited Marilyn Whitehead, who Adrian learned is one-half Muskogee. Her ancestors have lived in and around the Panhandle for twelve hundred years. Adrian told her he's one-quarter Catawba, on his mother's side. The next morning, Adrian and Dean squatted by the nest of a sea turtle, dug up her eggs, and toted them away to save them from the poison. Adrian watched Dean and Marilyn wash a Piping Plover in a basin, and the world seemed more surprising then than ever before.

His ankle is essentially healed. He stopped wearing his air cast five or six weeks after his accident, then moved on to support socks with regular shoes, and now his only remaining symptom is a slight numbness at the outer edge of the sole of his foot. Maybe that will always be there; he doesn't know. Jeff tells him he's got a limp. Though he can't see it himself, he assumes it's true.

Getting off the pills was painful. It's amazing how quickly the body and mind fall into addiction again, even after substantial time has passed. He weaned himself off very precisely, as if it were only science, not magic, and it took four months until he didn't think of it for a full day.

He thinks of nothing now, really, but the morning. The way it shows up without fail, dependable, often sunny, expecting nothing, offering everything.

Michaela, Zander, and Adrian hike high up Sugarloaf Mountain from the parking lot by Switzerland Trail. They start out

*early and walk until they're hungry, stopping to eat pimento-
cheese sandwiches and dill pickles by a creek that rushes by
them like quicksilver. There are wildflowers in the crevices of
the rocks, along the trail, and on the hillside.*

Everyone falls into that natural hush that overtakes an audience just before the lights go down. They sense it's going to happen. Sure enough, the lights go to half, and in a minute, quickly
fade.

A man and two women walk onto the stage in a little line, the
man carrying something large, a cello or an upright bass, one
woman with nothing in her hands, and Stella, carrying her oboe.
A smattering of audience members awkwardly applaud before
they realize they should have waited, as the musicians fan out to
find their places.

Once in their own brightening pools of light, they make their
small preparations. The man, who Adrian now sees is a cellist,
sits, lets out his end pin, and tightens the horsehairs of his bow.
The singer picks up her bottle of water, replaces it back on the
floor without drinking from it, and leans back against her stool.
Stella simply stands, the oboe held lightly in both hands, and
looks out across the bodies in their seats toward Adrian.

*By the time he and the kids get to the last spiral of the trail,
they are sweaty and winded, and their noses are burned.
Adrian tells them that the trail they are walking used to be
a mining road and how carts used to carry out gold, silver,
and coal along a track that was pulled up, cut into pieces,
and thrown away. The kids aren't too interested; they
just want to walk beside him. He doesn't know what he is*

teaching them—that it's okay to walk even when your body
wants to stop walking, how to look for things both far away
and near.

The cellist begins to play, his right hand so relaxed in posture he looks to be about to drop the bow, his left hand inching up and down the neck without frets, finding the notes. His bow saws long across the first two strings, sticky and thick, vibrating Adrian's rib cage.

The singer opens her mouth and sings one extended note, finally tripping forward into other notes that climb higher, then plateau, descend, then plateau, her brow furrowed, chest wide, singing only the sound of a vowel. Adrian waits for Stella, but she stands by, her face in rapt, unselfconscious attention, lips slightly open, waiting for her cue. Right now it's cello and voice, cello and voice, in a simple harmony even Adrian can recognize as such, the singer straddling the cello's sweet, sad melody in a tune you can almost remember.

They see it coming: the dry, rocky summit. The three of them
step upon it all at once and stand there in their sneakers. Miles
away, and clear as a bell, the Continental Divide rings like a
summons before them. From there, the waters of the land mass
flow, every day, down the west side toward the Pacific, down
the east toward the Atlantic. When Adrian's mother called, she
waited for a response but there was no answer, so she stilled her
fingers and stared straight ahead. As if stillness would make
a response more likely. As if her loneliness would make a re-
sponse more likely. As if wild fires and tsunamis and droughts
and earthquakes would make a response more likely.

Much of the audience is unaware of the moment Stella enters the song, the oboe's sound is so thin, but Adrian hears the very first whisper of its double-reeded tone, sustaining long and longer, then wavering and dipping into full sound.

Just when Adrian believes the singer has become the center of the song as usual, over the top of her voice now adventuring, over the top of the cello now lamenting, answers Stella again with her call—not like a songbird brightening the branches, more like an ivorybill, with the sweet rainy-day tone of a child's tin horn. It is oboe—and voice, then oboe—and voice, the cello omnipresent, like the earth underfoot. And the three instruments are inexorably intertwined, integral parts of the same true story.

Michaela steps away from the edge to retie her shoe. Her laces are a tangle of cotton and burrs, so Adrian kneels down to help sort them out.

They are surrounded, these children, on all sides—Fourmile Canyon snaking up from Boulder; the mushrooming communities of Denver to the south; the spine of the Rocky Mountains to the west, Indian Peaks, Longs Peak, Mount Meeker; and the Eastern Plains, a grassland with no grasses, stretching farther away than any of them can see—all lit within the canopy of the Colorado sky.

"Dad," Zander shouts, dangling a leg toward the blue abyss, sneaker full of sand. "Do you think we could find our way home from here?"

Acknowledgments

Grateful thanks to: my insightful, persistent, and always encouraging agent, Tim Wojcik of Levine Greenberg Rostan; my brave, generous, and talented editor, Lara Blackman; hawk-eyed copyeditor Peg Haller; inspired cover designer Sandra Chiu; production editor Kayley Hoffman; interior designer Jill Putorti; and to everyone at Touchstone Books and Simon & Schuster, with special thanks to Tara Parsons, for giving my book a shot and lending it their support and expertise.

To the great Larry Balch, Betsy Fikejs, Father Tom Pincelli, Tim Radford, Tim Manns, Bob Kantz, Carol Wallace, Peter Schoenberger, Barbara Heile, Dianne Hardin, and Betsy Thomas; to John Seginak, Mike Spaits, and Gregory Kemp; to Lee Anne Auerhan, MD, Matt Andry, MD, Barbara Malach, MD, and Richard Kalman, MD; and to the Cornell Lab of Ornithology, the American Birding Association, and the National Audubon Society for invaluable information and research assistance.

To Robert Boswell for the most perceptive, comprehensive set of notes imaginable; to Lili Wright, my traveling companion on the winding road to the novel; to David Field, Patti White, Barbara Bean, Hillary Kelleher, Susan Hahn, Martha Rainbolt, David Crouse, and Christie Cashner Alli for thorough and thoughtful reading. To Rosemary James, Joseph J. DeSalvo, Jr., John Gregory Brown, and the William Faulkner–William Wisdom Competition for welcoming my work and me. To De-Pauw University, my wonderful academic home, for helping me create the space and time to write.

Finally, heartfelt thanks to Griffin, Fiona, Gwendolyn, and Maia, dear ones. To my husband, writer Tom Chiarella, for his keen narrative eye and unwavering confidence in my seeing this project through, and for his daily love and illumination. And to the brilliant and inimitable Cathie Malach, dearest friend and reader, for her ever-lucid discernment, inexhaustible faith, and selfless devotion to helping me uncover, shape, and refine this story.

About the Author

Chris White is an award-winning playwright and screen-writer, with an MFA in dramatic writing from NYU's Tisch School of the Arts. Her plays have been produced nationally and internationally, and her play *Rhythms* won the Helen Hayes Award for Outstanding New Play. She received an Award of Merit at the Women's Independent Film Festival for her feature-length screenplay *Weasel in the Icebox*, and her short film *Mud Lotus* was an official selection at the New Hampshire, Albany, Copper Mountain, and Cincinnati Film Festivals. White is a professor of English at DePauw University teaching creative writing. She lives near the town of Bainbridge, Indiana, on Big Walnut Creek. *The Life List of Adrian Mandrick* is her first novel.

The
Life List of
Adrian Mandrick

— A Novel —

CHRIS WHITE

This reading group guide for The Life List of Adrian Mandrick *includes an introduction, discussion questions, ideas for enhancing your book club, and a Q&A with author Chris White. The suggested questions are intended to help your reading group find new and interesting angles and topics for your discussion. We hope that these ideas will enrich your conversation and increase your enjoyment of the book.*

Introduction

Adrian Mandrick seems to have the perfect life—a loving wife and family, an accomplished career as an anesthesiologist, and a serious passion for birding. But Adrian holds dark secrets about his childhood and pill addiction, secrets that threaten to consume him in the wake of his estranged mother's death and a deteriorating marriage. In the midst of this turmoil, Adrian attempts to add one more bird—the elusive Ivory-billed Woodpecker—to his "life list," the third-longest list of bird species in North America. His quest leads him to a discovery of something far more rare: a chance to confront the past, to seek forgiveness, and to change his life.

Topics & Questions for Discussion

1. In the prologue, Adrian and his mother set out in a rented canoe for a day of birdwatching when they happen to come across the rare Ivory-billed Woodpecker perched in a nearby tree—if Adrian remembers correctly. How does this moment—a defining moment in Adrian's life—contrast with the rest of the narrative? Is this early moment in Adrian's life like the description he gives morning time, "when plans were made and not yet botched" (1)? In what ways do Adrian's plans get "botched" later in his life?

2. A poignant moment occurs on page 9 when Adrian discovers his father crying alone in the kitchen in the middle of the night. How does this version of his father compare to the man Adrian describes throughout the story? How does Adrian's misunderstanding of his family affect his adult life?

3. Adrian's "life list" is impressive—the third-longest in North America—and extremely important to him, arguably more important than his career, family, or friendships. What significance do you think the list holds for Adrian?

4. Revisit the chain of events that lead to Adrian's relapse into pills. Do you agree with his logic on page 34 that "he should never have stopped pursuing the bird"?

5. Discuss the irony of discovering the accentor dead after accidentally abandoning Stella at a gas station and nearly killing them in a snowstorm. Do you think Adrian's apology warrants forgiveness? Does Stella ever really forgive him? Justify your response.

6. Discuss Adrian's relationship with his mother, June. Why do you think it was important for Adrian to "define the birds for himself" (68)?

7. Pain in many forms is discussed in the novel—emotional pain, physical pain, psychological pain, the pain of misunderstanding, the pain of desiring forgiveness, etc. Adrian even describes his medical specialty as dealing "exclusively in the avoidance of pain" (81). Why do you think pain figures so prominently into this story?

8. What draws Adrian to Deborah? Do you think he feels a particular kinship with her or is his affair a response to something else?

9. On page 120 Adrian muses to himself that he "has the sensation he's pulled the plug on something that's draining away at a rate he can't control." What exactly do you think he is "pulling the plug on"?

10. Discuss the notion of escapism. How does Adrian escape the realities of his life? How does Stella? Do you think the characters are successful in escaping their realities? Why or why not?

11. Answer Adrian's question to Deborah on page 173: "What's the most important thing about dying?"

12. Reread Adrian's assessment of himself at the top of page 185, the paragraph beginning "He hadn't been attentive, that's what it was. He had been arrogant . . ." Do you agree that his lack of attentiveness is why his marriage is crumbling?

13. Reread the last line of the Epilogue. In your opinion, does Adrian find his way back home in the end? Is he able to change?

Enhance Your Book Club

1. Adrian's birding is simultaneously deeply personal and deeply rooted in human history. He describes it as "a deep, primal impulse" and remarks that "birds and their characteristics show up in the illustrations and writings of all ancient societies" (104). Invite your book club on a nature walk. Pack binoculars and a birding book. See if your group can create your own "life list," locating as many different birds as possible. Afterward, discuss the experience. What did observing birds feel like? What about the experience do you think most appeals to Adrian? Do you think birding is an escape from life for Adrian, or a way to be part of something larger than himself?

2. *The Life List of Adrian Mandrick* is in part a love letter to mother nature. For Adrian, "the earth is a bed he can lie down on when he needs to, his entire body held" (178). It is a home we share with creatures big and small—birds among them—and one that is in grave danger. Now more than ever, care for the environment is crucial. As Adrian mentions, "global warming is driving 60 percent of . . . bird species . . . out of environments they've adapted to for

centuries" (54). Host an activist picnic lunch with your book club. Find a local park in your region (https://www.nps .gov/findapark/index.htm), and invite everyone to bring a dish for sharing and a pen, paper, envelope, and stamp. Over lunch, draft letters to your local government officials describing the beauty of your surroundings and urging them to vote on legislation to protect such parks in the future.

3. Adrian's addiction to pain medication is largely to blame for his failing marriage, mistakes at work, and strained relationship with his children. Countless Americans struggle with addiction in many forms, often resulting in even more serious consequences than Adrian suffered. Host a movie night with your book club and watch *Warning: This Drug May Kill You* (2017). After the film, discuss the families devastated by addiction, and see if you can draw any comparisons to Adrian's downward spiral.

A Conversation with Chris White

Q: This is your debut novel, though you are an accomplished playwright and screenwriter. How does writing prose compare with dramatic writing? Do you find one more challenging than the other? Explain.

A: When I first started writing prose after writing plays and screenplays for a number of years, it was like being set free. I could suddenly go anywhere in my writing, with any number of characters, and they could do anything (with no budgetary constraints!). I could describe things in detail and focus in on an image exactly as I saw it in my head, or explore what a character was thinking with as much intricacy as I liked. I love working on plays for their collaborative elements and their immediacy, for the magical relationship between writer and actor and audience. They require me to work like mad on dialogue and character, symbolism and metaphor. Plays are a kind of primordial mystery. Screenwriting is all muscle—outlining and planning and diagramming ahead of time and working draft after draft to get to a crisp and rich precision of image, character arc, and structure. Fiction brings all of these pursuits together for me.

Q: What prompted you to give your main character birding as a hobby? Are you a birder yourself?

A: Adrian would probably take umbrage at your calling birding his "hobby!" Unlike him, though, I'm no expert. I'm just learning. But the seed of the novel is completely bound up with birds. It came from a story a stranger told me on a plane about an avid birder who had taken his wife on a whirlwind trip to chase a rare bird. They stopped to get gas, and he forgot his wife at the gas station. There was so much in that story for me, a marriage in turmoil, a depth of obsession, an imperfect character somehow both devoted and blundering at once. It just lit me up like a light. I have always loved birds—their fragility juxtaposed against their amazing capacity for flight, their astounding variety, the companionship they share with us nearly everywhere we go. And my passion for nature and the environment couldn't be stronger.

Q: Throughout the novel there are several facts about the dangers of global warming on the environment, particularly for bird species. Do you hope to spread awareness about the dangers of global warming with this novel?

A: Climate change is at the beating heart of our current planetary condition and beyond urgent. This reality, this daily, hourly evidence of our excesses, shortsightedness, and losses is a huge current in the novel for me. I also think it's responsible in some way for the pace of the story—the sense that Adrian is running for his life, that there is no time to lose, and that the stakes are dire.

Q: Do you agree that at heart Adrian seems to want to escape the reality of his life, and that both the birds and the pills aid him in doing so? Would you diagnose your main character as an escapist? Why or why not?

A: I would diagnose most human beings as escapists, to be honest. We want to avoid pain and discomfort and push instead toward pleasure and an idealized self. It's what we do. That avoidance just gets us into more trouble, keeps us running, stumbling, wreaking havoc, like Adrian. But Adrian has a good heart, also like most of us. It takes a lot of courage to be willing to look at what's actually going on in our lives (or country), as a result of our choices. It often takes hitting bottom for us to change. But I believe it's possible!

Q: Describe the research that went into writing this novel. What was the process like? Did you uncover any facts that were particularly surprising?

A: I learned so much. When I began I knew almost nothing about the birding world and was aided by an amazing and diverse group of birders who were incredibly generous with their time and energies, some of them, like Larry Balch (former president of the American Birding Association) and Betsy Fikejs, for many years at various iterations of the novel's progress. The great store of information at the Cornell Lab of Ornithology was a godsend. I also had little knowledge of anesthesiology and got lots of help from doctors in different areas of specialty. The book presented research challenges in terms of its settings as well—from upstate New York and Boulder (where I lived for several years before beginning the book), to Texas and Washington State, to very particular areas of the Florida Panhandle. All of these required research, some of it more extensive. For me, research is more than a means to create greater authenticity or accuracy. It's a powerful creative engine that can shape the narrative in ways I never could have imagined beforehand. I did uncover facts that were particularly surprising, many of them having to do with climate change, extinction, and American history, some of which made it into the book directly, and some of which made it into the book in more covert ways.

Q: What is your favorite moment in the novel? What was the most difficult scene to write?

A: Probably my favorite moment in the novel was also the most difficult to write: the climactic scene in the swamp.

Q: In the end it is left unclear if Stella and Adrian work out their differences. Can you lend us insight into how you think their future plays out?

A: I wish I could! I have my own opinions, of course, but one can't be sure. I imagine Adrian will make his way to sharing what he's gone through with Stella, both in the recent past and in his childhood. There will surely be healing in that. What her response will be, I can't say.

Q: What was your process like in writing the novel? What were the biggest challenges and changes it went through?

A: The first draft of the novel was extremely different than the last (not to mention the many drafts in between). It began as a book from several characters' points of view, but the primary protagonist was the wife, the character that on some level I could identify with best. It was a very different story as well, with different thematic emphases, locations, plotline, and characters. At a certain point though, after working on that book for some time, I realized that Adrian's story was taking over, compelling me and driving me. I now believe that's because I needed to understand his story in an even more urgent way than Stella's. I completely redrafted the book at that point, attempting to hone in on his perspective. Then the book went through yet another major shift, when I realized I wanted to do away with all other perspectives and write it exclusively from Adrian's POV. I redrafted it yet again, finding ways of integrating what I had gained through the other characters' perspectives into the new version. The book was a great labor of love for me. It spanned many years.

Q: What is next for you as a writer? Can we expect to learn any more about Adrian in the future?

A: I'm working on a new novel. I'm not yet at a point where I'm ready to say much more. But I'm very excited about it and very much in the middle of the abyss of finding. It feels a little dangerous, which is usually a good thing. As for Adrian, I don't know whether we'll hear from him again or not! I miss working with him. He taught me a lot about myself. Sometimes I think about extracting threads from *The Life List of Adrian Mandrick* and weaving them into either this next novel or something in the future. But I guess I'll have to wait to find out.